BOOKS BY RICHARD FORD

A Piece of My Heart

The Ultimate Good Luck

The Sportswriter

Rock Springs

Wildlife

Independence Day

Women with Men

A Multitude of Sins

VINTAGE FORD

Richard Ford

VINTAGE BOOKS

A Division of Random House, Inc.

New York

Kristina

A VINTAGE ORIGINAL, JANUARY 2004

Copyright © 2004 by Richard Ford

All rights reserved under International and Pan-American
Copyright Conventions. Published in the United States by
Vintage Books, a division of Random House, Inc., New York,
and simultaneously in Canada by
Random House of Canada Limited, Toronto.

Vintage and colophon are registered trademarks
of Random House, Inc.

The pieces herein first appeared in collected form in the following works:
"Communist" was originally published in *Rock Springs,* copyright © 1987 by Richard Ford
(Vintage Books, 1988). "Reunion" was originally published in *A Multitude of Sins,*
copyright © 2001 by Richard Ford (Vintage Books, 2003). "Calling" was originally
published in *A Multitude of Sins,* copyright © 2001 by Richard Ford (Vintage Books, 2003).
Selection from *Independence Day,* copyright © 1995 by Richard Ford (Vintage Books, 1996).
"The Womanizer" was originally published in *Women with Men,* copyright © 1997
by Richard Ford (Vintage Books, 1998). "Rock Springs" was originally published in
Rock Springs, copyright © 1987 by Richard Ford (Vintage Books, 1988). "My Mother, In
Memory" was originally published in *Harper's Magazine.*

Library of Congress Cataloging-in-Publication Data
Ford, Richard, 1944–
Vintage Ford / Richard Ford.—1st Vintage Books ed.
p. cm.
Contents: "Communist" from Rock Springs—"Reunion" from A multitude of sins—
"Calling" from A multitude of sins—Selection from Independence Day—"The
womanizer" from Women with men—"Rock Springs" from Rock Springs—My
mother, in memory.
ISBN 1-4000-3392-6 (trade pbk.)
I. Title
PS3556.O713A6 2003
813'.54—dc22   2003060283

Book design by JoAnne Metsch

www.vintagebooks.com

Printed in the United States of America
10   9   8   7   6   5   4   3   2   1

CONTENTS

VINTAGE FORD

COMMUNIST

My mother once had a boyfriend named Glen Baxter. This was in 1961. We—my mother and I—were living in the little house my father had left her up the Sun River, near Victory, Montana, west of Great Falls. My mother was thirty-two at the time. I was sixteen. Glen Baxter was somewhere in the middle, between us, though I cannot be exact about it.

We were living then off the proceeds of my father's life insurance policies, with my mother doing some part-time waitressing work up in Great Falls and going to the bars in the evenings, which I know is where she met Glen Baxter. Sometimes he would come back with her and stay in her room at night, or she would call up from town and explain that she was staying with him in his little place on Lewis Street by the GN yards. She gave me his number every time, but I never called it. I think she probably thought that what she was doing was terrible, but simply couldn't help herself. I thought it was all right, though. Regular life it seemed, and still does. She was young, and I knew that even then.

Glen Baxter was a Communist and liked hunting, which he talked about a lot. Pheasants. Ducks. Deer. He killed all of them, he said. He had been to Vietnam as far back as then, and when he was in our house he often talked about shooting the animals over there—monkeys and beautiful parrots—using military guns just for sport. We did not know what Vietnam was then, and Glen, when he talked about that, referred to it only as "the Far East." I think now he must've been in the CIA and been disillusioned by something he saw or found out about and been thrown out, but that kind of thing did not matter to us. He was a tall, dark-eyed man with short black hair, and was usually in a good humor. He had gone halfway through college in Peoria, Illinois, he said, where he grew up. But when he was around our life he worked wheat farms as a ditcher, and stayed out of work winters and in the bars drinking with women like my mother, who had work and some money. It is not an uncommon life to lead in Montana.

What I want to explain happened in November. We had not been seeing Glen Baxter for some time. Two months had gone by. My mother knew other men, but she came home most days from work and stayed inside watching television in her bedroom and drinking beers. I asked about Glen once, and she said only that she didn't know where he was, and I assumed they had had a fight and that he was gone off on a flyer back to Illinois or Massachusetts, where he said he had relatives. I'll admit that I liked him. He had something on his mind always. He was a labor man as well as a Communist, and liked to say that the country was poisoned by the rich, and strong men would need to bring it to life again, and I liked that because my father had been a labor man, which was why we had a house to live in and money coming through. It was also true that I'd had a few boxing bouts by then—just with town boys and one with an Indian from Choteau—and there were some girlfriends I knew from that. I did not like my mother being around the house so much at night, and I wished Glen Baxter would come back, or that another man would come along and entertain her somewhere else.

At two o'clock on a Saturday, Glen drove up into our yard in a car. He had had a big brown Harley-Davidson that he rode most of the year, in his black-and-red irrigators and a baseball cap turned backwards. But this time he had a car, a blue Nash Ambassador. My mother and I went out on the porch when he stopped inside the olive trees my father had planted as a shelter belt, and my mother had a look on her face of not much pleasure. It was starting to be cold in earnest by then. Snow was down already onto the Fairfield Bench, though on this day a chinook was blowing, and it could as easily have been spring, though the sky above the Divide was turning over in silver and blue clouds of winter.

"We haven't seen you in a long time, I guess," my mother said coldly.

"My little retarded sister died," Glen said, standing at the door of his old car. He was wearing his orange VFW jacket and canvas shoes we called wino shoes, something I had never seen him wear before. He seemed to be in a good humor. "We buried her in Florida near the home."

"That's a good place," my mother said in a voice that meant she was a wronged party in something.

"I want to take this boy hunting today, Aileen," Glen said. "There're snow geese down now. But we have to go right away, or they'll be gone to Idaho by tomorrow."

"He doesn't care to go," my mother said.

"Yes I do," I said, and looked at her.

My mother frowned at me. "Why do you?"

"Why does he need a reason?" Glen Baxter said and grinned.

"I want him to have one, that's why." She looked at me oddly. "I think Glen's drunk, Les."

"No, I'm not drinking," Glen said, which was hardly ever true. He looked at both of us, and my mother bit down on the side of her lower lip and stared at me in a way to make you think she thought something was being put over on her and she didn't like you for it. She was very pretty, though when she was mad her features were sharpened and less pretty by a long way. "All right, then I don't care," she said to no one in particular. "Hunt, kill, maim. Your father did that too." She turned to go back inside.

"Why don't you come with us, Aileen?" Glen was smiling still, pleased.

"To do what?" my mother said. She stopped and pulled a package of cigarettes out of her dress pocket and put one in her mouth.

"It's worth seeing."

"See dead animals?" my mother said.

"These geese are from Siberia, Aileen," Glen said. "They're not like a lot of geese. Maybe I'll buy us dinner later. What do you say?"

"Buy what with?" my mother said. To tell the truth, I didn't know why she was so mad at him. I would've thought she'd be glad to see him. But she just suddenly seemed to hate everything about him.

"I've got some money," Glen said. "Let me spend it on a pretty girl tonight."

"Find one of those and you're lucky," my mother said, turning away toward the front door.

"I already found one," Glen Baxter said. But the door slammed behind her, and he looked at me then with a look I think now was helplessness, though I could not see a way to change anything.

My mother sat in the backseat of Glen's Nash and looked out the window while we drove. My double gun was in the seat between us beside Glen's Belgian pump, which he kept loaded with five shells in case, he said, he saw something beside the road he wanted to shoot. I had hunted rabbits before, and had ground-sluiced pheasants and other birds, but I had never been on an actual hunt before, one where you drove out to some special place and did it formally. And I was excited. I had a feeling that something important was about to happen to me, and that this would be a day I would always remember.

My mother did not say anything for a long time, and neither did I. We drove up through Great Falls and out the other side toward Fort Benton, which was on the benchland where wheat was grown.

"Geese mate for life," my mother said, just out of the blue, as we were driving. "I hope you know that. They're special birds."

"I know that," Glen said in the front seat. "I have every respect for them."

"So where were you for three months?" she said. "I'm only curious."

"I was in the Big Hole for a while," Glen said, "and after that I went over to Douglas, Wyoming."

"What were you planning to do there?" my mother asked.

"I wanted to find a job, but it didn't work out."

"I'm going to college," she said suddenly, and this was something I had never heard about before. I turned to look at her, but she was staring out her window and wouldn't see me.

"I knew French once," Glen said. "*Rosé's* pink. *Rouge's* red." He glanced at me and smiled. "I think that's a wise idea, Aileen. When are you going to start?"

"I don't want Les to think he was raised by crazy people all his life," my mother said.

"Les ought to go himself," Glen said.

"After I go, he will."

"What do you say about that, Les?" Glen said, grinning.

"He says it's just fine," my mother said.

"It's just fine," I said.

Where Glen Baxter took us was out onto the high flat prairie that was disked for wheat and had high, high mountains out to the east, with lower heartbreak hills in between. It was, I remember, a day for blues in the sky, and down in the distance we could see the small town of Floweree, and the state highway running past it toward Fort Benton and the Hi-line. We drove out on top of the prairie on a muddy dirt road fenced on both sides, until we had gone about three miles, which is where Glen stopped.

"All right," he said, looking up in the rearview mirror at my mother. "You wouldn't think there was anything here, would you?"

"*We're* here," my mother said. "You brought us here."

"You'll be glad though," Glen said, and seemed confident to me. I had looked around myself but could not see anything. No water or trees, nothing that seemed like a good place to hunt anything. Just wasted land. "There's a big lake out there, Les," Glen said. "You can't see it now from here because it's low. But the geese are there. You'll see."

"It's like the moon out here, I recognize that," my mother said, "only it's worse." She was staring out at the flat wheatland as if she could actually see something in particular, and wanted to know more about it. "How'd you find this place?"

"I came once on the wheat push," Glen said.

"And I'm sure the owner told you just to come back and hunt anytime you like and bring anybody you wanted. Come one, come all. Is that it?"

"People shouldn't own land anyway," Glen said. "Anybody should be able to use it."

"Les, Glen's going to poach here," my mother said. "I just want you to know that, because that's a crime and the law will get you for it. If you're a man now, you're going to have to face the consequences."

"That's not true," Glen Baxter said, and looked gloomily out over the steering wheel down the muddy road toward the mountains. Though for myself I believed it was true, and didn't care. I didn't care about anything at that moment except seeing geese fly over me and shooting them down.

"Well, I'm certainly not going out there," my mother said. "I like towns better, and I already have enough trouble."

"That's okay," Glen said. "When the geese lift up you'll get to see them. That's all I wanted. Les and me'll go shoot them, won't we, Les?"

"Yes," I said, and I put my hand on my shotgun, which had been my father's and was heavy as rocks.

"Then we should go on," Glen said, "or we'll waste our light."

We got out of the car with our guns. Glen took off his canvas shoes and put on his pair of black irrigators out of the trunk. Then we crossed the barbed wire fence, and walked out into the high, tilled field toward nothing. I looked back at my mother when we were still not so far away, but I could only see the small, dark top of her head, low in the backseat of the Nash, staring out and thinking what I could not then begin to say.

————

On the walk toward the lake, Glen began talking to me. I had
never been alone with him, and knew little about him except
what my mother said—that he drank too much, or other times
that he was the nicest man she had ever known in the world and
that someday a woman would marry him, though she didn't think
it would be her. Glen told me as we walked that he wished he had
finished college, but that it was too late now, that his mind was too
old. He said he had liked the Far East very much, and that people
there knew how to treat each other, and that he would go back
some day but couldn't go now. He said also that he would like to
live in Russia for a while and mentioned the names of people
who had gone there, names I didn't know. He said it would be
hard at first, because it was so different, but that pretty soon anyone would learn to like it and wouldn't want to live anywhere
else, and that Russians treated Americans who came to live there
like kings. There were Communists everywhere now, he said. You
didn't know them, but they were there. Montana had a large number, and he was in touch with all of them. He said that Communists were always in danger and that he had to protect himself all
the time. And when he said that he pulled back his VFW jacket
and showed me the butt of a pistol he had stuck under his shirt
against his bare skin. "There are people who want to kill me right
now," he said, "and I would kill a man myself if I thought I had
to." And we kept walking. Though in a while he said, "I don't
think I know much about you, Les. But I'd like to. What do you
like to do?"

"I like to box," I said. "My father did it. It's a good thing to
know."

"I suppose you have to protect yourself too," Glen said.

"I know how to," I said.

"Do you like to watch TV," Glen asked, and smiled.

"Not much."

"I love to," Glen said. "I could watch it instead of eating if I
had one."

I looked out straight ahead over the green tops of sage that
grew to the edge of the disked field, hoping to see the lake Glen

said was there. There was an airishness and a sweet smell that I
thought might be the place we were going, but I couldn't see it.
"How will we hunt these geese?" I said.

"It won't be hard," Glen said. "Most hunting isn't even hunting. It's only shooting. And that's what this will be. In Illinois you
would dig holes in the ground and hide and set out your decoys.
Then the geese come to you, over and over again. But we don't
have time for that here." He glanced at me. "You have to be sure
the first time here."

"How do you know they're here now," I asked. And I looked
toward the Highwood Mountains twenty miles away, half in snow
and half dark blue at the bottom. I could see the little town of
Floweree then, looking shabby and dimly lighted in the distance.
A red bar sign shone. A car moved slowly away from the scattered
buildings.

"They always come November first," Glen said.

"Are we going to poach them?"

"Does it make any difference to you," Glen asked.

"No, it doesn't."

"Well then, we aren't," he said.

We walked then for a while without talking. I looked back
once to see the Nash far and small in the flat distance. I couldn't
see my mother, and I thought that she must've turned on the
radio and gone to sleep, which she always did, letting it play all
night in her bedroom. Behind the car the sun was nearing the
rounded mountains southwest of us, and I knew that when the
sun was gone it would be cold. I wished my mother had decided
to come along with us, and I thought for a moment of how little
I really knew her at all.

Glen walked with me another quarter-mile, crossed another
barbed wire fence where sage was growing, then went a hundred
yards through wheatgrass and spurge until the ground went up
and formed a kind of long hillock bunker built by a farmer
against the wind. And I realized the lake was just beyond us. I
could hear the sound of a car horn blowing and a dog barking all

the way down in the town, then the wind seemed to move and all I could hear then and after then were geese. So many geese, from the sound of them, though I still could not see even one. I stood and listened to the high-pitched shouting sound, a sound I had never heard so close, a sound with size to it—though it was not loud. A sound that meant great numbers and that made your chest rise and your shoulders tighten with expectancy. It was a sound to make you feel separate from it and everything else, as if you were of no importance in the grand scheme of things.

"Do you hear them singing," Glen asked. He held his hand up to make me stand still. And we both listened. "How many do you think, Les, just hearing?"

"A hundred," I said. "More than a hundred."

"Five thousand," Glen said. "More than you can believe when you see them. Go see."

I put down my gun and on my hands and knees crawled up the earthwork through the wheatgrass and thistle, until I could see down to the lake and see the geese. And they were there, like a white bandage laid on the water, wide and long and continuous, a white expanse of snow geese, seventy yards from me, on the bank, but stretching far onto the lake, which was large itself—a half-mile across, with thick tules on the far side and wild plums farther and the blue mountain behind them.

"Do you see the big raft?" Glen said from below me, in a whisper.

"I see it," I said, still looking. It was such a thing to see, a view I had never seen and have not since.

"Are any on the land?" he said.

"Some are in the wheatgrass," I said, "but most are swimming."

"Good," Glen said. "They'll have to fly. But we can't wait for that now."

And I crawled backwards down the heel of land to where Glen was, and my gun. We were losing our light, and the air was purplish and cooling. I looked toward the car but couldn't see it, and I was no longer sure where it was below the lighted sky.

"Where do they fly to?" I said in a whisper, since I did not want anything to be ruined because of what I did or said. It was important to Glen to shoot the geese, and it was important to me.

"To the wheat," he said. "Or else they leave for good. I wish your mother had come, Les. Now she'll be sorry."

I could hear the geese quarreling and shouting on the lake surface. And I wondered if they knew we were here now. "She might be," I said with my heart pounding, but I didn't think she would be much.

It was a simple plan he had. I would stay behind the bunker, and he would crawl on his belly with his gun through the wheat-grass as near to the geese as he could. Then he would simply stand up and shoot all the ones he could close up, both in the air and on the ground. And when all the others flew up, with luck some would turn toward me as they came into the wind, and then I could shoot them and turn them back to him, and he would shoot them again. He could kill ten, he said, if he was lucky, and I might kill four. It didn't seem hard.

"Don't show them your face," Glen said. "Wait till you think you can touch them, then stand up and shoot. To hesitate is lost in this."

"All right," I said. "I'll try it."

"Shoot one in the head, and then shoot another one," Glen said. "It won't be hard." He patted me on the arm and smiled. Then he took off his VFW jacket and put it on the ground, climbed up the side of the bunker, cradling his shotgun in his arms, and slid on his belly into the dry stalks of yellow grass out of my sight.

Then, for the first time in that entire day, I was alone. And I didn't mind it. I sat squat down in the grass, loaded my double gun and took my other two shells out of my pocket to hold. I pushed the safety off and on to see that it was right. The wind rose a little, scuffed the grass and made me shiver. It was not the warm chinook now, but a wind out of the north, the one geese flew away from if they could.

Then I thought about my mother, in the car alone, and how much longer I would stay with her, and what it might mean to her for me to leave. And I wondered when Glen Baxter would die and if someone would kill him, or whether my mother would marry him and how I would feel about it. And though I didn't know why, it occurred to me that Glen Baxter and I would not be friends when all was said and done, since I didn't care if he ever married my mother or didn't.

Then I thought about boxing and what my father had taught me about it. To tighten your fists hard. To strike out straight from the shoulder and never punch backing up. How to cut a punch by snapping your fist inwards, how to carry your chin low, and to step toward a man when he is falling so you can hit him again. And most important, to keep your eyes open when you are hitting in the face and causing damage, because you need to see what you're doing to encourage yourself, and because it is when you close your eyes that you stop hitting and get hurt badly. "Fly all over your man, Les," my father said. "When you see your chance, fly on him and hit him till he falls." That, I thought, would always be my attitude in things.

And then I heard the geese again, their voices in unison, louder and shouting, as if the wind had changed again and put all new sounds in the cold air. And then a *boom*. And I knew Glen was in among them and had stood up to shoot. The noise of geese rose and grew worse, and my fingers burned where I held my gun too tight to the metal, and I put it down and opened my fist to make the burning stop so I could feel the trigger when the moment came. *Boom*, Glen shot again, and I heard him shuck a shell, and all the sounds out beyond the bunker seemed to be rising—the geese, the shots, the air itself going up. *Boom*, Glen shot another time, and I knew he was taking his careful time to make his shots good. And I held my gun and started to crawl up the bunker so as not to be surprised when the geese came over me and I could shoot.

From the top I saw Glen Baxter alone in the wheatgrass field, shooting at a white goose with black tips of wings that was on the ground not far from him, but trying to run and pull into the air. He shot it once more, and it fell over dead with its wings flapping.

Glen looked back at me and his face was distorted and strange. The air around him was full of white rising geese and he seemed to want them all. "Behind you, Les," he yelled at me and pointed. "They're all behind you now." I looked behind me, and there were geese in the air as far as I could see, more than I knew how many, moving so slowly, their wings wide out and working calmly and filling the air with noise, though their voices were not as loud or as shrill as I had thought they would be. And they were so close! Forty feet, some of them. The air around me vibrated and I could feel the wind from their wings and it seemed to me I could kill as many as the times I could shoot—a hundred or a thousand—and I raised my gun, put the muzzle on the head of a white goose, and fired. It shuddered in the air, its wide feet sank below its belly, its wings cradled out to hold back air, and it fell straight down and landed with an awful sound, a noise a human would make, a thick, soft, *hump* noise. I looked up again and shot another goose, could hear the pellets hit its chest, but it didn't fall or even break its pattern for flying. *Boom*, Glen shot again. And then again. "Hey," I heard him shout, "Hey, hey." And there were geese flying over me, flying in line after line. I broke my gun and reloaded, and thought to myself as I did: I need confidence here, I need to be sure with this. I pointed at another goose and shot it in the head, and it fell the way the first one had, wings out, its belly down, and with the same thick noise of hitting. Then I sat down in the grass on the bunker and let geese fly over me.

By now the whole raft was in the air, all of it moving in a slow swirl above me and the lake and everywhere, finding the wind and heading out south in long wavering lines that caught the last sun and turned to silver as they gained a distance. It was a thing to see, I will tell you now. Five thousand white geese all in the air around you, making a noise like you have never heard before. And I thought to myself then: this is something I will never see again. I will never forget this. And I was right.

Glen Baxter shot twice more. Once he missed, but with the other he hit a goose flying away from him, and knocked it half falling and flying into the empty lake not far from shore, where it began to swim as though it was fine and make its noise.

Glen stood in the stubby grass, looking out at the goose, his gun lowered "I didn't need to shoot that one, did I, Les?"

"I don't know," I said, sitting on the little knoll of land, looking at the goose swimming in the water.

"I don't know why I shoot 'em. They're so beautiful." He looked at me.

"I don't know either," I said.

"Maybe there's nothing else to do with them." Glen stared at the goose again and shook his head. "Maybe this is exactly what they're put on earth for."

I did not know what to say because I did not know what he could mean by that, though what I felt was embarrassment at the great numbers of geese there were, and a dulled feeling like a hunger because the shooting had stopped and it was over for me now.

Glen began to pick up his geese, and I walked down to my two that had fallen close together and were dead. One had hit with such an impact that its stomach had split and some of its inward parts were knocked out. Though the other looked unhurt, its soft white belly turned up like a pillow, its head and jagged bill-teeth, its tiny black eyes looking as they would if they were alive.

"What's happened to the hunters out here?" I heard a voice speak. It was my mother, standing in her pink dress on the knoll above us, hugging her arms. She was smiling though she was cold. And I realized that I had lost all thought of her in the shooting. "Who did all this shooting? Is this your work, Les?"

"No," I said.

"Les is a hunter, though, Aileen," Glen said. "He takes his time." He was holding two white geese by their necks, one in each hand, and he was smiling. He and my mother seemed pleased.

"I see you didn't miss too many," my mother said and smiled. I could tell she admired Glen for his geese, and that she had done some thinking in the car alone. "It *was* wonderful, Glen," she said. "I've never seen anything like that. They were like snow."

"It's worth seeing once, isn't it?" Glen said. "I should've killed more, but I got excited."

My mother looked at me then. "Where's yours, Les?"

"Here," I said and pointed to my two geese on the ground beside me.

My mother nodded in a nice way, and I think she liked everything then and wanted the day to turn out right and for all of us to be happy. "Six, then. You've got six in all."

"One's still out there," I said, and motioned where the one goose was swimming in circles on the water.

"Okay," my mother said and put her hand over her eyes to look. "Where is it?"

Glen Baxter looked at me then with a strange smile, a smile that said he wished I had never mentioned anything about the other goose. And I wished I hadn't either. I looked up in the sky and could see the lines of geese by the thousands shining silver in the light, and I wished we could just leave and go home.

"That one's my mistake there," Glen Baxter said and grinned. "I shouldn't have shot that one, Aileen. I got too excited."

My mother looked out on the lake for a minute, then looked at Glen and back again. "Poor goose." She shook her head. "How will you get it, Glen?"

"I can't get that one now," Glen said.

My mother looked at him. "What do you mean?"

"I'm going to leave that one," Glen said.

"Well, no. You can't leave one," my mother said. "You shot it. You have to get it. Isn't that a rule?"

"No," Glen said.

And my mother looked from Glen to me. "Wade out and get it, Glen," she said in a sweet way, and my mother looked young then, like a young girl, in her flimsy short-sleeved waitress dress and her skinny, bare legs in the wheatgrass.

"No." Glen Baxter looked down at his gun and shook his head. And I didn't know why he wouldn't go, because it would've been easy. The lake was shallow. And you could tell that anyone could've walked out a long way before it got deep, and Glen had on his boots.

My mother looked at the white goose, which was not more than thirty yards from the shore, its head up, moving in slow circles, its wings settled and relaxed so you could see the black tips. "Wade out and get it, Glenny, won't you, please?" she said. "They're special things."

"You don't understand the world, Aileen," Glen said. "This can happen. It doesn't matter."

"But that's so cruel, Glen," she said, and a sweet smile came on her lips.

"Raise up your own arms, 'Leeny," Glen said. "I can't see any angel's wings, can you, Les?" He looked at me, but I looked away.

"Then you go on and get it, Les," my mother said. "You weren't raised by crazy people." I started to go, but Glen Baxter suddenly grabbed me by my shoulder and pulled me back hard, so hard his fingers made bruises in my skin that I saw later.

"Nobody's going," he said. "This is over with now."

And my mother gave Glen a cold look then. "You don't have a heart, Glen," she said. "There's nothing to love in you. You're just a son of a bitch, that's all."

And Glen Baxter nodded at my mother, then, as if he understood something he had not understood before, but something that he was willing to know. "Fine," he said, "that's fine." And he took his big pistol out from against his belly, the big blue revolver I had only seen part of before and that he said protected him, and he pointed it out at the goose on the water, his arm straight away from him, and shot and missed. And then he shot and missed again. The goose made its noise once. And then he hit it dead, because there was no splash. And then he shot it three times more until the gun was empty and the goose's head was down and it was floating toward the middle of the lake where it was empty and dark blue. "Now who has a heart?" Glen said. But my mother was not there when he turned around. She had already started back to the car and was almost lost from sight in the darkness. And

Glen smiled at me then and his face had a wild look on it. "Okay, Les?" he said.

"Okay," I said.

"There're limits to everything, right?"

"I guess so," I said.

"Your mother's a beautiful woman, but she's not the only beautiful woman in Montana." And I did not say anything. And Glen Baxter suddenly said, "Here," and he held the pistol out at me. "Don't you want this? Don't you want to shoot me? Nobody thinks they'll die. But I'm ready for it right now." And I did not know what to do then. Though it is true that what I wanted to do was to hit him, hit him as hard in the face as I could, and see him on the ground bleeding and crying and pleading for me to stop. Only at that moment he looked scared to me, and I had never seen a grown man scared before—though I have seen one since—and I felt sorry for him, as though he was already a dead man. And I did not end up hitting him at all.

A light can go out in the heart. All of this happened years ago, but I still can feel now how sad and remote the world was to me. Glen Baxter, I think now, was not a bad man, only a man scared of something he'd never seen before—something soft in himself—his life going a way he didn't like. A woman with a son. Who could blame him there? I don't know what makes people do what they do, or call themselves what they call themselves, only that you have to live someone's life to be the expert.

My mother had tried to see the good side of things, tried to be hopeful in the situation she was handed, tried to look out for us both, and it hadn't worked. It was a strange time in her life then and after that, a time when she had to adjust to being an adult just when she was on the thin edge of things. Too much awareness too early in life was her problem, I think.

And what I felt was only that I had somehow been pushed out into the world, into the real life then, the one I hadn't lived yet. In a year I was gone to hard-rock mining and no-paycheck jobs and not to college. And I have thought more than once about my mother saying that I had not been raised by crazy people, and I don't know what that could mean or what difference it could make, unless it means that love is a reliable commodity, and even that is not always true, as I have found out.

Late on the night that all this took place I was in bed when I heard my mother say, "Come outside, Les. Come and hear this." And I went out onto the front porch barefoot and in my underwear, where it was warm like spring, and there was a spring mist in the air. I could see the lights of the Fairfield Coach in the distance, on its way up to Great Falls.

And I could hear geese, white birds in the sky, flying. They made their high-pitched sound like angry yells, and though I couldn't see them high up, it seemed to me they were everywhere. And my mother looked up and said, "Hear them?" I could smell her hair wet from the shower. "They leave with the moon," she said. "It's still half wild out here."

And I said, "I hear them," and I felt a chill come over my bare chest, and the hair stood up on my arms the way it does before a storm. And for a while we listened.

"When I first married your father, you know, we lived on a street called Bluebird Canyon, in California. And I thought that was the prettiest street and the prettiest name. I suppose no one brings you up like your first love. You don't mind if I say that, do you?" She looked at me hopefully.

"No," I said.

"We have to keep civilization alive somehow." And she pulled her little housecoat together because there was a cold vein in the air, a part of the cold that would be on us the next day. "I don't feel part of things tonight, I guess."

"It's all right," I said.

"Do you know where I'd like to go?"

"No," I said. And I suppose I knew she was angry then, angry with life, but did not want to show me that.

"To the Straits of Juan de Fuca. Wouldn't that be something? Would you like that?"

"I'd like it," I said. And my mother looked off for a minute, as if she could see the Straits of Juan de Fuca out against the line of mountains, see the lights of things alive and a whole new world.

"I know you liked him," she said after a moment. "You and I both suffer fools too well."

"I didn't like him too much," I said. "I didn't really care."

"He'll fall on his face. I'm sure of that," she said. And I didn't say anything because I didn't care about Glen Baxter anymore, and was happy not to talk about him. "Would you tell me something if I asked you? Would you tell me the truth?"

"Yes," I said.

And my mother did not look at me. "Just tell the truth," she said.

"All right," I said.

"Do you think I'm still very feminine? I'm thirty-two years old now. You don't know what that means. But do you think I am?"

And I stood at the edge of the porch, with the olive trees before me, looking straight up into the mist where I could not see geese but could still hear them flying, could almost feel the air move below their white wings. And I felt the way you feel when you are on a trestle all alone and the train is coming, and you know you have to decide. And I said, "Yes, I do." Because that was the truth. And I tried to think of something else then and did not hear what my mother said after that.

And how old was I then? Sixteen. Sixteen is young, but it can also be a grown man. I am forty-one years old now, and I think about that time without regret, though my mother and I never talked in that way again, and I have not heard her voice now in a long, long time.

REUNION

When I saw Mack Bolger he was standing beside the bottom of the marble steps that bring travelers and passersby to and from the balcony of the main concourse in Grand Central. It was before Christmas last year, when the weather stayed so warm and watery the spirit seemed to go out of the season.

I was cutting through the terminal, as I often do on my way home from the publishing offices on Forty-first Street. I was, in fact, on my way to meet a new friend at Billy's. It was four o'clock on Friday, and the great station was athrong with citizens on their way somewhere, laden with baggage and precious packages, shouting good-byes and greetings, flagging their arms, embracing, gripping each other with pleasure. Others, though, simply stood, as Mack Bolger was when I saw him, staring rather vacantly at the crowds, as if whomever he was there to meet for some reason hadn't come. Mack is a tall, handsome, well-put-together man who seems to see everything from a height. He was wearing a long, well-fitted gabardine overcoat of some deep-olive twill—an expensive coat, I thought, an Italian coat. His brown shoes were polished to a high gloss; his trouser cuffs hit them just right. And because he was without a hat, he seemed even taller than what he was—perhaps six-three. His hands were in his coat pockets, his smooth chin slightly elevated the way a middle-aged man would, and as if he thought he was extremely visible there. His hair was thinning a little in front, but it was carefully cut, and he was tanned, which caused his square face and prominent brow to appear heavy, almost artificially so, as though in a peculiar way the man I saw was not Mack Bolger but a good-looking effigy situated precisely there to attract my attention.

For a while, a year and a half before, I had been involved with Mack Bolger's wife, Beth Bolger. Oddly enough—only because all events that occur outside New York seem odd and fancifully unreal to New Yorkers—our affair had taken place in the city of St. Louis, that largely overlookable red-brick abstraction that is neither West nor Middlewest, neither South nor North; the city lost in the middle, as I think of it. I've always found it interesting that it was both the boyhood home of T. S. Eliot, and only eighty-five years before that, the starting point of westward expansion. It's a place, I suppose, the world can't get away from fast enough.

What went on between Beth Bolger and me is hardly worth the words that would be required to explain it away. At any distance but the close range I saw it from, it was an ordinary adultery—spirited, thrilling and then, after a brief while, when we had crossed the continent several times and caused as many people as possible unhappiness, embarrassment and heartache, it became disappointing and ignoble and finally almost disastrous to those same people. Because it is the truth and serves to complicate Mack Bolger's unlikeable dilemma and to cast him in a more sympathetic light, I will say that at some point he was forced to confront me (and Beth as well) in a hotel room in St. Louis—a nice, graceful old barn called the Mayfair—with the result that I got banged around in a minor way and sent off into the empty downtown streets on a warm, humid autumn Sunday afternoon, without the slightest idea of what to do, ending up waiting for hours at the St. Louis airport for a midnight flight back to New York. Apart from my dignity, I left behind and never saw again a brown silk Hermès scarf with tassels that my mother had given me for Christmas in 1971, a gift she felt was the nicest thing she'd ever seen and perfect for a man just commencing life as a book editor. I'm glad she didn't have to know about my losing it, and how it happened.

I also did not see Beth Bolger again, except for one sorrowful and bitter drink we had together in the theater district last spring, a nervous, uncomfortable meeting we somehow felt obligated to have, and following which I walked away down Forty-seventh Street, feeling that all of life was a sorry mess, while Beth went along to see *The Iceman Cometh*, which was playing then. We have not seen each other since that leave-taking, and, as I said, to tell more would not be quite worth the words.

But when I saw Mack Bolger standing in the crowded, festive holiday-bedecked concourse of Grand Central, looking rather vacant-headed but clearly himself, so far from the middle of the country, I was taken by a sudden and strange impulse—which was to walk straight across through the eddying sea of travelers and speak to him, just as one might speak to anyone you casually knew and had unexpectedly yet not unhappily encountered. And not to impart anything, or set in motion any particular action (to clarify history, for instance, or make amends), but simply to create an event where before there was none. And not an unpleasant event, or a provocative one. Just a dimensionless, unreverberant moment, a contact, unimportant in every other respect. Life has few enough of these moments—the rest of it being so consumed by the predictable and the obligated.

I knew a few things about Mack Bolger, about his life since we'd last confronted each other semi-violently in the Mayfair. Beth had been happy to tell me during our woeful drink at the Espalier Bar in April. Our—Beth's and my—love affair was, of course, only one feature in the long devaluation and decline in her and Mack's marriage. This I'd always understood. There were two children, and Mack had been frantic to hold matters together for their sakes and futures; Beth was a portrait photographer who worked at home, but craved engagement with the wide world outside of University City—craved it in the worst way, and was therefore basically unsatisfied with everything in her life. After my sudden departure, she moved out of their house, rented an apartment near the Gateway Arch and, for a time, took a much younger lover. Mack, for his part in their upheaval, eventually quit his job as an executive for a large agri-biz company, considered studying for the ministry, considered going on a missionary journey to

Senegal or French Guiana, briefly took a young lover himself. One child had been arrested for shoplifting; the other had gotten admitted to Brown. There were months of all-night confrontations, some combative, some loving and revelatory, some derisive from both sides. Until everything that could be said or expressed or threatened was said, expressed and threatened, after which a standstill was achieved whereby they both stayed in their suburban house, kept separate schedules, saw new and different friends, had occasional dinners together, went to the opera, occasionally even slept together, but saw little hope (in Beth's case, certainly) of things turning out better than they were at the time of our joyless drink and the O'Neill play. I'd assumed at that time that Beth was meeting someone else that evening, had someone in New York she was interested in, and I felt completely fine about it.

"It's really odd, isn't it?" Beth said, stirring her long, almost pure-white finger around the surface of her Kir Royale, staring not at me but at the glass rim where the pink liquid nearly exceeded its vitreous limits. "We were so close for a little while." Her eyes rose to me, and she smiled almost girlishly. "You and me, I mean. Now, I feel like I'm telling all this to an old friend. Or to my brother."

Beth is a tall, sallow-faced, big-boned, ash-blond woman who smokes cigarettes and whose hair often hangs down in her eyes like a forties Hollywood glamour girl. This can be attractive, although it often causes her to seem to be spying on her own conversations.

"Well," I said, "it's all right to feel that way." I smiled back across the little round black-topped café table. It *was* all right. I had gone on. When I looked back on what we'd done, none of it except for what we'd done in bed made me feel good about life, or that the experience had been worth it. But I couldn't undo it. I don't believe the past can be repaired, only exceeded. "Sometimes, friendship's all we're after in these sorts of things," I said. Though this, I admit, I did not really believe.

"Mack's like a dog, you know," Beth said, flicking her hair away from her eyes. He was on her mind. "I kick him, and he tries to bring me things. It's pathetic. He's very interested in Tantric sex now, whatever that is. Do you know what that even is?"

"I really don't like hearing this," I said stupidly, though it was true. "It sounds cruel."

"You're just afraid I'll say the same thing about you, Johnny." She smiled and touched her damp fingertip to her lips, which were wonderful lips.

"Afraid," I said. "Afraid's really not the word, is it?"

"Well, then, whatever the word is." Beth looked quickly away and motioned the waiter for the check. She didn't know how to be disagreed with. It always frightened her.

But that was all. I've already said our meeting wasn't a satisfying one.

Mack Bolger's pale gray eyes caught me coming toward him well before I expected them to. We had seen each other only twice. Once at a fancy cocktail party given by an author I'd come to St. Louis to wrest a book away from. It was the time I'd met his wife. And once more, in the Mayfair Hotel, when I'd taken an inept swing at him and he'd slammed me against a wall and hit me in the face with the back of his hand. Perhaps you don't forget people you knock around. That becomes their place in your life. I, myself, find it hard to recognize people when they're not where they belong, and Mack Bolger belonged in St. Louis. Of course, he was an exception.

Mack's gaze fixed on me, then left me, scanned the crowd uncomfortably, then found me again as I approached. His large tanned face took on an expression of stony unsurprise, as if he'd known I was somewhere in the terminal and a form of communication had already begun between us. Though, if anything, really, his face looked resigned—resigned to me, resigned to the situations the world foists onto you unwilling; resigned to himself. Resignation was actually what we had in common, even if neither of us had a language which could express that. So as I came into his presence, what I felt for him, unexpectedly, was

sympathy—for having to see me now. And if I could've, I would
have turned and walked straight away and left him alone. But I
didn't.

"I just saw you," I said from the crowd, ten feet before I ever
expected to speak. My voice isn't loud, so that the theatrically
nasal male voice announcing the arrival from Poughkeepsie on
track 34 seemed to have blotted it out.

"Did you have something special in mind to tell me?" Mack
Bolger said. His eyes cast out again across the vaulted hall, where
Christmas shoppers and overbundled passengers were moving in
all directions. It occured to me at that instant—and shockingly—
that he was waiting for Beth, and that in a moment's time I would
be standing here facing her and Mack together, almost as we had
in St. Louis. My heart struck two abrupt beats deep in my chest,
then seemed for a second to stop altogether. "How's your face?"
Mack said with no emotion, still scanning the crowd. "I didn't
hurt you too bad, did I?"

"No," I said.

"You've grown a moustache." His eyes did not flicker toward me.

"Yes," I said, though I'd completely forgotten about it, and for
some reason felt ashamed, as if it made me look ridiculous.

"Well," Mack Bolger said. "Good." His voice was the one you
would use to speak to someone in line beside you at the post
office, someone you'd never see again. Though there was also, just
barely noticeable, a hint of what we used to call *juiciness* in his
speech, some minor, undispersable moisture in his cheek that one
heard in his *s*'s and *f*'s. It was unfortunate, since it robbed him of a
small measure of gravity. I hadn't noticed it before in the few
overheated moments we'd had to exchange words.

Mack looked at me again, hands in his expensive Italian coat
pockets, a coat that had heavy, dark, bone buttons and long, wide
lapels. Too stylish for him, I thought, for the solid man he was.
Mack and I were nearly the same height, but he was in every way
larger and seemed to look down to me—something in the way
he held his chin up. It was almost the opposite of the way Beth
looked at me.

"I live here now," Mack said, without really addressing me. I noticed he had long, dark almost feminine eyelashes, and small, perfectly shaped ears, which his new haircut put on nice display. He might've been forty—younger than I am—and looked more than anything like an army officer. A major. I thought of a letter Beth had shown me, written by Mack to her, containing the phrase, "I want to kiss you all over. Yes I do. Love, Macklin." Beth had rolled her eyes when she showed it to me. At another time she had talked to Mack on the telephone while we were in bed together naked. On that occasion, too, she'd *kept* rolling her eyes at whatever he was saying—something, I gathered, about difficulties he was having at work. Once we even engaged in a sexual act while she talked to him. I could hear his tiny, buzzing, fretful-sounding voice inside the receiver. But that was now gone. Everything Beth and I had done was gone. All that remained was this—a series of moments in the great train terminal, moments which, in spite of all, seemed correct, sturdy, almost classical in character, as if this later time was all that really mattered, whereas the previous, briefly passionate, linked but now-distant moments were merely preliminary.

"Did you buy a place?" I said, and all at once felt a widely spreading vacancy open all around inside me. It was such a preposterous thing to say.

Mack's eyes moved gradually to me, and his impassive expression, which had seemed to signify one thing—resignation—began to signify something different. I knew this because a small cleft appeared in his chin.

"Yes," he said and let his eyes stay on me.

People were shouldering past us. I could smell some woman's heavy, warm-feeling perfume around my face. Music commenced in the rotunda, making the moment feel suffocating, clamorous: "We three kings of Orient are, bearing gifts we traverse afar . . ."

"Yes," Mack Bolger said again, emphatically, spitting the word from between his large straight, white, nearly flawless teeth. He had grown up on a farm in Nebraska, gone to a small college in Minnesota on a football scholarship, then taken an MBA at Wharton, had done well. All that life, all that experience was now being brought into play as self-control, dignity. It was strange that anyone would call him a dog when he wasn't that at all. He was extremely admirable. "I bought an apartment on the Upper East Side," he said, and he blinked his eyelashes very rapidly. "I moved out in September. I have a new job. I'm living alone. Beth's not here. She's in Paris where she's miserable—or rather I hope she is. We're getting divorced. I'm waiting for my daughter to come down from boarding school. Is that all right? Does that seem all right to you? Does it satisfy your curiosity?"

"Yes," I said. "Of course." Mack was not angry. He was, instead, a thing that anger had no part in, or at least had long been absent from, something akin to exhaustion, where the words you say are the only true words you *can* say. Myself, I did not think I'd ever felt that way. Always for me there had been a choice.

"Do you understand me?" Mack Bolger's thick athlete's brow furrowed, as if he was studying a creature he didn't entirely understand, an anomaly of some kind, which perhaps I was.

"Yes," I said. "I'm sorry."

"Well then," he said, and seemed embarrassed. He looked away, out over the crowd of moving heads and faces, as if he'd sensed someone coming.

I looked toward where he seemed to be looking. But no one was approaching us. Not Beth, not a daughter. Not anyone. Perhaps, I thought, this was all a lie, or possibly even that I'd, for an instant, lost consciousness, and this was not Mack Bolger at all, and I was dreaming everything.

"Do you think there could be someplace else you could go now?" Mack said. His big, tanned, handsome face looked imploring and exhausted. Once Beth had said Mack and I looked alike. But we didn't. That had just been her fantasy. Without really looking at me again he said, "I'll have a hard time introducing you to my daughter. I'm sure you can imagine that."

"Yes," I said. I looked around again, and this time I saw a pretty blond girl standing in the crowd, watching us from several steps away. She was holding a red nylon backpack by its straps. Something was causing her to stay away. Possibly her father had signaled her not to come near us. "Of course," I said. And by speaking I somehow made the girl's face break into a wide smile, a smile I recognized.

"Nothing's happened here," Mack said unexpectedly to me, though he was staring at his daughter. From the pocket of his overcoat he'd produced a tiny white box wrapped and tied with a red bow.

"I'm sorry?" People were swirling noisily around us. The music seemed louder. I was leaving, but I thought perhaps I'd misunderstood him. "I didn't hear you," I said. I smiled in an involuntary way.

"Nothing's happened today," Mack Bolger said. "Don't go away thinking anything happened here. Between you and me, I mean. *Nothing* happened. I'm sorry I ever met you, that's all. Sorry I ever had to touch you. You make me feel ashamed." He still had the unfortunate dampness with his *s*'s.

"Well," I said. "All right. I can understand that."

"Can you?" he said. "Well, that's very good." Then Mack simply stepped away from me, and began saying something to the blond girl standing in the crowd smiling. What he said was, "Wow-wee, boy, oh boy, do *you* look like a million bucks."

And I walked on toward Billy's then, toward the new arrangement I'd made that would take me into the evening. I had, of course, been wrong about the linkage of moments, and about what was preliminary and what was primary. It was a mistake, one I would not make again. None of it was a good thing to have done. Though it is such a large city here, so much larger than, say, St. Louis, I knew I would not see him again.

CALLING

A year after my father departed, moved to St. Louis, and left my mother and me behind in New Orleans to look after ourselves in whatever manner we could, he called on the telephone one afternoon and asked to speak to me. This was before Christmas, 1961. I was home from military school in Florida. My mother had begun her new singing career, which meant taking voice lessons at a local academy, and also letting a tall black man who was her accompanist move into our house and into her bedroom, while passing himself off to the neighborhood as the yard man. William Dubinion was his name, and together he and my mother drank far too much and filled up the ashtrays and played jazz recordings too loud and made unwelcome noise until late, which had not been how things were done when my father was there. However, it was done *because* he was not there, and because he had gone off to St. Louis with another man, an ophthalmologist named Francis Carter, never to come back. I think it seemed to my mother that in view of these facts it didn't matter what she did or how she lived, and that doing the worst was finally not much different from doing the best.

They're all dead now. My father. My mother. Dr. Carter. The black accompanist, Dubinion. Though occasionally I'll still see a man on St. Charles Avenue, in the business district, a man entering one of the new office buildings they've built—a tall, handsome, long-strided, flaxen-haired, youthful, slightly ironic-looking man in a seersucker suit, bow tie and white shoes, who will remind me of my father, or how he looked, at least, when these events occurred. He must've looked that way, in fact, all of his years, into his sixties. New Orleans produces men like my father, or once did: clubmen, racquets players, deft, balmy-day sailors, soft-handed Episcopalians with progressive attitudes, good educations, effortless manners, but with secrets. These men, when you meet them on the sidewalk or at some uptown dinner, seem like the very best damn old guys you could ever know. You want to call them up the very next day and set some plans going. It seems you always knew about them, that they were present in the city but you just hadn't seen a lot of them—a glimpse here and there. They seem exotic, and your heart expands with the thought of a long friendship's commencement and your mundane life taking a new and better turn. So you do call, and you do see them. You go *spec* fishing off Pointe a la Hache. You stage a dinner and meet their pretty wives. You take a long lunch together at Antoine's or Commander's and decide to do this every week from now on to never. Yet someplace along late in the lunch you hit a flat spot. A silent moment occurs, and your eyes meet in a way that could signal a deep human understanding you'd never ever have to speak about. But what you see is, suddenly—and it *is* sudden and fleeting—you see this man is far, far away from you, so far in fact as not even to realize it. A smile could be playing on his face. He may just have said something charming or incisive or flatteringly personal to you. But then the far, far away awareness dawns, and you know you're nothing to him and will probably never even see him again, never take the trouble. Or, if you do chance to see him, you'll cross streets midblock, cast around for exits in crowded dining rooms, sit longer than you need to in the front seat of your car to let such a man go around a corner or disappear into the very building I mentioned. You avoid him. And it is not that there is anything so wrong with him, nothing unsavory or misaligned. Nothing sexual. You just know he's not for you. And that is an end to it. It's simple really. Though of course it's more complicated when the man in question is your father.

When I came to the telephone and my father's call—my mother
had answered, and they had spoken some terse words—my father
began right away to talk. "Well, let's see, is it Van Cliburn, or
Mickey Mantle?" These were two heroes of the time whom I had
gone on and on about and alternately wanted to be when my
father was still in our lives. I had already forgotten them.

"Neither one," I said. I was in the big front hall, where the
telephone alcove was. I could see outside through the glass door
to where William Dubinion was on his knees in the monkey grass
that bordered my mother's camellias. It was a fine situation, I
thought—staring at my mother's colored boyfriend while talking
to my father in his far-off city, living as he did. "Oh, of course,"
my father said. "Those were our last year's fascinations."

"It was longer ago," I said. My mother made a noise in the next
room. I breathed her cigarette smoke, heard the newspaper crackle.
She was listening to everything, and I didn't want to seem friendly
to my father, which I did not in any case feel. I felt he was a bastard.

"Well now, see here, ole Buck Rogers," my father continued.
"I'm calling up about an important matter to the future of mankind.
I'd like to know if you'd care to go duck hunting in the fabled
Grand Lake marsh. With me, that is. I have to come to town in
two days to settle some legal business. My ancient father had a
trusted family retainer named Renard Theriot, a disreputable old
yat. But Renard could unquestionably blow a duck call. So, I've
arranged for his son, Mr. Renard, Jr., to put us both in a blind and
call in several thousand ducks for our pleasure." My father cleared
his throat in the stagy way he always did when he talked like
this—high-falutin'. "I mean if you're not over-booked, of course,"
he said, and cleared his throat again.

"I might be," I said, and felt strange even to be talking to him.
He occasionally called me at military school, where I had to con-
verse with him in the orderly room. Naturally, he paid all my school
bills, sent an allowance, and saw to my mother's expenses. He no

doubt paid for William Dubinion's services, too, and wouldn't have cared what their true nature was. He had also conceded us the big white Greek Revival raised cottage on McKendall Street in uptown. (McKendall is our family name—*my* name. It is such a family as that.) But still it was very odd to think that your father was living with another man in a distant city, and was calling up to ask you to go duck hunting. And then to have my mother listening, sitting and smoking and reading the *States Item*, in the very next room and thinking whatever she must've been thinking. It was nearly too much for me.

And yet, I *wanted* to go duck hunting, to go by boat out into the marsh that makes up the vast, brackish tidal land south and east of our city. I had always imagined I'd go with my father when I was old enough. And I *was* old enough now, and had been taught to fire a rifle—though not a shotgun—in my school. Also, when we spoke that day, he didn't sound to me like some man who was living with another man in St. Louis. He sounded much as he always had in our normal life when I had gone to Jesuit and he had practiced law in the Hibernia Bank building, and we were a family. Something I think about my father—whose name was Boatwright McKendall and who was only forty-one years old at the time—something about him must've wanted things to be as they had been before he met his great love, Dr. Carter. Though you could also say that my father just wanted not to have it be that he couldn't do whatever he wanted; wouldn't credit that anything he did might be deemed wrong, or be the cause of hard feeling or divorce or terrible scandal such as what sees you expelled from the law firm your family started a hundred years ago and that bears your name; or that you conceivably caused the early death of your own mother from sheer disappointment. And in fact if anything he did *had* caused someone difficulty, or ruined a life, or set someone on a downward course—well, then he just largely ignored it, or agreed to pay money about it, and afterward tried his level best to go on as if the world was a smashingly great place for everyone and we could all be wonderful friends. It was the absence I mentioned before, the skill he had to not be where he exactly was, but yet to seem to be present to any but the most practiced observer. A son, for instance.

"Well, now look-it here, Mr. Buck-a-roo," my father said over the telephone from—I guessed—St. Louis. Buck is what I was called and still am, to distinguish me from him (our name is the same). And I remember becoming nervous, as if by agreeing to go with him, and to see him for the first time since he'd left from a New Year's party at the Boston Club and gone away with Dr. Carter—as if by doing these altogether natural things (going hunting) I was crossing a line, putting myself at risk. And not the risk you might think, based on low instinct, but some risk you don't know exists until you feel it in your belly, the way you'd feel running down a steep hill and at the bottom there's a deep river or a canyon, and you realize you can't stop. Disappointment was what I risked, I know now. But I wanted what I wanted and would not let such a feeling stop me.

"I want you to know," my father said, "that I've cleared all this with your mother. She thinks it's a wonderful idea."

I pictured his yellow hair, his handsome, youthful, unlined face talking animatedly into the receiver in some elegant, sunny, high-ceilinged room, beside an expensive French table with some fancy art objects on top, which he would be picking up and inspecting as he talked. In my picture he was wearing a purple smoking jacket and was happy to be doing what he was doing. "Is somebody else going?" I said.

"Oh, God no," my father said and laughed. "Like who? Francis is too refined to go duck hunting. He'd be afraid of getting his beautiful blue eyes put out. Wouldn't you, Francis?"

It shocked me to think Dr. Carter was right there in the room with him, listening. My mother, of course, was still listening to me.

"It'll just be you and me and Renard Junior," my father said, his voice going away from the receiver. I heard a second voice then, a soft, cultured voice, say something there where my father was, some possibly ironic comment about our plans. "Oh Christ," my father said in an irritated voice, a voice I didn't know any better than I knew Dr. Carter's. "Just don't say that. This is not that kind of conversation. This is Buck here." The voice said something else, and in my mind I suddenly saw Dr. Carter in a very unkind light, one I will not even describe. "Now you raise your bones at four a.m. on Thursday, Commander Rogers," my father said in his high-falutin' style. "Ducks are early risers. I'll collect you at your house. Wear your boots and your Dr. Dentons and nothing bright-colored. I'll supply our artillery."

It seemed odd to think that my father thought of the great house where we had all lived, and that his own father and grandfather had lived in since after the Civil War, as *my* house. It was not my house, I felt. The most it was was my mother's house, because she had married him in it and then taken it in their hasty divorce.

"How's school, by the way," my father said distractedly.

"How's what?" I was so surprised to be asked that. My father sounded confused, as if he'd been reading something and lost his place on a page.

"School. You know? Grades? Did you get all A's? You should. You're smart. At least you have a smart mouth."

"I hate school," I said. I had liked Jesuit where I'd had friends. But my mother had made me go away to Sandhearst because of all the upset with my father's leaving. There I wore a khaki uniform with a blue stripe down the side of my pants leg, and a stiff blue doorman's hat. I felt a fool at all times.

"Oh well, who cares," my father said. "You'll get into Harvard the same way I did."

"What way," I asked, because even at fifteen I wanted to go to Harvard.

"On looks," my father said. "That's how southerners get along. That's the great intelligence. Once you know that, the rest is pretty simple. The world *wants* to operate on looks. It only uses brains if looks aren't available. Ask your mother. It's why she married me when she shouldn't have. She'll admit it now."

"I think she's sorry about it," I said. I thought about my mother listening to half our conversation.

"Oh yes. I'm sure she is, Buck. We're all a little sorry *now*. I'll

testify to that." The other voice in the room where he was spoke
something then, again in an ironic tone. "Oh you shut up," my
father said. "You just shut up that talk and stay out of this. I'll see
you Thursday morning, son," my father said, and hung up before
I could answer.

This conversation with my father occurred on Monday, the eigh-
teenth of December, three days before we were supposed to go
duck hunting. And for the days in between then and Thursday,
my mother more or less avoided me, staying in her room upstairs
with the door closed, often with William Dubinion, or going away
in the car to her singing lessons with him driving and acting as
her chauffeur (though she rode in the front seat). It was still the
race times then, and colored people were being lynched and
trampled on and burnt out all over the southern states. And yet it
was just as likely to cause no uproar if a proper white woman
appeared in public with a Negro man in our city. There was no
rule or logic to any of it. It was New Orleans, and if you could
carry it off you did. Plus Dubinion didn't mind working in the
camellia beds in front of our house, just for the record. In truth, I
don't think he minded anything very much. He had grown up in
the cotton patch in Pointe Coupee Parish, between the rivers,
had somehow made it to music school at Wilberforce in Ohio,
been to Korea, and had played in the Army band. Later he barged
around playing the clubs and juke joints in the city for a decade
before he somehow met my mother at a society party where he
was the paid entertainment, and she was putting herself into the
public eye to make the case that when your husband abandons
you for a rich queer, life will go on.

Mr. Dubinion never addressed a great deal to me. He had arrived
in my mother's life after I had gone away to military school, and
was simply a fait accompli when I came home for Thanksgiving.
He was a tall, skinny, solemnly long yellow-faced Negro with sal-
low, moist eyes, a soft lisp and enormous, bony, pink-nailed hands
he could stretch up and down a piano keyboard. I don't think my

mother could have thought he was handsome, but possibly that didn't matter. He often parked himself in our living room, drinking scotch whiskey, smoking cigarettes and playing tunes he made up right on my grandfather's Steinway concert grand. He would hum under his breath and grunt and sway up and back like the jazzman Erroll Garner. He usually looked at me only out of the corner of his yellow Oriental-looking eye, as if neither of us really belonged in such a dignified place as my family's house. He knew, I suppose, he wouldn't be there forever and was happy for a reprieve from his usual life, and to have my mother as his temporary girlfriend. He also seemed to think I would not be there much longer either, and that we had this in common.

The one thing I remember him saying to me was during the days before I went with my father to the marsh that Christmas— Dubinion's only Christmas with us, as it turned out. I came into the great shadowy living room where the piano sat beside the front window and where my mother had established a large Christmas tree with blinking lights and a gold star on top. I had a copy of *The Inferno*, which I'd decided I would read over the holidays because the next year I hoped to leave Sandhearst and be admitted to Lawrenceville, where my father had gone before Harvard. William Dubinion was again in his place at the piano, smoking and drinking. My mother had been singing "You've Changed" in her thin, pretty soprano and had left to take a rest because singing made her fatigued. When he saw the red jacket on my book he frowned and turned sideways on the bench and crossed one long thin leg over the other so his pale hairless skin showed above his black patent leather shoes. He was wearing black trousers with a white shirt, but no socks, which was his normal dress around the house.

"That's a pretty good book," he said in his soft lisping voice, and stared right at me in a way that felt accusatory.

"It's written in Italian," I said. "It's a poem about going to hell."

"So is that where you expect to go?"

"No," I said. "I don't."

" '*Per me si va nella citta dolente. Per me si va nell'eterno dolore.*'

That's all I remember," he said, and he played a chord in the bass clef, a spooky, rumbling chord like the scary part in a movie.

I assumed he was making this up, though of course he wasn't. "What's that supposed to mean?" I said.

"Same ole," he said, his cigarette still dangling in his mouth. "Watch your step when you take a guided tour of hell. Nothing new."

"When did you read this book?" I said, standing between the two partly closed pocket doors. This man was my mother's boyfriend, her Svengali, her impresario, her seducer and corrupter (as it turned out). He was a strange, powerful man who had seen life I would never see. And I'm sure I was both afraid of him and equally afraid he would detect it, which probably made me appear superior and insolent and made him dislike me.

Dubinion looked above the keyboard at an arrangement of red pyracanthas my mother had placed there. "Well, I could say something nasty. But I won't." He took a breath and let it out heavily. "You just go ahead on with your readin'. I'll go on with my playin'." He nodded but did not look at me again. We didn't have too many more conversations after that. My mother sent him away in the winter. Once or twice he returned but, at some point, he disappeared. Though by then her life had changed in the bad way it probably had been bound to change.

The only time I remember my mother speaking directly to me during these three days, other than to inform me dinner was ready or that she was leaving at night to go out to some booking Dubinion had arranged, which I'm sure she paid him to arrange (and paid for the chance to sing as well), was on Wednesday afternoon, when I was sitting on the back porch poring over the entrance requirement information I'd had sent from Lawrenceville. I had never seen Lawrenceville, or been to New Jersey, never been farther away from New Orleans than to Yankeetown, Florida, where my military school was located in the buildings of a former Catholic hospital for sick and crazy priests. But I thought that Lawrenceville—just the word itself—could save me from the impossible situation I deemed myself to be in. To go to Lawrenceville, to travel the many train miles, and to enter whatever strange, complex place New Jersey was—all that coupled to the fact that my father had gone there and my name and background meant something—all that seemed to offer escape and relief and a future better than the one I had at home in New Orleans.

My mother had come out onto the back porch, which was glassed in and gave a prospect down onto the backyard grass. On the manicured lawn was an arrangement of four wooden Adirondack chairs and a wooden picnic table, all painted pink. The yard was completely walled in and no one but our neighbors could see—if they chose to—that William Dubinion was lying on top of the pink picnic table with his shirt off, smoking a cigarette and staring sternly up at the warm blue sky.

My mother stood for a while watching him. She was wearing a pair of men's white silk pajamas, and her voice was husky. I'm sure she was already taking the drugs that would eventually disrupt her reasoning. She was holding a glass of milk, which was probably not just milk but milk with gin or scotch or something in it to ease whatever she felt terrible about.

"What a splendid idea to go hunting with your father," she said sarcastically, as if we were continuing a conversation we'd been having earlier, though in fact we had said nothing about it, despite my wanting to talk about it, and despite thinking I ought to not go and hoping she wouldn't permit it. "Do you even own a gun?" she asked, though she knew I didn't. She knew what I did and didn't own. I was fifteen.

"He's going to give me one," I said.

She glanced at me where I was sitting, but her expression didn't change. "I just wonder what it's like to take up with another man of your social standing," my mother said as she ran her hand through her hair, which was newly colored ash-blond and done in a very neat bob, which had been Dubinion's idea. My mother's father had been a pharmacist on Prytania Street and had done well catering to the needs of rich families like the McKendalls. She had gone to Newcombe, married *up* and come to be at ease with the society my father introduced her into (though I have never thought she really cared about New Orleans society one way or the other—unlike my father, who cared about it enough to spit in its face).

"I always assume," she said, "that these escapades usually involve someone on a lower rung. A stevedore, or a towel attendant at your club." She was watching Dubinion. He must've qualified in her mind as a lower-rung personage. She and my father had been married twenty years, and at age thirty-nine she had taken Dubinion into her life to wipe out any trace of the way she had previously conducted her affairs. I realize now, as I tell this, that she and Dubinion had just been in bed together, and he was enjoying the dreamy aftermath by lying half-naked out on our picnic table while she roamed around the house in her pajamas alone and had to end up talking to me. It's sad to think that in a little more than a year, when I was just getting properly adjusted at Lawrenceville, she would be gone. Thinking of her now is like hearing the dead speak.

"But I don't hold it against your father. The *man* part anyway," my mother said. "Other things, of course, I do." She turned, then stepped over and took a seat on the striped-cushion wicker chair beside mine. She set her milk down and took my hand in her cool hands, and held it in her lap against her silky leg. "What if I became a very good singer and had to go on the road and play in Chicago and New York and possibly Paris? Would that be all right? You could come and see me perform. You could wear your school uniform." She pursed her lips and looked back at the yard, where William Dubinion was laid out on the picnic table like a pharaoh.

"I wouldn't enjoy that," I said. I didn't lie to her. She was going out at night and humiliating herself and making me embarrassed and afraid. I wasn't going to say I thought this was all fine. It was a disaster and soon would be proved so.

"No?" she said. "You wouldn't come see me perform in the *Quartier Latin*?"

"No," I said. "I never would."

"Well." She let go of my hand, crossed her legs and propped her chin on her fist. "I'll have to live with that. Maybe you're right." She looked around at her glass of milk as if she'd forgotten where she'd left it.

"What other things do you hold against him?" I asked, referring to my father. The *man* part seemed enough to me.

"Oh," my mother said, "are we back to him now? Well, let's just say I hold his entire self against him. And not for my sake, certainly, but for yours. He could've kept things together here. Other men do. It's perfectly all right to have a lover of whatever category. So, he's no worse than a lot of other men. But that's what I hold against him. I hadn't really thought about it before. He fails to be any better than most men would be. That's a capital offense in marriage. You'll have to grow up some more before you understand that. But you will."

She picked up her glass of milk, rose, pulled her loose white pajamas up around her scant waist and walked back inside the house. In a while I heard a door slam, then her voice and Dubinion's, and I went back to preparing myself for Lawrenceville and saving my life. Though I think I knew what she meant. She meant my father did only what pleased him, and believed that doing so permitted others the equal freedom to do what they wanted. Only that isn't how the world works, as my mother's life and mine were living proof. Other people affect you. It's really no more complicated than that.

My father sat slumped in the bow of the empty skiff at the end of the plank dock. It was the hour before light. He was facing the silent, barely moving surface of Bayou Baptiste, beyond which (though I couldn't see it) was the vacant marshland that stretched as far as the Mississippi River itself, west of us and miles away. My father was bareheaded and seemed to be wearing a tan raincoat. I had not seen him in a year.

The place we were was called Reggio dock, and it was only a rough little boat camp from which fishermen took their charters out in the summer months, and duck hunters like us departed into the marsh by way of the bayou, and where a few shrimpers stored their big boats and nets when their season was off. I had never been to it, but I knew about it from boys at Jesuit who came here with their fathers, who leased parts of the marsh and had built wooden blinds and stayed in flimsy shacks and stilt-houses along the single-lane road down from Violet, Louisiana. It was a famous place to me in the way that hunting camps can be famously mysterious and have a danger about them, and represent the good and the unknown that so rarely combine in life.

My father had not come to get me as he'd said he would. Instead a yellow taxi with a light on top had stopped in front of our house and a driver came to the door and rang and told me that Mr. McKendall had sent him to drive me to Reggio—which was in St. Bernard Parish, and for all its wildness not really very far from the Garden District.

"And is that really you?" my father said from in the boat, turning around, after I had stood on the end of the dock for a minute waiting for him to notice me. A small stunted-looking man with a large square head and wavy black hair and wearing coveralls was hauling canvas bags full of duck decoys down to the boat. Around the camp there was activity. Cars were arriving out of the darkness, their taillights brightening. Men's voices were heard laughing. Someone had brought a dog that barked. And it was not cold, in spite of being the week before Christmas. The morning air felt heavy and velvety, and a light fog had risen off the bayou, which smelled as if oil or gasoline had been let into it. The mist clung to my hands and face, and made my hair under my cap feel soiled. "I'm sorry about the taxi ride," my father said from the bow of the aluminum skiff. He was smiling in an exaggerated way. His teeth were very white, though he looked thin. His pale, fine hair was cut shorter and seemed yellower than I remembered it, and had a wider part on the side. It was odd, but I remember thinking—standing looking down at my father—that if he'd had an older brother, this would be what that brother would look like. Not good. Not happy or wholesome. And of course I realized he was drinking, even at that hour. The man in the coveralls brought down three shotgun cases and laid them in the boat. "This little *yat* rascal is Mr. Rey-nard Theriot, Junior," my father said, motioning at the small, wavy-haired man. "There're some people, in New Orleans, who know him as Fabrice, or the Fox. Or Fabree-chay. Take your pick."

I didn't know what all this meant. But Renard Junior paused after setting the guns in the boat and looked at my father in an unfriendly way. He had a heavy, rucked brow, and even in the poor light his dark complexion made his eyes seem small and penetrating. Under his coveralls he was wearing a red shirt with tiny gold stars on it.

"Fabree-chay is a duck caller of surprising subtlety," my father said too loudly. "Among, that is to say, his other talents. Isn't that right, Mr. Fabrice? Did you say hello to my son, Buck, who's a very fine boy?" My father flashed his big white-toothed smile around at me, and I could tell he was taunting Renard Junior, who did not speak to me but continued his job to load the boat. I wondered how much he knew about my father, and what he thought if he knew everything.

"I couldn't locate my proper hunting attire," my father said, and looked down at the open front of his topcoat. He pulled it apart, and I could see he was wearing a tuxedo with a pink shirt, a bright-red bow tie and a pink carnation. He was also wearing white-and-black spectator shoes which were wrong for the Christmas season and in any case would be ruined once we were in the marsh. "I had them stored in the garage at mother's," he said, as if talking to himself. "This morning quite early I found I'd lost the key." He looked at me, still smiling. "You have on very good brown things," he said. I had just worn my khaki pants and shirt from school—minus the brass insignias—and black tennis shoes and an old canvas jacket and cap I found in a closet. This was not exactly duck hunting in the way I'd heard about from my school friends. My father had not even been to bed, and had been up drinking and having a good time. Probably he would've preferred staying wherever he'd been, with people who were his friends now.

"What important books have you been reading?" my father asked for some reason, from down in the skiff. He looked around as a boat full of hunters and the big black Labrador dog I'd heard barking motored slowly past us down Bayou Baptiste. Their guide had a sealed-beam light he was shining out on the water's misted surface. They were going to shoot ducks. Though I couldn't see where, since beyond the opposite bank of the bayou was only a flat black treeless expanse that ended in darkness. I couldn't tell where ducks might be, or which way the city lay, or even which way east was.

"I'm reading *The Inferno*," I said, and felt self-conscious for saying "Inferno" on a boat dock.

"Oh, that," my father said. "I believe that's Mr. Fabrice's favorite book. Canto Five: those who've lost the power of restraint. I think you should read Yeats's autobiography, though. I've been reading it in St. Louis. Yeats says in a letter to his friend the great John Synge that we should unite stoicism, asceticism and ecstasy. I think that would be good, don't you?" My father seemed to be assured and challenging, as if he expected me to know what he meant by these things, and who Yeats was, and Synge. But I didn't know. And I didn't care to pretend I did to a drunk wearing a tuxedo and a pink carnation, sitting in a duck boat.

"I don't know them. I don't know what those things are," I said and felt terrible to have to admit it.

"They're the perfect balance for life. All I've been able to arrange are two, however. Maybe one and a half. And how's your mother?" My father began buttoning his overcoat.

"She's fine," I lied.

"I understand she's taken on new household help." He didn't look up, just kept fiddling with his buttons.

"She's learning to sing," I said, leaving Dubinion out of it.

"Oh well," my father said, getting the last button done and brushing off the front of his coat. "She always had a nice little voice. A sweet church voice." He looked up at me and smiled as if he knew I didn't like what he was saying and didn't care.

"She's gotten much better now." I thought about going home right then, though of course there was no way to get home.

"I'm sure she has. Now get us going here, Fabree-chay," my father said suddenly.

Renard was behind me on the dock. Other boats full of hunters had already departed. I could see their lights flicking this way and that over the water, heading away from where we were still tied up, the soft putt-putts of their outboards muffled by the mist. I stepped down into the boat and sat on the middle thwart. But when Renard scooted into the stern, the boat tilted dramatically to one side just as my father was taking a long, uninterrupted drink out of a pint bottle he'd had stationed between his feet, out of sight.

"Don't go fallin' in, baby," Renard said to my father from the rear of the boat as he was giving the motor cord a strong pull. He had a deep, mellow voice, tinged with sarcasm. "I don't think nobody'll pull ya'll out."

My father, I think, didn't hear him. But I heard him. And I thought he was certainly right.

I cannot tell you how we went in Renard Junior's boat that morning, only that it was out into the dark marshy terrain that is the Grand Lake and is in Plaquemines Parish and seems the very end of the earth. Later, when the sun rose and the mist was extinguished, what I saw was a great surface of gray-brown water broken by low, yellow-grass islands where it smelled like tar and vegetation decomposing, and where the mud was blue-black and adhesive and rank-smelling. Though on the horizon, illuminated by the morning light, were the visible buildings of the city—the Hibernia Bank where my father's office had been—nudged just above the earth's curve. It was strange to feel so outside of civilization, and yet to see it so clearly.

Of course at the beginning it was dark. Renard Junior, being small, could stand up in the rear of the skimming boat, and shine

his own light over me in the middle and my father hunched in the
boat's bow. My father's blond hair shone brightly and stayed back
off his face in the breeze. We went for a ways down the bayou,
then turned and went slowly under a wooden bridge and then
out along a wide canal bordered by swamp hummocks where
white herons were roosting and the first ducks of those we hoped
to shoot went swimming away from the boat out of the light,
suddenly springing up into the shadows and disappearing. My
father pointed at these startled ducks, made a gun out of his fingers and jerked one-two-three silent shots as the skiff hurtled
along through the marsh.

Naturally, I was thrilled to be there—even in my hated military
school clothes, with my drunk father dressed in his tuxedo and
the little monkey that Renard was, operating our boat. I believed,
though, that this had to be some version of what the real thing
felt like—hunting ducks with your father and a guide—and that
anytime you went, even under the most perfect circumstances,
there would always be something imperfect that would leave you
feeling not exactly good. The trick was to get used to that feeling,
or risk missing what little happiness there really was.

At a certain point when we were buzzing along the dark slick
surface of the lake, Renard Junior abruptly backed off on the
motor, cut his beam light, turned the motor hard left, and let the
wake carry us straight into an island of marsh grass I hadn't made
out. Though I immediately saw it wasn't simply an island but was
also a grass-fronted blind built of wood palings driven into the
mud, with peach crates lined up inside where hunters would sit
and not be seen by flying ducks. As the boat nosed into the grass
bank, Renard, now in a pair of hip waders, was out heeling us
farther up onto the solider mud. "It's duck heaven out here," my
father said, then densely coughed, his young man's smooth face
becoming stymied by a gasp, so that he had to shake his head and
turn away.

"He means it's the place where ducks *go* to heaven," Renard
said. It was the first thing he'd said to me, and I noticed now how
much his voice didn't sound much like the *yat* voices I'd heard

and that supposedly sound like citizens of New York or Boston—
cities of the North. Renard's voice was cultivated and mellow and
inflected, I thought, like some uptown funeral director's, or a
florist. It seemed to be a voice better suited to a different body
than the muscular, gnarly little man up to his thighs just then in
filmy, strong-smelling water, and wearing a long wavy white-
trash hairstyle.

"When do the ducks come?" I said, only to have something to
say back to him. My father was recovering himself, spitting in the
water and taking another drink off his bottle.

Renard laughed a little private laugh he must've thought my
father would hear. "When they ready to come. Just like you and
me," he said, then began dragging out the big canvas decoy sacks
and seemed to quit noticing me entirely.

Renard had a wooden pirogue hidden back in the thick grass, and
when he had covered our skiff with a blanket made of straw mats,
he used the pirogue to set out decoys as the sky lightened, though
where we were was still dark. My father and I sat side by side on
the peach boxes and watched him tossing out the weighted duck
bodies to make two groups in front of our blind with a space of
open water in between. I could begin to see now that what I'd
imagined the marsh to look like was different from how it was.
For one thing, the expanse of water around us was smaller than I
had thought. Other grass islands gradually came into view a quarter mile off, and a line of green trees appeared in the distance,
closer than I'd expected. I heard a siren, and then music that
must've come from a car at the Reggio dock, and eventually there
was the sun, a white disk burning behind the mist, and from a
part of the marsh opposite from where I expected it. In truth,
though, all of these things—these confusing and disorienting and
reversing features of where I was—seemed good, since they made
me feel placed, so that in time I forgot the ways I was feeling
about the day and about life and about my future, none of which
had seemed so good.

Inside the blind, which was only ten feet long and four feet wide and had spent shells and candy wrappers and cigarette butts on the planks, my father displayed the pint bottle of whiskey, which was three-quarters empty. He sat for a time, once we were arranged on our crates, and said nothing to me or to Renard when he had finished distributing the decoys and had climbed into the blind to await the ducks. Something seemed to have come over my father, a great fatigue or ill feeling or a preoccupying thought that removed him from the moment and from what we were supposed to be doing there. Renard unsheathed the guns from their cases. Mine was the old A. H. Fox twenty-gauge double gun, that was heavy as lead and that I had seen in my grandmother's house many times and had handled enough to know the particulars of without ever shooting it. My grandmother had called it her "ladies gun," and she had shot it when she was young and had gone hunting with my father's father. Renard gave me six cartridges, and I loaded the chambers and kept the gun muzzle pointed up from between my knees as we watched the silver sky and waited for the ducks to try our decoys.

My father did not load up, but sat slumped against the wooden laths, with his shotgun leaned on the matted front of the blind. After a while of sitting and watching the sky and seeing only a pair of ducks operating far out of range, we heard the other hunters on the marsh begin to take their shots, sometimes several at a terrible burst. I could then see that two other blinds were across the pond we were set down on—three hundred yards from us, but visible when my eyes adjusted to the light and the distinguishing irregularities of the horizon. A single duck I'd watched fly across the sky at first flared when the other hunters shot, but then abruptly collapsed and fell straight down, and I heard a dog bark and a man's voice, high-pitched and laughing through the soft air. "Hoo, hoo, hoo, lawd oooh lawdy," the man's voice said very distinctly in spite of the distance. "Dat mutha-scootcha was all the way to Terre Bonne Parish when I popped him." Another man laughed. It all seemed very close to us, even though we hadn't shot and were merely scanning the milky skies.

"Coon-ass bastards," my father said. "Jumpin' the shooting time. They have to do that. It's genetic." He seemed to be addressing no one, just sitting leaned against the blind's sides, waiting.

"Already *been* shootin' time," Renard Junior said, his gaze fixed upwards. He was wearing two wooden duck calls looped to his neck on leather thongs. He had yet to blow one of the calls, but I wanted him to, wanted to see a V of ducks turn and veer and come into our decoy-set, the way I felt they were supposed to.

"Now is that so, Mr. Grease-Fabrice, Mr. Fabree-chay." My father wiped the back of his hand across his nose and up into his blond hair, then closed his eyes and opened them wide, as if he was trying to fasten his attention to what we were doing, but did not find it easy. The blind smelled sour but also smelled of his whiskey, and of whatever ointment Renard Junior used on his thick hair. My father had already gotten his black-and-white shoes muddy and scratched, and mud on his tuxedo pants and his pink shirt and even onto his forehead. He was an unusual-looking figure to be where he was. He seemed to have been dropped out of an airplane on the way to a party.

Renard Junior did not answer back to my father calling him "Grease-Fabrice," but it was clear he couldn't have liked a name like that. I wondered why he would even be here to be talked to that way. Though of course there was a reason. Few things in the world are actually mysterious. Most things have disappointing explanations somewhere behind them, no matter how strange they seem at first.

After a while, Renard produced a package of cigarettes, put one in his mouth, but did not light it—just held it between his damp lips, which were big and sensuous. He was already an odd-looking man, with his star shirt, his head too big for his body—a man who was probably in his forties and had just missed being a dwarf.

"Now there's the true sign of the *yat*," my father said. He was leaning on his shotgun, concentrating on Renard Junior. "Notice the unlit cigarette pooched out the front of the too expressive mouth. If you drive the streets of Chalmette, Louisiana, sonny, you'll see men and women and children who're all actually blood-related to Mr. Fabrice, standing in their little postage-stamp yards wearing hip boots with unlighted Picayunes in their mouths just like you see now. *Ecce Homo.*"

Renard Junior unexpectedly opened his mouth with his cigarette somehow stuck to the top of his big ugly purple tongue. He cast an eye at my father, leaning forward against his shotgun, smirking, then flicked the cigarette backward into his mouth and swallowed it without changing his expression. Then he looked at me, sitting between him and my father, and smiled. His teeth were big and brown-stained. It was a lewd act. I didn't know how it was lewd, but I was sure that it was.

"Pay no attention to him," my father said. "These are people we have to deal with. French acts, carny types, brutes. Now I want you to tell me about yourself, Buck. Are there any impossible situations you find yourself in these days? I've become expert in impossible situations lately." My father shifted his spectator shoes on the muddly floor boards, so that suddenly his shotgun, which was a beautiful Beretta over-under with silver inlays, slipped and fell right across my feet with a loud clatter—the barrels ending up pointed right at Renard Junior's ankles. My father did not even try to grab the gun as it fell.

"Pick that up right now," he said to me in an angry voice, as if I'd dropped his gun. But I did. I picked the gun up and handed it back to him, and he pinned it to the side of the blind with his knee. Something about this almost violent act of putting his gun where he wanted it reminded me of my father before a year ago. He had always been a man for abrupt moves and changes of attitude, unexpected laughter and strong emotion. I had not always liked it, but I'd decided that was what men did and accepted it.

"Do you ever hope to travel?" my father said, ignoring his other question, looking up at the sky as if he'd just realized he was in a duck blind and for a second at least was involved in the things we were doing. His topcoat had sagged open again, and his tuxedo front was visible, smudged with mud. "You should," he said before I could answer.

Renard Junior began to blow on his duck call then, and crouched forward in front of his peach crate. And because he did, I crouched in front of mine, and my father—noticing us—squatted on his knees too and averted his face downwards. And after a few moments of Renard calling, I peered over the top of the straw wall and could see two black-colored ducks flying right in front of our blind, low and over our decoys. Renard Junior changed his calling sound to a broken-up cackle, and when he did the ducks swerved to the side and began winging hard away from us, almost as if they could fly backwards.

"You let 'em see you," Renard said in a hoarse whisper. "They seen that white face."

Crouched beside him, I could smell his breath—a smell of cigarettes and sour meat that must've tasted terrible in his mouth.

"Call, goddamn it, Fabrice," my father said then—shouted, really. I twisted around to see him, and he was right up on his two feet, his gun to his shoulder, his topcoat lying on the floor so that he was just in his tuxedo. I looked out at our decoys and saw four small ducks just cupping their wings and gliding toward the water where Renard had left it open. Their wings made a pinging sound.

Renard Junior immediately started his cackle call again, still crouched, his face down, in front of his peach crate. "Shoot 'em, Buck, shoot 'em," my father shouted, and I stood up and got my heavy gun to my shoulder and, without meaning to, fired both barrels, pulled both triggers at once, just as my father (who at some moment had loaded his gun) also fired one then the other of his barrels at the ducks, which had briefly touched the water but were already heading off, climbing up and up as the others had, going backwards away from us, their necks outstretched, their eyes—or so it seemed to me who had never shot at a duck—wide and frightened.

My two barrels, fired together, had hit one of Renard's decoys and shattered it to several pieces. My father's two shots had hit, it seemed, nothing at all, though one of the gray paper wads drifted back toward the water while the four ducks grew small in the distance until they were shot at by the other hunters across the pond and two of them dropped.

"That was completely terrible," my father said, standing at the end of the blind in his tuxedo, his blond hair slicked close down on his head in a way to make him resemble a child. He instantly broke his gun open and replaced the spent shells with new ones out of his tuxedo-coat pocket. He seemed no longer drunk, but completely engaged and sharp-minded, except for having missed everything.

"Y'all shot like a coupla 'ole grandmas," Renard said, disgusted, shaking his head.

"Fuck you," my father said calmly, and snapped his beautiful Italian gun shut in a menacing way. His blue eyes widened, then narrowed, and I believed he might point his gun at Renard Junior. White spit had collected in the corners of his mouth, and his face had gone quickly from looking engaged to looking pale and damp and outraged. "If I need your services for other than calling, I'll speak to your owner," he said.

"Speak to yo' own owner, snooky," Renard Junior said, and when he said this he looked at me, raised his eyebrows and smiled in a way that pushed his heavy lips forward in a cruel, simian way.

"That's *enough*," my father said loudly. "That *is* absolutely enough." I thought he might reach past me and strike Renard in the mouth he was smiling through. But he didn't. He just slumped back on his peach crate, faced forward and held his newly reloaded shotgun between his knees. His white-and-black shoes were on top of his overcoat and ruined. His little pink carnation lay smudged in the greasy mud.

I could hear my father's hard breathing. Something had happened that wasn't good, but I didn't know what. Something had risen up in him, some force of sudden rebellion, but it had been defeated before it could come out and act. Or so it seemed to me. Silent events, of course, always occur between our urges and our actions. But I didn't know what event had occurred, only that one had, and I could feel it. My father seemed tired now, and to be considering something. Renard Junior was no longer calling ducks, but was just sitting at his end staring at the misty sky, which was turning a dense, warm luminous red at the horizon, as if a fire was burning at the far edge of the marsh. Shooting in the other blinds had stopped. A small plane inched across the sky. I heard a dog bark. I saw a fish roll in the water in front of the blind. I thought I saw an alligator. Mosquitoes appeared, which is never unusual in Louisiana.

"What do you do in St. Louis," I said to my father. It was the thing I wanted to know.

"Well," my father said thoughtfully. He sniffed, "Golf. I play quite a bit of golf. Francis has a big house across from a wonderful park. I've taken it up." He felt his forehead, where a mosquito had landed on a black mud stain that was there. He rubbed it and looked at his fingertips.

"Will you practice law up there?"

"Oh lord no," he said and shook his head and sniffed again. "They requested me to leave the firm here. You know that."

"Yes," I said. His breathing was easier. His face seemed calm. He looked handsome and youthful. Whatever silent event that had occurred had passed off of him, and he seemed settled about it. I thought I might talk about going to Lawrenceville. Duck blinds were where people had such conversations. Though it would've been better, I thought, if we'd been alone, and didn't have Renard Junior to overhear us. "I'd like to ask you . . ." I began.

"Tell me about your girlfriend situation," my father interrupted me. "Tell me the whole story there."

I knew what he meant by that, but there wasn't a story. I was in military school, and there were only other boys present, which was not a story to me. If I went to Lawrenceville, I knew there could be a story. Girls would be nearby. "There isn't any story . . ." I started to say, and he interrupted me again.

"Let me give you some advice." He was rubbing his index finger around the muzzle of his Italian shotgun. "Always try to imagine how you're going to feel *after* you fuck somebody *before* you fuck somebody. *Comprendes?* There's the key to everything. History. Morality. Philosophy. You'll save yourself a lot of misery." He nodded as if this wisdom had just become clear to him all over again. "Maybe you already know that," he said. He looked above the front of the blind where the sky had turned to fire, then looked at me in a way to seem honest and to say (so I thought) that he liked me. "Do you ever find yourself saying things in conversations that you absolutely don't believe?" He reached with his two fingers and plucked a mosquito off my cheek. "Do you?" he said distractedly. "Do ya, do ya?"

I thought of conversations I'd had with Dubinion, and some I'd had with my mother. They were that kind of conversation—memorable if only for the things I didn't say. But what I said to my father was "no."

"Convenience must not matter to you much then," he said in a friendly way.

"I don't know if it does or not," I said because I didn't know what convenience meant. It was a word I'd never had a cause to use.

"Well, convenience matters to me very much. Too much, I think," my father said. I, of course, thought of my mother's assessment of him—that he was not better than most men. I assumed that caring too much for convenience led you there, and that my fault in later life could turn out to be the same one because he was my father. But I decided, at that moment, to see to it that my fault in life would not be his.

"There's one ducky duck," my father said. He was watching the sky and seemed bemused. "Fabrice, would you let me apologize for acting ugly to you, and ask you to call? How generous that would be of you. How nice." My father smiled strangely at Renard Junior, who I'd believed to be brooding.

And Renard Junior did call. I didn't see a duck, but when my father squatted down on the dirty planking where his topcoat was smeared and our empty shell casings were littered, I did too, and turned my face toward the floor. I could hear my father's breathing, could smell the whiskey on his breath, could see his pale wet knuckles supporting him unsteadily on the boards, could even smell his hair, which was warm and musty smelling. It was as close as I would come to him. And I understood that it would have to do, might even be the best there could be.

"Wait now, wait on 'im," my father said, hunkered on the wet planks, but looking up out of the tops of his eyes. He put his fingers on my hand to make me be still. I still had not seen anything. Renard Junior was blowing the long, high-pitched rasping call, followed by short bursts that made him grunt heavily down in his throat, and then the long highball call again. "Not quite yet," my father whispered. "Not yet. Wait on him." I turned my face sideways to see up, my eyes cut to the side to find *something*. "No," my father said, close to my ear. "Don't look up." I inhaled deeply and breathed in all the smells again that came off my father. And then Renard Junior said loudly, "Go on, Jesus! Go on! Shoot 'im. Shoot now. Whatchyouwaitin'on?"

I just stood up, then, without knowing what I would see, and brought my shotgun up to my shoulder before I really looked. And what I saw, coming low over the decoys, its head turning to the side and peering down at the brown water, was one lone duck. I could distinguish its green head and dark bullet eyes in the haze-burnt morning light and could hear its wings pinging. I didn't think it saw me or heard my father and Renard Junior shouting, "Shoot, shoot, oh Jesus, shoot 'im Buck." Because when my face and gun barrel appeared above the front of the blind, it didn't change its course or begin the backward-upward maneuvering I'd already seen, which was its way to save itself. It just kept looking down and flying slowly and making its noise in the reddened air above the water and all of us.

And as I found the duck over my barrel tops, my eyes opened wide in the manner I knew was the way you shot such a gun, and yet I thought: it's only one duck. There may not be any others. What's the good of one duck shot down? In my dreams there'd been hundreds of ducks, and my father and I shot them so that they fell out of the sky like rain, and how many there were would not have mattered because we were doing it together. But I was doing this alone, and one duck seemed wrong, and to matter in a way a hundred ducks wouldn't have, at least if I was going to be the one to shoot. So that what I did was not shoot and lowered my gun.

"What's wrong?" my father said from the floor just below me, still on all fours in his wrecked tuxedo, his face turned down expecting a gun's report. The lone duck was past us now and out of range.

I looked at Renard Junior, who was seated on his peach crate, small enough not to need to hunker. He looked at me, and made a strange face, a face I'd never seen but will never forget. He smiled and began to bat his eyelids in fast succession, and then he raised his two hands, palms up to the level of his eyes, as if he expected something to fall down into them. I don't know what that gesture meant, though I have thought of it often—sometimes in the middle of a night when my sleep is disturbed. Derision, I think; or possibly it meant he merely didn't know why I hadn't shot the duck and was awaiting my answer. Or possibly it was something else, some sign whose significance I would never know. Fabrice was a strange man. No one would've doubted it.

My father had gotten up onto his muddy feet by then, although with difficulty. He had his shotgun to his shoulder, and he shot once at the duck that was then only a speck in the sky. And of course it did not fall. He stared for a time with his gun to his shoulder until the speck of wings disappeared.

"What the hell happened?" he said, his face red from kneeling and bending. "Why didn't you shoot that duck?" His mouth was opened into a frown. I could see his white teeth, and one hand was gripping the sides of the blind. He seemed in jeopardy of falling down. He was, after all, still drunk. His blond hair shone in the misty light.

"I wasn't close enough," I said.

My father looked around again at the decoys as if they could prove something. "Wasn't close enough?" he said. "I heard the damn duck's wings. How close do you need it? You've got a gun there."

"You couldn't hear it," I said.

"Couldn't hear it?" he said. His eyes rose off my face and found Renard Junior behind me. His mouth took on an odd expression. The scowl left his features, and he suddenly looked amused, the damp corners of his mouth revealing a small, flickering smile I was sure was derision, and represented his view that I had balked at a crucial moment, made a mistake, and therefore didn't have to be treated so seriously. This from a man who had left my mother and me to fend for ourselves while he disported without dignity or shame out of sight of those who knew him.

"You don't know anything," I suddenly said. "You're only . . ." And I don't know what I was about to say. Something terrible and hurtful. Something to strike out at him and that I would've regretted forever. So I didn't say any more, didn't finish it. Though I did that for myself, I think now, and not for him, and in order that I not have to regret more than I already regretted. I didn't really care what happened to him, to be truthful. Didn't and don't.

And then my father said, the insinuating smile still on his handsome lips, "Come on, sonny boy. You've still got some growing up to do, I see." He reached for me and put his hand behind my neck, which was rigid in anger and loathing. And without seeming to notice, he pulled me to him and kissed me on my forehead, and put his arms around me and held me until whatever he was thinking had passed and it was time for us to go back to the dock.

My father lived thirty years after that morning in December, on the Grand Lake, in 1961. By any accounting he lived a whole life after that. And I am not interested in the whys and why nots of what he did and didn't do, or in causing that day to seem life-changing for me, because it surely wasn't. Life had already changed. That morning represented just the first working out of particulars I would evermore observe. Like my father, I am a lawyer. And the law is a calling which teaches you that most of life is about adjustments, the seatings and reseatings we perform to accommodate events occurring outside our control and over which we might not have sought control in the first place. So that when we are tempted, as I was for an instant in the duck blind, or as I was through all those thirty years, to let myself become preoccupied and angry with my father, or when I even see a man who reminds me of

him, stepping into some building in a seersucker suit and a bright
bow tie, I try to realize again that it is best just to offer myself
release and to realize I am feeling anger all alone, and that there is
no redress. We want it. Life can be seen to be about almost nothing else sometimes than our wish for redress. As a lawyer who was
the son of a lawyer and the grandson of another, I know this. And
I also know not to expect it.

For the record—because I never saw him again—my father
went back to St. Louis and back to the influence of Dr. Carter,
who I believe was as strong a character as my father was weak.
They lived on there for a time until (I was told) Dr. Carter quit
the practice of medicine entirely. Then they left America and
traveled first to Paris and after that to a bright white stucco house
near Antibes, which I in fact once saw, completely by accident,
on a side tour of a business trip, and somehow knew to be his
abode the instant I came to it, as though I had dreamed it—but
then couldn't get away from it fast enough, though they were
both dead and buried by then.

Once, in our newspaper, early in the nineteen-seventies, I saw
my father pictured in the society section amid a group of smiling,
handsome crew-cut men, once again wearing tuxedos and red
sashes of some foolish kind, and holding champagne glasses. They
were men in their fifties, all of whom seemed, by their smiles, to
want very badly to be younger.

Seeing this picture reminded me that in the days after my
father had taken me to the marsh, and events had ended not altogether happily, I had prayed for one of the few times, but also for
the last time, in my life. And I prayed quite fervently for a while
and in spite of all, that he would come back to us and that our life
would begin to be as it had been. And then I prayed that he
would die, and die in a way I would never know about, and his
memory would cease to be a memory, and all would be erased.
My mother died a rather sudden, pointless and unhappy death not
long afterward, and many people including myself attributed her
death to him. In time, my father came and went in and out of
New Orleans, just as if neither of us had ever known each other.

And so the memory was not erased. Yet because I can tell this now, I believe that I have gone beyond it, and on to a life better than one might've imagined for me. Of course, I think of life—mine—as being part of their aftermath, part of the residue of all they risked and squandered and ignored. Such a sense of life's connectedness can certainly occur, and conceivably it occurs in some places more than in others. But it is survivable. I am the proof, inasmuch as since that time, I have never imagined my life in any way other than as it is.

from INDEPENDENCE DAY

My clients the Markhams, whom I'm meeting at nine-fifteen, are from tiny Island Pond, Vermont, in the far northeast corner, and their dilemma is now the dilemma of many Americans. Sometime in the indistinct Sixties, each with a then-spouse, they departed unpromising flatlander lives (Joe was a trig teacher in Aliquippa, Phyllis a plump, copper-haired, slightly bulgy-eyed housewife from the D.C. area) and trailered up to Vermont in search of a sunnier, less predictable *Weltansicht.* Time and fate soon took their unsurprising courses: spouses wandered off with other people's spouses; their kids got busily into drugs, got pregnant, got married, then disappeared to California or Canada or Tibet or Wiesbaden, West Germany. Joe and Phyllis each floated around uneasily for two or three years in intersecting circles of neighborhood friends and off-again, on-again *Weltansicht*s, taking classes, starting new degrees, trying new mates and eventually giving in to what had been available and obvious all along: true and eyes-open love for each other. Almost immediately, Joe Markham—who's a stout, aggressive little bullet-eyed, short-armed, hairy-backed Bob Hoskins type of about my age, who played nose guard for the Aliquippa Fighting Quips and who's not obviously "creative"—started having good luck with the pots and sand-cast sculptures in abstract forms he'd been making, projects he'd only fiddled around with before and that his first wife, Melody, had made vicious fun of before moving back to Beaver Falls, leaving him alone with his regular job for the Department of Social Services. Phyllis meanwhile began realizing she, in fact, had an untapped genius for designing slick, lush-looking pamphlets on fancy paper she could actually make herself (she designed Joe's first big mailing). And before they knew it they were shipping Joe's art and Phyllis's sumptuous descriptive booklets all over hell. Joe's pots began showing up in big department stores in Colorado and California and as expensive specialty items in ritzy mail-order catalogs, and to both their amazement were winning prizes at prestigious crafts fairs the two of them didn't even have time to attend, they were so busy.

Pretty soon they'd built themselves a big new house with cantilevered cathedral ceilings and a hand-laid hearth and chimney, using stones off the place, the whole thing hidden at the end of a private wooded road behind an old apple orchard. They started teaching free studio classes to small groups of motivated students at Lyndon State as a way of giving something back to the community that had nurtured them through assorted rough periods, and eventually they had another child, Sonja, named for one of Joe's Croatian relatives.

Both of them, of course, realized they'd been lucky as snake charmers, given the mistakes they'd made and all that had gone kaflooey in their lives. Though neither did they view "the Vermont life" as necessarily the ultimate destination. Each of them had pretty harsh opinions about professional dropouts and trust-fund hippies who were nothing more than nonproducers in a society in need of new ideas. "I didn't want to wake up one morning," Joe said to me the first day they came in the office, looking like bedraggled, wide-eyed missionaries, "and be a fifty-five-year-old asshole with a bandanna and a goddamn earring and nothing to talk about but how Vermont's all fucked up since a lot of people just like me showed up to ruin it."

Sonja needed to go to a better school, they decided, so she could eventually get into an even better school. Their previous batch of kids had all trooped off in serapes and Sorels and down jackets to the local schools, and that hadn't worked out very well. Joe's oldest boy, Seamus, had already done time for armed robbery, toured three detoxes and was learning-disabled; a girl, Dot, got married to a Hell's Commando at sixteen and hadn't been heard from in a long time. Another boy, Federico, Phyllis's son, was making the Army a career. And so, based on these sobering but instructive experiences, they understandably wanted something more promising for little Sonja.

They therefore made a study of where schools were best and the lifestyle pretty congenial, and where they could have some access to NYC markets for Joe's work, and Haddam came at the top in every category. Joe blanketed the area with letters and résumés and found a job working on the production end for a new textbook publisher, Leverage Books in Hightstown, a job that took advantage of his math and computer background. Phyllis found out there were several paper groups in town, and that they could go on making pots and sculptures in a studio Joe would build or renovate or rent, and could keep sending his work out with Phyllis's imaginative brochures, yet embark on a whole new adventure where schools were good, streets safe and everything basked in a sunny drug-free zone.

Their first visit was in March—which they correctly felt was when "everything" came on the market. They wanted to take their time, survey the whole spectrum, work out a carefully reasoned decision, make an offer on a house by May first and be out watering the lawn by the 4th. They realized, of course, as Phyllis Markham told me, that they'd probably need to "scale back" some. The world had changed in many ways while they were plopped down in Vermont. Money wasn't worth as much, and you needed more of it. Though all told they felt they'd had a good life in Vermont, saved some money over the past few years and wouldn't have done anything—divorce, wandering alone at loose ends, kid troubles—one bit differently.

They decided to sell their own new hand-built house at the first opportunity, and found a young movie producer willing to take it on a ten-year balloon with a small down. They wanted, Joe told me, to create a situation with no fallback. They put their furniture in some friends' dry barn, took over some other friends' cabin while they were away on vacation, and set off for Haddam in their old Saab one Sunday night, ready to present themselves as home buyers at somebody's desk on Monday morning.

Only they were in for the shock of their lives!

What the Markhams were in the market for—as I told them—was absolutely clear and they were dead right to want it: a modest three-bedroom with charm and maybe a few nice touches, though in keeping with the scaled-back, education-first ethic they'd opted for. A house with hardwood floors, crown moldings, a small carved mantel, plain banisters, mullioned windows, perhaps a window seat. A Cape or a converted saltbox set back on a small chunk of land bordering some curmudgeonly old farmer's cornfield or else a little pond or stream. Pre-war, or just after. Slightly out of the way. A lawn with maybe a healthy maple tree, some mature plantings, an attached garage possibly needing improvement. Assumable note or owner-finance, something they could live with. Nothing ostentatious: a sensible home for the recast nuclear family commencing life's third quartile with a kid on board. Something in the 148K area, up to three thousand square feet, close to a middle school, with a walk to the grocery.

The only problem was, and is, that houses like that, the ones the Markhams still google-dream about as they plow down the Taconic, mooning out at the little woods-ensconced rooftops and country lanes floating past, with mossy, overgrown stone walls winding back to mysterious-wondrous home possibilities in Columbia County—those houses are history. Ancient history. And those prices quit floating around at about the time Joe was saying good-bye to Melody and turning his attentions to plump, round-breasted and winsome Phyllis. Say 1976. Try four-fifty today if you can find it.

And I *maybe* could come close if the buyer weren't in a big hurry and didn't faint when the bank appraisal came in at thirty-under-asking, and the owner wanted 25% as earnest money and hadn't yet heard of a concept called owner-finance.

The houses I *could* show them all fell significantly below their dream. The current median Haddam-area house goes for 149K, which buys you a builder-design colonial in an almost completed development in not-all-that-nearby Mallards Landing: 1,900 sq ft, including garage, three-bedroom, two-bath, expandable, no fplc, basement or carpets, sited on a 50-by-200-foot lot "clustered" to preserve the theme of open space and in full view of a fiberglass-bottom "pond." All of which cast them into a deep gloom pit and, after three weeks of looking, made them not even willing to haul out of the car and walk through most of the houses where I'd made appointments.

Other than that, I showed them an assortment of older village-in houses inside their price window—mostly small, dark two-bedrooms with vaguely Greek facades, originally built for the servants of the rich before the turn of the century and owned now either by descendants of immigrant Sicilians who came to New Jersey to be stonemasons on the chapel at the Theological Institute, or else by service-industry employees, shopkeepers or Negroes. For the most part those houses are unkempt, shrunken versions of grander homes across town—I know because Ann and I rented one when we moved in eighteen years ago—only the rooms are square with few windows, low-ceilinged and connected in incongruous ways so that inside you feel as closed in and on edge as you would in a cheap chiropractor's office. Kitchens are all on the back, rarely is there more than one bath (unless the place has been fixed up, in which case the price is double); most of the houses have wet basements, old termite damage, unsolvable structural enigmas, cast-iron piping with suspicions of lead, subcode wiring and postage-stamp yards. And for this you pay full price just to get anybody to break wind in your direction. Sellers are always the last line of defense against reality and the first to feel their soleness threatened by mysterious market corrections. (Buyers are the second.)

On two occasions I actually ended up showing houses to *Sonja* (who's my daughter's age!) in hopes she'd see something she liked (a primly painted "pink room" that could be hers, a particularly nifty place to snug a VCR, some kitchen built-ins she thought were neat), then go traipsing back down the walk burbling that this was the place she'd dreamed of all her little life and her Mom and Dad simply had to see it.

Only that never happened. On both of these charades, as Sonja went clattering around the empty rooms, wondering, I'm sure, how a twelve-year-old is supposed to buy a house, I peeked through the curtains and saw Joe and Phyllis waging a corrosive argument inside my car—something that'd been brewing all day—both of them facing forward, he in the front, she in the back, snarling but not actually looking at each other. Once or twice Joe'd whip his head around, focus in his dark little eyes as intent as an ape, growl something withering, and Phyllis would cross her plump arms and stare out hatefully at the house and shake her head without bothering to answer. Pretty soon we were out and headed to our next venue.

Unhappily, the Markhams, out of ignorance and pigheadedness, have failed to intuit the one gnostic truth of real estate (a truth impossible to reveal without seeming dishonest and cynical): that people never find or buy the house they say they want. A market economy, so I've learned, is not even remotely premised on anybody getting what he wants. The premise is that you're presented with what you might've thought you didn't want, but what's available, whereupon you give in and start finding ways to feel good about it and yourself. And not that there's anything wrong with that scheme. Why should you only get what you think you want, or be limited by what you can simply plan on? Life's never like that, and if you're smart you'll decide it's better the way it is.

My own approach in all these matters and specifically so far as the Markhams are concerned has been to make perfectly clear who pays my salary (the seller) and that my job is to familiarize them with our area, let them decide if they want to settle here, and then use my accumulated goodwill to sell them, in fact, a house. I've also impressed on them that I go about selling houses the way I'd want one sold to me: by not being a realty wind sock; by not advertising views I don't mostly believe in; by not showing

clients a house they've already said they won't like by pretending
the subject never came up; by not saying a house is "interesting" or
"has potential" if I think it's a dump; and finally by not trying to
make people believe in *me* (not that I'm untrustworthy—I simply
don't invite trust) but by asking them to believe in whatever they
hold dearest—themselves, money, God, permanence, progress, or
just a house they see and like and decide to live in—and to act
accordingly.

All told today, the Markhams have looked at forty-five houses—
dragging more and more grimly down from and back to Vermont—
though many of these listings were seen only from the window of
my car as we rolled slowly along the curbside. "I wouldn't live in
that particular shithole," Joe would say, fuming out at a house
where I'd made an appointment. "Don't waste your time here,
Frank," Phyllis would offer, and away we'd go. Or Phyllis would
observe from the backseat: "Joe can't stand stucco construction.
He doesn't want to be the one to say so, so I'll just make it easier.
He grew up in a stucco house in Aliquippa. Also, we'd rather not
share a driveway."

And these weren't bad houses. There wasn't a certifiable "fixer-
upper," "handyman special," or a "just needs love" in the lot (Haddam doesn't have these anyway). I haven't shown them one yet
that the three of them couldn't have made a damn good fresh start
in with a little elbow grease, a limited renovation budget and some
spatial imagination.

Since March, though, the Markhams have yet to make a pur-
chase, tender an offer, write an earnest-money check or even see a
house twice, and consequently have become despondent as we've
entered the dog days of midsummer. In my own life during this
period, I've made eight satisfactory home sales, shown a hundred
other houses to thirty different people, gone to the Shore or off
with my kids any number of weekends, watched (from my bed)
the Final 4, opening day at Wrigley, the French Open and three
rounds of Wimbledon; and on the more somber side, I've watched
the presidential campaigns grind on in disheartening fashion,
observed my forty-fourth birthday, and sensed my son gradually

become a source of worry and pain to himself and me. There have also been, in this time frame, two fiery jetliner crashes far from our shores, Iraq has poisoned many Kurdish villagers, President Reagan has visited Russia, there's been a coup in Haiti, drought has crippled the country's midsection and the Lakers have won the NBA crown. Life, as noted, has gone on.

Meanwhile, the Markhams have begun "eating into their down" from the movie producer now living in their dream house and, Joe believes, producing porn movies using local teens. Likewise Joe's severance pay at Vermont Social Services has come and gone, and he's nearing the end of his piled-up vacation money. Phyllis, to her dismay, has begun suffering painful and possibly ominous female problems that have required midweek trips to Burlington for testing, plus two biopsies and a discussion of surgery. Their Saab has started overheating and sputtering on the daily commutes Phyllis makes to Sonja's dance class in Craftsbury. And as if that weren't enough, their friends are now home from their geological vacation to the Great Slave Lake, so that Joe and Phyllis are having to give thought to moving into the original and long-abandoned "home place" on their own former property and possibly applying for welfare.

Beyond all that, the Markhams have had to face the degree of unknown involved in buying a house—unknown likely to affect their whole life, even if they were rich movie stars or the keyboardist for the Rolling Stones. Buying a house will, after all, partly determine what they'll be worrying about but don't yet know, what consoling window views they'll be taking (or not), where they'll have bitter arguments and make love, where and under what conditions they'll feel trapped by life or safe from the storm, where those spirited parts of themselves they'll eventually leave behind (however overprized) will be entombed, where they might die or get sick and wish they were dead, where they'll return after funerals or after they're divorced, like I did.

After which all these unknown facts of life to come have then to be figured into what they still don't know about a house itself, right along with the potentially grievous certainty that they *will* know a *great* deal the instant they sign the papers, walk in, close the door and it's theirs; and then later will know even a great deal more that's possibly not good, though they want none of it to turn out badly for them or anyone they love. Sometimes I don't understand why anybody buys a house, or for that matter does anything with a tangible downside.

As part of my service to the Markhams, I've tried to come up with some stopgap accommodations. Addressing that feeling of not knowing *is*, after all, my job, and I'm aware what fears come quaking and quivering into most clients' hearts after a lengthy, unsatisfactory realty experience: Is this guy a crook? Will he lie to me and steal my money? Is this street being rezoned C-1 and he's in on the ground floor of a new chain of hospices or drug rehab centers? I know also that the single biggest cause of client "jumps" (other than realtor rudeness or blatant stupidity) is the embittering suspicion that the agent isn't paying any attention to your wishes. "He's just showing us what he hasn't already been able to unload and trying to make us like it"; or "She's never shown us anything like what we said we were interested in"; or "He's just pissing away our time driving us around town and letting us buy him lunch."

In early May I came up with a furnished condominium in a remodeled Victorian mansion on Burr Street, behind the Haddam Playhouse, complete with utilities and covered off-street parking. It was steep at $1,500, but it was close to schools and Phyllis could've managed without a second car if they'd stayed put till Joe started work. Joe, though, swore he'd lived in his last "shitty cold-water flat" in 1964, when he was a sophomore at Duquesne, and didn't intend to start Sonja off in some oppressive new school environment with a bunch of rich, neurotic suburban kids while the three of them lived like transient apartment rats. She'd never outlive it. He'd rather, he said, forget the whole shittaree. A week later I turned up a perfectly workable brick-and-shingle bunga-low on a narrow street behind Pelcher's—a bolt-hole, to be sure, but a place they could get into with some lease-to-buy furniture and a few odds and ends of their own, exactly the way Ann and I and everybody else used to live when we were first married and thought everything was great and getting greater. Joe, however, refused to even drive by.

Since early June, Joe has grown increasingly sullen and mean-spirited, as though he's begun to see the world in a whole new way he doesn't like and is working up some severe defense mechanisms. Phyllis has called me twice late at night, once when she'd been crying, and hinted Joe was not an easy man to live with. She said he'd begun disappearing for parts of the day and had started throwing pots at night over in a woman artist friend's studio, drinking a lot of beer and coming home after midnight. Among her other worries, Phyllis is convinced he might just forget the whole damn thing—the move, Sonja's schooling, Leverage Books, even their marriage—and sink back into an aimless noncon-formist's life he lived before they got together and charted a new path to the waterfall. It was possible, she said, that Joe couldn't stand the consequences of real intimacy, which to her meant shar-ing your troubles as well as your achievements with the person you loved, and it seemed also possible that the art of trying to buy a house had opened the door on some dark corridors in herself that she was fearful of going down, though she thankfully seemed unready to discuss which these might be.

In so many words, the Markhams are faced with a potentially calamitous careen down a slippery socio-emotio-economic slope, something they could never have imagined six months ago. Plus, I know they have begun to brood about all the other big missteps they've taken in the past, the high cost of these, and how they don't want to make any more like that. As regret goes, theirs, of course, is not unusual in kind. Though finally the worst thing about regret is that it makes you duck the chance of suffering new regret just as you get a glimmer that nothing's worth doing unless it has the potential to fuck up your whole life.

THE WOMANIZER

1

Martin Austin turned up the tiny street—rue Sarrazin—at the head of which he hoped he would come to a larger one he knew, rue de Vaugirard, possibly, a street he could take all the way to Joséphine Belliard's apartment by the Jardin du Luxembourg. He was on his way to sit with Joséphine's son, Léo, while Joséphine visited her lawyers to sign papers divorcing her husband. Later in the evening, he was taking her for a romantic dinner. Joséphine's husband, Bernard, was a cheap novelist who'd published a scandalous book in which Joséphine figured prominently; her name used, her parts indelicately described, her infidelity put on display in salacious detail. The book had recently reached the stores. Everybody she knew was reading it.

"Okay. Maybe it is not so bad to *write* such a book," Joséphine had said the first night Austin had met her, only the week before, when he had also taken her to dinner. "It is his choice to write it. I cause him unhappiness. But to publish this? In Paris? No." She had shaken her head absolutely. "I'm sorry. This is too much. My husband—he is a shit. What can I do? I say good-bye to him."

Austin was from Chicago. He was married, with no children, and worked as a sales representative for an old family-owned company that sold expensive specially treated paper to foreign textbook publishers. He was forty-four and had worked for the same company, the Lilienthal Company of Winnetka, for fifteen years. He'd met Joséphine Belliard at a cocktail party given by a publisher he regularly called on, for one of its important authors. He'd been invited only as a courtesy, since his company's paper had not been used for the author's book, a sociological text that calculated the suburban loneliness of immigrant Arabs by the use of sophisticated differential equations. Austin's French was lacking—he'd always been able to speak much more than he could understand—and as a consequence he'd stood by himself at the edge of the party, drinking champagne, smiling pleasantly and hoping he'd hear English spoken and find someone he could talk to instead of someone who would hear him speak a few words of French and then start a conversation he could never make sense of.

Joséphine Belliard was a sub-editor at the publishing house. She was a small, slender dark-haired Frenchwoman in her thirties and of an odd beauty—a mouth slightly too wide and too thin; her chin soft, almost receding; but with a smooth caramel skin and dark eyes and dark eyebrows that Austin found appealing. He had caught a glimpse of her earlier in the day when he'd visited the publisher's offices in the rue de Lille. She was sitting at her desk in a small, shadowy office, rapidly and animatedly speaking English into the telephone. He'd peered in as he passed but had forgotten about her until she came up to him at the party and smiled and asked in English how he liked Paris. Later that night they had gone to dinner, and at the end of the evening he'd taken her home in a taxi, then returned to his hotel alone and gone to sleep.

The next day, though, he'd called her. He had nothing special in mind, just an aimless, angling call. Maybe he could sleep with her—not that he even thought that. It was just a possibility, an inevitable thought. When he asked if she would like to see him again, she said she would if he wanted to. She didn't say she'd had a good time the night before. She didn't mention that at all—almost, Austin felt, as if that time had never happened. But it was an attitude he found attractive. She was smart. She judged things.

It wasn't an American attitude. In America a woman would have
to seem to care—more, probably, than she did or could after one
harmless encounter.

That evening they had gone to a small, noisy Italian restaurant
near the Gare de l'Est, a place with bright lights and mirrors on
the walls and where the food was not very good. They'd ordered
light Ligurian wine, gotten a little drunk and engaged in a long
and in some ways intimate conversation. Joséphine told him she
had been born in the suburb of Aubervilliers, north of Paris, and
couldn't wait to leave home. She had gone to a university and
studied sociology while living with her parents, but now had no
relationship with her mother, or with her father, who had moved
to America in the late seventies and not been heard from. She said
she had been married eight years to a man she once liked and had
had one child with but did not especially love, and that two years
ago she had begun an affair with another man, a younger man,
which lasted only a short time, then ended, as she had expected it
might. Afterwards she had believed she could simply resume married life more or less as she'd left it, a lifelong bourgeois muddle of
continuance. But her husband had been shocked and incensed by
his wife's infidelity and had moved out of their apartment, quit
his job at an advertising firm, found a woman to live with and
gone to work writing a novel which had as its only subject his
wife's supposed indiscretions—some of which, she told Austin,
he'd obviously made up, though others, amusingly enough, were
surprisingly accurate.

"It's not so much I blame him, you know?" Joséphine had said
and laughed. "These things come along. They happen. Other
people do what they please." She looked out the restaurant window at the row of small parked cars along the street. "So?"

"But what's happening now?" Austin said, trying to find a part
of the story that would allow him into it. A phrase, a niche that
could be said to invite his closer interest—though there didn't
seem to be such a phrase.

"Now? Now I am living with my child. Alone. That is all of
my life." She unexpectedly looked up at Austin, her eyes opened

wide, as though to say, What else is there? "What more else?" she in fact did say.

"I don't know," Austin said. "Do you think you'll go back with your husband?" This was a question he was quite happy to ask.

"Yes. I don't know. No. Maybe," Joséphine said, extending her lower lip slightly and raising one shoulder in a gesture of careless ness Austin believed was typical of French women. He didn't mind it in Joséphine, but he usually disliked people for affecting this gesture. It was patently false and always came at the service of important matters a person wished to pretend were not important.

Joséphine, though, did not seem like a woman to have an affair and then talk about it matter-of-factly to someone she barely knew; she seemed more like an unmarried woman looking for someone to be interested in. Obviously she was more complicated, maybe even smarter, than he'd thought, and quite realistic about life, though slightly disillusioned. Probably, if he wanted to press the matter of intimacy, he could take her back to his room—a thing he'd done before on business trips, and even if not so many times, enough times that to do so now wouldn't be extraordinary or meaningful, at least not to him. To share an unexpected intimacy might intensify both their holds on life.

Yet there was a measure of uncertainty surrounding that very thought—a thought he was so used to having he couldn't keep from it. Maybe it was true that even though he liked her, liked the frankness and direct nature of her conduct toward him, intimacy was not what he wanted. She appealed to him in a surprising way, but he was not physically attracted to her. And maybe, he thought, looking at her across the table, an intimacy with him was the last thing on earth *she* was interested in. She was French. He didn't know anything about them. An illusion of potential intimacy was probably what all French women broadcast, and everyone knew it. Probably she had no interest in him at all and was just passing the time. It made him feel pleased even to entertain such a multi-layered view.

They finished dinner in thoughtful, weighted silence. Austin felt ready to begin a discourse on his own life—his marriage, its

length and intensity, his feelings about it and himself. He was willing to talk about the uneasy, unanchored sensation he'd had lately
of not knowing exactly how to make the next twenty-five years of
life as eventful and important as the previous twenty-five, a sensation buttressed by the hope that he wouldn't fail of courage if
courage was required, and by the certainty that everybody had his
life entirely in his hands and was required to live with his own ter-
rors and mistakes, etc. Not that he was unhappy with Barbara or
lacked anything. He was not the conventionally desperate man on
the way out of a marriage that had grown tiresome. Barbara, in
fact, was the most interesting and beautiful woman he'd ever
known, the person he admired most. He wasn't looking for a better life. He wasn't looking for anything. He loved his wife, and he
hoped to present to Joséphine Belliard a different human perspec-
tive from the ones she might be used to.

"No one thinks your thoughts for you when you lay your head
on the pillow at night" was a sobering expression Austin often
used in addressing himself, as well as when he'd addressed the few
women he'd known since being married—including Barbara. He
was willing to commence a frank discussion of this sort when
Joséphine asked him about himself.

But the subject did not come up. She didn't ask about his
thoughts, or about himself. And not that she talked about *her*self.
She talked about her job, about her son, Léo, about her husband
and about friends of theirs. He had told her he was married. He
had told her his age, that he had gone to college at the University
of Illinois and grown up in the small city of Peoria. But to know
no more seemed fine to her. She was perfectly nice and seemed to
like him, but she was not very responsive, which he felt was
unusual. She seemed to have more serious things on her mind and
to take life seriously—a quality Austin liked. In fact, it made her
appealing in a way she had not seemed at first, when he was only
thinking about how she looked and whether he wanted to sleep
with her.

But when they were walking to her car, down the sidewalk at
the end of which were the bright lights of the Gare de l'Est and

the Boulevard Strasbourg, swarming with taxis at eleven o'clock, Joséphine put her arm through his arm and pulled close to him, put her cheek against his shoulder and said, "It's all confusion to me."

And Austin wondered: *what* was all confusion? Not him. He was no confusion. He'd decided he was a good-intentioned escort for her, and that was a fine thing to be under the circumstances. There was already plenty of confusion in her life. An absent husband. A child. Surviving alone. That was enough. Though he took his arm from her grip and reached it around her shoulder and pulled her close to him until they reached her little black Opel and got in, where touching stopped.

When they reached his hotel, a former monastery with a walled-in courtyard garden, two blocks from the great lighted confluence of St.-Germain and the rue de Rennes, she stopped the car and sat looking straight ahead as if she were waiting for Austin to get out. They had made no mention of another meeting, and he was scheduled to leave in two days.

Austin sat in the dark without speaking. A police station occupied the next corner down the shadowy street. A police van had pulled up with blinking lights, and several uniformed officers in shiny white Sam Browne belts were leading a line of handcuffed men inside, the prisoners' heads all bowed like penitents. It was April, and the street surface glistened in the damp spring air.

This was the point, of course, to ask her to come inside with him if such a thing were ever to be. But it was clearly the furthest thing from possibility, and each of them knew it. And apart from privately acknowledging that much, Austin had no real thought of it. Although he wanted to do *something* good, something unusual that would please her and make them both know an occurrence slightly out of the ordinary had taken place tonight—an occurrence they could both feel good about when they were alone in bed, even if in fact nothing much had taken place.

His mind was working on what that extraordinary something might be, the thing you did if you didn't make love to a woman. A gesture. A word. What?

All the prisoners were finally led into the police station, and

the officers had gotten back in their van and driven it straight up
rue de Mézières, where Austin and Joséphine Belliard were sitting
in the silent darkness. Obviously she was waiting for him to get
out, and he was in a quandary about what to do. Though it was a
moment he relished, the exquisite moment before anything is
acted on and when all is potential, before life turns this way or
that—toward regret or pleasure or happiness, toward one kind of
permanence or another. It was a wonderful, tantalizing, important moment, one worth preserving, and he knew she knew it as
well as he did and wanted it to last as long as he wanted it to.

Austin sat with his hands in his lap, feeling large and cumber-
some inside the tiny car, listening to himself breathe, conscious he
was on the verge of what he hoped would be the right—rightest—
gesture. She hadn't moved. The car was idling, its headlights shining
weakly on the empty street, the dashboard instruments turning
the interior air faintly green.

Austin abruptly—or so it felt to him—reached across the space
between them, took Joséphine's small, warm hand off the steering wheel and held it between his two large equally warm ones
like a sandwich, though in a way that would also seem protective.
He would be protective of her, guard her from some as yet
unnamed harm or from her own concealed urges, though most
immediately from himself, since he realized it was her reluctance
more than his that kept them apart now, kept them from parking
the car and going inside and spending the night in each other's
arms.

He squeezed her hand tightly, then eased up.

"I'd like to make you happy somehow," he said in a sincere
voice, and waited while Joséphine said nothing. She did not remove
her hand, but neither did she answer. It was as if what he'd said
didn't mean anything, or that possibly she wasn't even listening to
him. "It's just human," Austin said, as though she *had* said something back, had said, "Why?" or "Don't try," or "You couldn't
possibly," or "It's too late."

"What?" She looked at him for the first time since they'd
stopped. "It's what?" She had not understood him.

"It's only human to want to make someone happy," Austin said, holding her warm, nearly weightless hand. "I like you very much, you know that." These were the right words, as ordinary as they sounded.

"Yes. Well. For what?" Joséphine said in a cold voice. "You are married. You have a wife. You live far away. In two days, three days, I don't know, you will leave. So. For what do you like me?" Her face seemed impenetrable, as though she were addressing a cab driver who'd just said something inappropriately familiar. She left her hand in his hand but looked straight ahead.

Austin wanted to speak again. He wished to say something— likewise absolutely correct—into this new void she'd opened between them, words no one could plan to say or even know in advance, but something that admitted to what she'd said, conceded his acquiescence to it, yet allowed another moment to occur during which the two of them would enter onto new and uncharted ground.

Though the only thing that Austin could say—and he had no idea why, since it sounded asinine and ruinous—was: *People have paid a dear price for getting involved with me.* Which were definitely the wrong words, since to his knowledge they weren't particularly true, and even if they were, they were so boastful and melodramatic as to cause Joséphine or anyone else to break out laughing.

Still, he could say that and immediately have it all be over between them and forget about it, which might be a relief. Though relief was not what he wanted. He wanted something to go forward between them, something definite and realistic and in keeping with the facts of their lives; to advance into that area where nothing actually seemed possible at the moment.

Austin slowly let go of Joséphine's hand. Then he reached both of his hands to her face and turned it toward him, and leaned across the open space and said, just before he kissed her, "I'm at least going to kiss you. I feel like I'm entitled to do that, and I'm going to."

Joséphine Belliard did not resist him at all, though she did not in any way concur. Her face was soft and compliant. She had a plain, not in the least full, mouth, and when Austin put his lips against hers she did not move toward him. She let herself be kissed, and Austin was immediately, cruelly aware of it. This is what was taking place: he was forcing himself on this woman, and a feeling came over him as he pressed his lips more completely onto hers that he was delusionary and foolish and pathetic—the kind of man he would make fun of if he heard himself described using only these facts as evidence. It was an awful feeling, like being old, and he felt his insides go hollow and his arms become heavy as cudgels. He wanted to disappear from this car seat and remember none of the idiotic things he had just an instant before been thinking. *This* had now been the first permanent move, when potentiality ended, and it had been the wrong one, the worst one possible. It was ludicrous.

Though before he could move his lips away, he realized Joséphine Belliard was saying something, speaking with her lips against his lips, faintly, and that by not resisting him she was in fact kissing him, her face almost unconsciously giving up to his intention. What she was saying all the while Austin was kissing her thin mouth was—whisperingly, almost dreamily—*"Non, non, non, non, non.* Please. I can't. I can't. *Non, non."*

Though she didn't stop. *No* was not what she meant exactly—she let her lips slightly part in a gesture of recognition. And after a moment, a long suspended moment, Austin inched away, sat back in his seat and took a deep breath. He put his hands back in his lap, and let the kiss fill the space between them, a space he had somehow hoped to fill with words. It was the most unexpected and enticing thing that could've come of his wish to do right.

She did not take an audible breath. She merely sat as she'd sat before he'd kissed her, and did not speak or seem to have anything in her mind to say. Things were mostly as they had been before he'd kissed her, only he *had* kissed her—*they* had kissed—and that made all the difference in the world.

"I'd like to see you tomorrow," Austin said very resolutely.

"Yes," Joséphine said almost sorrowfully, as if she couldn't help agreeing. "Okay."

And he was satisfied then that there was nothing else to say. Things were as they should be. Nothing would go wrong.

"Good night," Austin said with the same resolution as before. He opened the car door and hauled himself out onto the street.

"Okay," she said. She didn't look out the door, though he leaned back into the opening and looked at her. She had her hands on the steering wheel, staring straight ahead, appearing no different really from when she'd stopped to let him out five minutes before—only slightly more fatigued.

He wanted to say one more good word that would help balance how she felt at that moment—not that he had the slightest idea how she felt. She was opaque to him, completely opaque, and that was not even so interesting. Though all he could think to say was something as inane as the last thing had been ruinous. *Two people don't see the same landscape.* These were the terrible words he thought, though he didn't say them. He just smiled in at her, stood up, pushed the door closed firmly and stepped slowly back so Joséphine could turn and start down rue de Mézières. He watched her drive away and could tell that she did not look at him in the rearview mirror. It was as though in a moment he did not exist.

2

What Austin hoped would be the rue de Vaugirard, leading around and up to Joséphine's apartment, turned out instead to be the rue St.-Jacques. He had walked much too far and was now near the medical college, where there were only lightless shop windows containing drab medical texts and dusty, passed-over antiques.

He did not know Paris well—only a few hotels he'd stayed in and a few restaurants he didn't want to eat in again. He couldn't keep straight which arrondissement was which, what direction anything was from anything else, how to take the metro, or even how to leave town, except by airplane. All the large streets looked the same and traveled at confusing angles to one another, and all the famous landmarks seemed to be in unexpected locations when they peeked up into view above the building tops. In the two days he'd been back in Paris—after leaving home in a fury and taking the plane to Orly—he'd tried to make a point of remembering in which direction on the Boulevard St.-Germain the numbers got larger. But he couldn't keep it straight, and in fact he couldn't always find the Boulevard St.-Germain when he wanted to.

At rue St.-Jacques he looked down toward where he thought would be the river and the Petit Pont bridge, and there they were. It was a warm spring day, and the sidewalks along the riverbanks were jammed with tourists cruising the little picture stalls and gaping at the vast cathedral on the other side.

The prospect down the rue St.-Jacques seemed for an instant familiar—a pharmacy front he recognized, a café with a distinctive name. Horloge. He looked back up the street he'd come down and saw that he was only half a block away from the small hotel he'd once stayed in with his wife, Barbara. The Hôtel de la Tour de Notre Dame, which had advertised a view of the cathedral but from which no such view was possible. The hotel was run by Pakistanis and had rooms so small you couldn't have your suitcase open and also reach the window. He'd brought Barbara with him on business—it was four years ago—and she had shopped and visited museums and eaten lunch along the Quai de la Tournelle while he made his customer calls. They had stayed out of the room as long as possible until fatigue dumped them in bed in front of the indecipherable French TV, which eventually put them to sleep.

Austin remembered very clearly now, standing on the busy sidewalk on his way to Joséphine Belliard's apartment, that he and Barbara had left Paris on the first of April—intending to take a direct flight back to Chicago. Though, once they'd struggled their heavy luggage out of the room, crammed themselves into the tiny, airless elevator and emerged into the lobby, looking like beleaguered refugees but ready to settle their bill and depart, the

Pakistani room clerk, who spoke crisp British English, looked across the reception desk in an agitated way and said, "Oh, Mr. Austin, have you not heard the bad news? I'm sorry."

"What's that?" Austin had said, out of breath. "What bad news?" He looked at Barbara, who was holding a garment bag and a hat-box, not wanting to hear any bad news now.

"There is a quite terrible strike," the clerk said and looked very grave. "The airport's closed down completely. No one can leave Paris today. And, I'm sorry to say, we have already booked your room for another guest. A Japanese. I'm so, so sorry."

Austin had stood amid his suitcases, breathing in the air of defeat and frustration and anger he felt certain it would be useless to express. He stared out the lobby window at the street. The sky was cloudy and the wind slightly chilled. He heard Barbara say behind him, as much to herself as to him, "Oh well. We'll do something. We'll find another place. It's too bad. Maybe it'll be an adventure."

Austin looked at the clerk, a little beige man with neat black hair and a white cotton jacket, standing behind his marble desk. The clerk was smiling. This was all the same to him, Austin realized: that they had no place to go; that they were tired of Paris; that they had brought too much luggage and bought too much to take home; that they had slept badly every night; that the weather was inexplicably changing to colder; that they were out of money and sick of the arrogant French. None of this mattered to this man—in some ways, Austin sensed, it may even have pleased him, pleased him enough to make him smile.

"What's so goddamned funny?" Austin had said to the smug little subcontinental. "Why's my bad luck a source of such goddamned amusement to you?" This man would be the focus of his anger. He couldn't help himself. Anger couldn't make anything worse. "Doesn't it matter that we're guests of this hotel and we're in a bit of a bad situation here?" He heard what he knew was a pleading voice.

"April fool!" the clerk said and broke out in a squeaking little laughter. "Ha, ha, ha, ha, ha, ha, ha. It is only a joke, *monsieur*," the man said, so pleased with himself, even more than when he'd told Austin the lie. "The airport is perfectly fine. It is open. You can leave. There is no trouble. It's fine. It was only a joke. *Bon voyage*, Mr. Austin. *Bon voyage*."

3

For the two days after she had left him standing in the street at midnight, after he had kissed her the first time and felt that he had done something exactly right, Austin saw a great deal of Joséphine Belliard. He'd had plans to take the TGV to Brussels and then go on to Amsterdam, and from there fly to Chicago and home. But the next morning he sent messages to his customers and to the office, complaining of "medical problems" which had inexplicably "recurred," although he felt it was "probably nothing serious." He would conclude his business by fax when he was home the next week. He told Barbara he'd decided to stay in Paris a few extra days—to relax, to do things he'd never taken the time to do. Visit Balzac's house, maybe. Walk the streets like a tourist. Rent a car. Drive to Fontainebleau.

As to Joséphine Belliard, he decided he would spend every minute he could with her. He did not for an instant think that he loved her, or that keeping each other's company would lead him or her to anything important. He was married; he had nothing to give her. To get deluded about such a thing was to bring on nothing but trouble—the kind of trouble that when you're younger you glance away from, but when you're older you ignore at risk. Hesitancy in the face of trouble, he felt, was probably a virtue.

But short of that he did all he could. Together they went to a movie. They went to a museum. They visited Notre Dame and the Palais Royal. They walked together in the narrow streets of the Faubourg St.-Germain. They looked in store windows. They acted like lovers. Touched. She allowed him to hold her hand.

They exchanged knowing looks. He discovered what made her laugh, listened carefully for her small points of pride. She stayed as she had been—seemingly uninterested, but willing—as if it was all his idea and her duty, only a duty she surprisingly liked. Austin felt this very reluctance in her was compelling, attractive. And it caused him to woo her in a way that made him admire his own intensity. He took her to dinner in two expensive places, went with her to her apartment, met her son, met the country woman she paid to care for him during the week, saw where she lived, slept, ate, then stood gazing out her apartment windows to the Jardin du Luxembourg and down the peaceful streets of her neighborhood. He saw her life, which he found he was curious about, and once he'd satisfied that curiosity he felt as though he'd accomplished something, something that was not easy or ordinary.

She told him not much more about herself and, again, asked nothing about him, as if his life didn't matter to her. She told him she had once visited America, had met a musician in California and decided to live with him in his small wooden house by the beach in Santa Cruz. This was in the early seventies. She had been a teenager. Only one morning—it was after four months—she woke up on a mattress on the floor, underneath a rug made out of a tanned cowhide, got up, packed her bag and left.

"This was too much," Joséphine said, sitting in the window of her apartment, looking out at the twilight and the street where children were kicking a soccer ball. The musician had been disturbed and angry, she said, but she had come back to France and her parents' house. "You cannot live a long time where you don't belong. It's true?" She looked at him and elevated her shoulders. He was sitting in a chair, drinking a glass of red wine, contemplating the rooftops, enjoying how the tawny light burnished the delicate scrollwork cornices of the apartment buildings visible from the one he was in. Jazz was playing softly on the stereo, a sinuous saxophone solo. "It's true, no?" she said. "You can't."

"Exactly right," Austin said. He had grown up in Peoria. He

lived on the northwest side of Chicago. He'd attended a state U. He felt she was exactly right, although he saw nothing wrong in being here at this moment, enjoying the sunlight as it gradually faded then disappeared from the rooftops he could see from this woman's rooms. That seemed permissible.

She told him about her husband. His picture was on the wall in Léo's room—a bulbous-faced, dark-skinned Jew, with a thick black mustache that made him look like an Armenian. Slightly disappointing, Austin had thought. He'd imagined Bernard as being handsome, a smooth-skinned Louis Jourdan type with the fatal flaw of being boring. The real man looked like what he was—a fat man who once wrote French radio jingles.

Joséphine said that her affair had proved to her that she did not love her husband, although perhaps she once had, and that while for some people to live with a person you did not love was possible, it was not possible for her. She looked at Austin as if to underscore the point. This was not, of course, how she had first explained her feelings for her husband, when she said she'd felt she could resume their life after her affair but that her husband had left her flat. This was how she felt now, Austin thought, and the truth certainly lay somewhere in the middle. In any case, it didn't matter to him. She said her husband gave her very little money now, saw his son infrequently, had been seen with a new girlfriend who was German, and of course had written the terrible book, which everyone she knew was reading, causing her immense pain and embarrassment.

"But," she said, and shook her head as if shaking the very thoughts out of her mind. "What I can do, yes? I live my life now, here, with my son. I have twenty-five more years to work, then I'm finished."

"Maybe something better'll come along," Austin said. He didn't know what that might be, but he disliked her being so pessimistic. It felt like she was somehow blaming him, which he thought was very French. A more hopeful, American point of view, he thought, would help.

"What is it? What will be better?" Joséphine said, and she looked at him not quite bitterly, but helplessly. "What is going to happen? Tell me. I want to know."

Austin set his wineglass carefully on the polished floor, climbed out of his chair and walked to the open window where she sat, and below which the street was slowly being cast into grainy darkness. There was the bump of the soccer ball still being kicked aimlessly against a wall over and over, and behind that the sound of a car engine being revved down the block. Austin put his arms around her arms and put his mouth against her cool cheek and held her to him tightly.

"Maybe someone will come along who loves you," he said. He was offering encouragement, and he knew she knew that and would take it in a good spirit. "You wouldn't be hard to love. Not at all." He held her more tightly to him. "In fact," he said, "you'd be very easy to love."

Joséphine let herself be pulled, be gathered in. She let her head fall against his shoulder. It was perilous to be where she was, Austin thought, in the window, with a man holding her. He could feel the cool outside air on the backs of his hands and against his face, half in, half out. It was thrilling, even though Joséphine did not put her arms around him, did not reciprocate his touch in any way, only let him hold her as if pleasing him was easy but did not matter to her a great deal.

That night he took her to dinner at the Closerie des Lilas, a famous bistro where writers and artists had been frequenters in the twenties—a bright, glassy and noisy place where the two of them drank champagne, held hands, but did not talk much. They seemed to be running out of things to say. The next most natural things would be subjects that connected them, subjects with some future built in. But Austin was leaving in the morning, and those subjects didn't seem to interest either of them, though Austin could feel their pull, could imagine below the surface of unyielding facts that there could be a future for them. Certainly under different, better circumstances they would be lovers, would immediately begin to spend more time together, discover what there was to discover between them. Austin had a strong urge to say these very things to her as they sat silently over their champagne, just to go ahead and put that much on the table from his side and see what it called forth from hers. But the restaurant was too noisy. Once he tried to begin, the words sounded too loud. And these were not that kind of words. These were important words and needed to be said respectfully, even solemnly, with their inevitable sense of loss built in.

The words, though, had stayed in his mind as Joséphine again drove the short distance back to rue de Mézières and to the corner where she'd left him the first night. The words seemed to have missed their moment. They needed another context, a more substantial setting. To say them in the dark, in a crummy Opel with the motor running, at the moment of parting, would give them a sentimental weightiness they didn't mean to have, since they were, for all their built-in sorrow, an expression of optimism.

When Joséphine stopped the car, the gate into the hotel only a few steps away, she kept her hands on the steering wheel and stared straight ahead, as she had two nights before. She did not offer him anything, a word, a gesture, even a look. To her, this night, their last one, the night before Austin left for Chicago and home and his wife, possibly never to come back again, never to try to pick up from where they were at that moment—this night was just like their first, one Joséphine would forget as soon as the door slammed shut and her headlights swung onto the empty street toward home.

Austin looked out her window at the hotel's rustic wooden gate, beyond which was a ferny, footlit courtyard, a set of double glass doors, the lobby and the stairs up two flights to his small room. What he wanted was to take her there, lock the door, close the curtains and make sorrowful love until morning, until he had to call a cab to leave for the airport. But that was the wrong thing to do, having gotten this far without complication, without greater confusion or harm being caused to either of them. Harm *could* be caused by getting involved with him, Austin thought. They both knew it, and it didn't require saying. She wouldn't think of sleeping with him in any case. *No* did mean *no* to her. And that was the right way to play this.

Austin sat with his hands in his lap and said nothing. It was the way he'd known this moment of leaving would occur. Somberly on his part. Coldly on hers. He didn't think he should reach across and take her hands again as he had before. That became playacting the second time you did it, and he had already touched her that way plenty of times—sweetly, innocently, without trying anything more except possibly a brief, soft kiss. He would let this time—the last time—go exactly according to her wishes, not his.

He waited. He thought Joséphine might say something, something ironic or clever or cold or merely commonplace, something that would break her little rule of silence and that he could then reply to and perhaps have the last good word, one that would leave them both puzzled and tantalized and certain that a small but important moment had not entirely been missed. But she did not speak. She was intent on there being nothing that would make her do anything different from what she did naturally. And Austin knew if he had simply climbed out of the car right then, without a good-bye, she would've driven straightaway. Maybe this was why her husband had written a book about her, Austin thought. At least he'd known he'd gotten her attention.

Joséphine seemed to be waiting for the seat beside her to become empty. Austin looked across at her in the car darkness, and she for an instant glanced at him but did not speak. This was annoying, Austin thought; annoying and stupid and French to be so closed to the world, to be so unwilling to let a sweet and free moment cause you happiness—when happiness was in such short supply. He realized he was on the verge of being angry, of saying nothing else, of simply getting out of the car and walking away.

"You know," he said, more irritably than he wanted to sound, "we could be lovers. We're interested in each other. This isn't a sidetrack for me. This is real life. I like you. You like me. All I've wanted to do is take advantage of that in some way that makes you glad, that puts a smile on your face. Nothing else. I don't need to sleep with you. That would cause me as much trouble as it would cause you. But that's no reason we can't just like each other." He looked at her intently, her silhouette softened against the lights above the hotel gate across the street. She said nothing. Though he thought he heard a faint laugh, hardly more than an exhaled breath, intended, he presumed, to express what she'd thought of all he'd just said. "Sorry," Austin said, angry now, swiveling his knees into the doorway to get out. "Really, I am."

But Joséphine put her hand on his wrist and held him back, not looking at him, but speaking toward the cold windshield. "I am not so strong enough," she whispered, and squeezed his wrist.

"For what?" Austin said, also whispering, one foot already on the paving stones, but looking back at her in the darkness.

"I am not so strong enough to have something with you," she said. "Not now." She looked at him, her eyes soft and large, her one hand holding his wrist, the other in her lap, half curled.

"Do you mean you don't feel strongly enough, or you aren't strong enough in yourself?" Austin said, overassertive but feeling good about it.

"I don't know," Joséphine said. "It is still very confusing for me now. I'm sorry."

"Well, that's better than nothing," Austin said. "At least you gave me that much. That makes me glad." He reached across and squeezed her wrist where she was holding his tightly. Then he got out of the car into the street. She put her hand on the gearshift and pushed it forward with a loud rasp.

"If you come back," she said in a husky voice through the doorway, "call me."

"Sure," Austin said, "I'll call you. I don't know what else I'd do in Paris."

He closed the door firmly, and she drove away, spinning her tires on the slick stones. Austin walked across the street to the hotel without looking back at her taillights as they disappeared.

At one a.m., when it was six p.m. in Chicago, he had called Barbara, and they had come close to having a serious argument. It had made Austin angry, because when he had dialed the number, his own familiar number, and heard its reassuring ring, he'd felt happy—happy to be only hours away from leaving Paris, happy to be coming home and to have not just a wife to come home to but this wife—Barbara, whom he both loved and revered. And happy, also, to have effected his "contact" with Joséphine Belliard (that was the word he was using; at first it had been "rapprochement," but that had given way). Happy that there were no bad consequences to rue—no false promises inspiring false hopes, no tearful partings, no sense of entrapping obligations or feelings of being in over your boot tops. No damage to control.

Which was not to say nothing had taken place, because plenty had—things he and Joséphine Belliard both knew about and that had been expressed when she held his wrist in the car and admitted she wasn't strong enough, or that something was too strong for her.

What does one want in the world? Austin thought, propped against the headboard of the bed that night, having a glass of warm champagne from the minibar. He was in his blue pajama bottoms, on top of the covers, barefoot, staring across the room at his own image in the smoky mirror that occupied one entire wall—a man in a bed with a lighted bed lamp beside him, a glass on his belly. What does one want most of all, when one has experienced much, suffered some, persevered, tried to do good when good was within reach? What does this experience teach us that we can profit from? That the memory of pain, Austin thought, mounts up and lays a significant weight upon the present—a sobering weight—and the truth one has to discover is: exactly what's possible but also valuable and desirable between human beings, on a low level of event.

No easy trick, he thought. Certainly not everyone could do it. But he and Joséphine Belliard had in an admittedly small way brought it off, found the point of contact whose consequences were only positive for each of them. No hysteria. No confusion. Yet not insignificant, either. He realized, of course, that if he'd had his own way, Joséphine would be in bed beside him right now; though in God knows what agitated state of mind, the late hours ticking by, sex their sole hope of consolation. It was a distasteful thought. *There* was trouble, and nothing would've been gained—only something lost. But the two of them had figured out a better path to take, which had eventuated in his being alone in his room and feeling quite good about everything. Even virtuous. He almost raised his glass to himself in the mirror, only it seemed ridiculous.

He waited awhile before phoning Barbara, because he thought Joséphine might call—a drowsy late-night voice from bed, an opportunity for her to say something more to him, something interesting, maybe serious, something she hadn't wanted to say when they were together in the car and could reach each other.

But she didn't call, and Austin found himself staring at the foreign-looking telephone, willing it to ring. He'd had a lengthy conversation between himself and Joséphine playing in his mind for several minutes: he wished she was here now—that's what he wanted to say to her, even though he'd already decided that was distasteful. Still, he thought of her lying in bed asleep, alone, and it gave him a hollow, almost nauseated feeling. Then, for some reason, he thought of her meeting the younger man she'd had the calamitous affair with, the one that had ended her marriage. He picked up the receiver to see if the telephone was working. Then he put it down. Then he picked it up again and called Barbara.

"What did you do tonight, sweetheart? Did you have some fun?" Barbara was in jolly spirits. She was in the kitchen, fixing dinner for herself. He heard pots and pans rattling. He pictured her in his mind, tall and beautiful, confident about life.

"I took a woman to dinner," he said bluntly. There was no delay on the line—it was as if he were calling from the office. Something, though, was making him feel irritated. The sound of the pans, he thought; the fact that Barbara considered fixing her dinner to be important enough to keep doing it as she was talking to him. His feeling of virtue was fading.

"Well, that's wonderful," Barbara said. "Anybody special, or just somebody you met on a street corner who looked hungry?" She wasn't serious.

"A woman who works at Éditions Périgord," Austin said sternly. "An editor."

"That's nice," Barbara said, and what seemed like a small edge rose in her voice. He wondered if there was a signal in *his* voice, something that alerted her no matter how hard he tried to seem natural, something she'd heard before over the years and that couldn't be hidden.

"It *was* nice," Austin said. "We had a good time. But I'm coming home tomorrow."

"Well, we're waiting for you," Barbara said brightly.

"Who's we?" Austin said.

"Me. And the house. And the plants and the windows. The cars. Your life. We're all waiting with big smiles on our faces."

"That's great," Austin said.

"It *is* great," Barbara said. Then there was silence on the line—expensive, transoceanic silence. Austin felt the need to reorganize his good mood. He had nothing to be mad about. Or uncomfortable. All was well. Barbara hadn't done anything, but neither had he. "What time is it there?" she said casually. He heard another pot clatter, then water turn on in the sink. His champagne glass had gotten warmer, the champagne flat and sweet.

"After one," he said. "I'm sleepy now. I've got a long day tomorrow."

"So go to sleep," Barbara said.

"Thanks," Austin said.

There was more silence. "Who *is* this woman?" Barbara said somewhat brittlely.

"Just a woman I met," Austin said. "She's married. She has a baby. It's just *la vie moderne.*"

"*La vie moderne,*" Barbara said. She was tasting something now. Whatever she was cooking she was tasting.

"Right," Austin said. "Modern life."

"I understand," Barbara said. "*La vie moderne.* Modern life." She tapped a spoon hard on the rim of a pan.

"Are you glad I'm coming home?"

"Of course," Barbara said, and paused again while Austin tried to particularize for himself the look that was on her face now. All the features in her quite beautiful face seemed to get thinner when she got angry. He wondered if they were thin now. "Do you think," Barbara said, trying to sound merely curious, "that you might just possibly have taken me for granted tonight?" Silence. She was going on cooking. She was alone in their house, cooking for herself, and he was in a nice hotel in Paris—a former monastery—drinking champagne in his pajamas. There was some discrepancy. He had to admit that. Though it finally wasn't very important, since each of them was well fixed. But he felt sorry for her, sorry that she thought he took her for granted, when he didn't think he did; when in fact he loved her and was eager to see her. He was sorry she didn't know how he felt right now, how much regard he had for her. If she did, he thought, it would make her happy.

"No," Austin said, finally answering her question. "I don't think I do. I really don't think so. Do you think I ever do?"

"No? It's fine, then," Barbara said. He heard a cabinet door close. "I wouldn't want you to think that you took me for granted, that's all."

"Why do we have to talk about this now?" Austin said plaintively. "I'm coming home tomorrow. I'm eager to see you. I'm not mad about anything. Why are you?"

"I'm not," Barbara said. "Never mind. It doesn't matter. I just think things and then they go away." More spoon banging.

"I love you," Austin said. The rim of his ear had begun to ache from the receiver being pressed into it with his shoulder.

"Good," Barbara said. "Go to sleep loving me."

"I don't want to argue."

"Then don't argue," Barbara said. "Maybe I'm just in a bad mood. I'm sorry."

"Why are you mad?" Austin said.

"Sometimes," Barbara said. Then she stopped. "I don't know. Sometimes you just piss me off."

"Well, shit," Austin said.

"Shit is right. Shit," Barbara said. "It's nothing. Go to sleep."

"Fine. I will," Austin said.

"I'll see you tomorrow, sweetheart."

"Sure," Austin said, wanting to sound casual. He started to say something else. To tell her he loved her, again in the casual voice. But Barbara had hung up the phone.

Austin sat in bed in his pajamas, staring at himself in the smoky mirror. It was a different picture from before. He looked grainy, displeased, the light beside his bed harsh, intrusive, his champagne glass empty, the night he'd just spent unsuccessful, unpromising, vaguely humiliating. He looked like he was on drugs. That was the true picture, he thought. Later, he knew, he would think differently, would see events in a kinder, more flattering light. His spirits would rise as they always did and he would feel very, very encouraged by something, anything. But now was the time to take a true reading, he thought, when the tide was out and everything exposed—including himself—as it really, truly was. *There* was the real life, and he wasn't deluded about it. It was this picture you had to act on.

He sat in bed and felt gloomy, drank the rest of his champagne and thought about Barbara in the house alone, probably doing something to prepare for his arrival the next afternoon—arranging some fresh flowers or preparing to cook something he especially liked. Maybe that's what she was doing when they were talking, in which case he was certainly wrong to have been annoyed. After thinking along these lines for a while, he reached over and began to dial Joséphine's number. It was two a.m. He would wake her up, but that was all right. She'd be glad he had. He would tell her the truth—that he couldn't keep from calling her, that she was on his mind, that he wished she was here with him, that he already missed her, that there was more to this than seemed. But when he'd dialed her number the line was busy. And it was busy in five minutes. And in fifteen. And in thirty. So that after a while he dispiritedly turned off the light beside the bed, put his head on the crisp pillow and passed quickly into sleep.

4

In the small suburban community of Oak Grove, Illinois, Austin meant to take straight aim on his regular existence—driving to and from the Lilienthal office in nearby Winnetka; helping coach a Little League team sponsored by a friend's Oak Grove linoleum company; spending evenings at home with Barbara, who was a broker for a big firm that sold commercial real estate and who was herself having an excellent selling season.

Austin, however, could sense that something was wrong, which bewildered him. Although Barbara had decided to continue everyday life as if that were not true, or as if whatever was bothering him was simply outside her control and because she loved him, eventually his problem would either be solved privately or be carried away by the flow of ordinary happy life. Barbara's was a systematically optimistic view: that with the right attitude, everything works out for the best. She possessed this view, she said, because her family had all been Scottish Presbyterians. And it was a view Austin admired, though it was not always the way he saw things. He thought ordinary life had the potential to grind you into dust—his parents' life in Peoria, for instance, a life he couldn't have stood—and sometimes unusual measures were called for. Barbara said this point of view was typically shanty Irish.

On the day Austin returned—into a hot, springy airport sunshine, jet-lagged and forcibly good-spirited—Barbara had cooked venison haunch in a rich secret fig sauce, something she'd had to sleuth the ingredients for in a Hungarian neighborhood on West Diversey, plus Brabant potatoes and roasted garlics (Austin's favorite), plus a very good Merlot that Austin had drunk too much of while earnestly, painstakingly lying about all he'd done in Paris. Barbara had bought a new spring dress, had her hair restreaked and generally gone to a lot of trouble to orchestrate a happy homecoming and to forget about their unpleasant late-night phone conversation. Though Austin felt it should be his responsibility to erase that uncomfortable moment from memory and see to it his married life of long standing was once again the source of seamless, good-willed happiness.

Late that night, a Tuesday, he and Barbara made brief, boozy love in the dark of their thickly curtained bedroom, to the sound of a neighbor's springer spaniel barking unceasingly one street over. Theirs was practiced, undramatic lovemaking, a set of protocols and assumptions lovingly followed like a liturgy which points to but really has little connection with the mysteries and chaos that had once made it a breathless necessity. Austin noticed by the digital clock on the chest of drawers that it all took nine minutes, start to finish. He wondered bleakly if this was of normal or less than normal duration for Americans his and Barbara's age. Less, he supposed, though no doubt the fault was his.

Lying in the silent dark afterwards, side by side, facing the white plaster ceiling (the neighbor's dog had shut up as if on cue from an unseen observer of their act), he and Barbara sought to find something to say. Each knew the other's mind was seeking it; an upbeat, forward-sounding subject that conjured away the past couple or maybe it was three years, which hadn't been so wonderful between the two of them—a time of wandering for Austin and patience from Barbara. They wished for something unprovoking that would allow them to go to sleep thinking of themselves the way they assumed they were.

"Are you tired? You must be pretty exhausted," Barbara said matter-of-factly into the darkness. "You poor old thing." She reached and patted him on his chest. "Go to sleep. You'll feel better tomorrow."

"I feel fine now. I'm not tired," Austin said alertly. "Do I seem tired?"

"No. I guess not."

They were silent again, and Austin felt himself relaxing to the sound of her words. He was, in fact, corrosively tired. Yet he wanted to put a good end to the night, which he felt had been a nice one, and to the homecoming itself, and to the time he'd been gone and ridiculously infatuated with Joséphine Belliard. That encounter—there *was* no encounter, of course—but in any case those pronouncements and preoccupations could be put to rest. They could be disciplined away. They were not real life—at least not the bedrock, real*est* life, the one everything depended on—no matter how he'd briefly felt and protested. He wasn't a fool. He wasn't stupid enough to lose his sense of proportion. He was a survivor, he thought, and survivors always knew which direction the ground was.

"I just want to see what's possible now," Austin said unexpectedly. He was half asleep and had been having two conversations at once—one with Barbara, his wife, and one with himself about Joséphine Belliard—and the two were getting mixed up. Barbara hadn't asked him anything to which what he'd just mumbled was even a remotely logical answer. She hadn't, that he remembered, asked him anything at all. He was just babbling, talking in his near sleep. But a cold, stiffening fear gripped him, a fear that he'd said something, half asleep and half drunk, that he'd be sorry for, something that would incriminate him with the truth about Joséphine. Though in his current state of mind, he wasn't at all sure what that truth might be.

"That shouldn't be hard, should it?" Barbara said out of the dark.

"No," Austin said, wondering if he was awake. "I guess not."

"We're together. And we love each other. Whatever we want to make possible we ought to be able to do." She touched his leg through his pajamas.

"Yes," Austin said. "That's right." He wished Barbara would go to sleep now. He didn't want to say anything else. Talking was a minefield, since he wasn't sure what he would say.

Barbara was silent, while his insides contracted briefly, then slowly began to relax again. He resolved to say nothing else. After a couple of minutes Barbara turned and faced the curtains. The streetlight showed palely between the fabric closings, and Austin wondered if he had somehow made her cry without realizing it.

"Oh well," Barbara said. "You'll feel better tomorrow, I hope. Good night."

"Good night," Austin said. And he settled himself helplessly into sleep, feeling that he had not pleased Barbara very much, and that not only was he a man who probably pleased no one very much now, but that in his own life—among the things that should and always had made him happy—very little pleased him at all.

In the next days Austin went to work as he usually did. He made make-up calls to his accounts in Brussels and Amsterdam. He told a man he'd known for ten years and deeply respected that doctors had discovered a rather "mysterious inflammation" high in the upper quadrant of his stomach but that there was reasonable hope surgery could be averted with the aid of drugs. He tried to think of the name of the drug he was "taking" but couldn't. Afterwards he felt gloomy about having told such a pointless falsehood and worried that the man might mention something to his boss.

He wondered, staring at the elegantly framed azimuth map Barbara had given him when he'd been awarded the prestigious European accounts, and which he'd hung behind his desk with tiny red pennants attached, denoting where he'd increased the company's market share—Brussels, Amsterdam, Düsseldorf, Paris— wondered if his life, his normal carrying-on, was slipping out of control, yet so gradually as not to be noticed. But he decided it wasn't, and as proof he offered the fact that he was entertaining this idea in his office, on an ordinary business day, with everything in his life arrayed in place and going forward, rather than enter- taining it in some Parisian street café in the blear aftermath of calamity: a man with soiled lapels, in need of a shave and short of cash, scribbling his miserable thoughts into a tiny spiral notebook like all the other morons he'd seen who'd thrown their lives away. This feeling now, this sensation of heaviness, of life's coming unmoored, was actually, he believed, a feeling of vigilance, the weight of responsibility accepted, the proof that carrying life to a successful end was never an easy matter.

On Thursday, the moment he arrived in the office he put in a call to Joséphine at work. She'd been on his mind almost every minute: her little oddly matched but inflaming features, her boyish way of walking with her toes pointed out like a country bumpkin. But also her soft, shadowy complexion and soft arms, her whispered voice in his memory: *"Non, non, non, non, non."*

"Hi, it's me," Austin said. This time a bulky delay clogged his connection, and he could hear his voice echo on the line. He didn't sound like he wanted to sound. His voice was higher pitched, like a kid's voice.

"Okay. Hi," was all Joséphine said. She was rustling papers, a sound that annoyed him.

"I was just thinking about you," he said. A long pause opened after this announcement, and he endured it uncomfortably.

"Yes," she said. Another pause. "Me, too. How are you?"

"I'm fine," Austin said, though he didn't want to stress that. He wanted to stress that he missed her. "I miss you," he said, and felt feeble hearing his voice inside the echo.

"Yeah," she said finally though flatly. "Me, too."

He wasn't sure if she'd actually heard what he'd said. Possibly she was talking to someone else, someone in her office. He felt disoriented and considered hanging up. Though he knew how he'd feel if that happened. Wretched beyond imagining. In fact, he needed to persevere now or he'd end up feeling wretched anyway.

"I'd like to see you very much," Austin said, his ear pressed to the receiver.

"Yeah," Joséphine said. "Come and take me to dinner tonight." She laughed a harsh, ironic laugh. He wondered if she was saying this for someone else's benefit, someone in her office who knew all about him and thought he was stupid. He heard more papers rustle. He felt things spinning.

"I mean it," he said. "I would."

"When are you coming back to Paris?"

"I don't know. But very soon, I hope." He didn't know why

he'd said that, since it wasn't true, or at least wasn't in any plans he currently had. Only in that instant it seemed possible. Anything was possible. And indeed *this* seemed imminently possible. He simply had no idea how. You couldn't decide to go for the weekend. France wasn't Wisconsin.

"So. Call me, I guess," Joséphine said. "I would see you."

"I will," Austin said, his heart beginning to thump. "When I come I'll call you."

He wanted to ask her something. He didn't know what, though. He didn't know anything to ask. "How's Leo?" he said, using the English pronunciation.

Joséphine laughed, but not ironically. "How is Leo?" she said, using the same pronunciation. "Léo is okay. He is at home. Soon I'm going there. That's all."

"Good," Austin said. "That's great." He swiveled quickly and stared at Paris on the map. As usual, he was surprised at how much nearer the top of France it was instead of perfectly in the middle, the way he always thought of it. He wanted to ask her why she hadn't called him the last night he'd seen her, to let her know he'd hoped she would. But then he remembered her line had been busy, and he wanted to know who she'd been talking to. Although he couldn't ask that. It wasn't his business.

"Fine," he said. And he knew that in five seconds the call would be over and Paris would instantly be as far from Chicago as it ever was. He almost said "I love you" into the receiver. But that would be a mistake, and he didn't say it, though part of him furiously wanted to. Then he nearly said it in French, thinking possibly it might mean less than it meant in English. But again he refrained. "I want to see you very much," he said as a last, weak, compromise.

"So. See me. I kiss you," Joséphine Belliard said, but in a strange voice, a voice he'd never heard before, almost an emotional voice. Then she quietly hung up.

Austin sat at his desk, staring at the map, wondering what that voice had been, what it meant, how he was supposed to interpret it. Was it the voice of love, or some strange trick of the phone line? Or was it a trick of his ear to confect something he wanted to hear and so allow him not to feel as wretched as he figured he'd feel but in fact didn't feel. Because how he felt was wonderful. Ebullient. The best he'd felt since the last time he'd seen her. Alive. And there was nothing wrong with that, was there? If something makes you feel good for a moment and no one is crushed by it, what's the use of denying yourself? Other people denied. And for what? The guys he'd gone to college with, who'd never left the track once they were on it, never had a moment of ebullience, and maybe even never knew the difference. But he *did* know the difference, and it was worth it, no matter the difficulties you endured living with the consequences. You had one life, Austin thought. Use it up. He'd heard what he'd heard.

That evening he picked Barbara up at the realty offices and drove them to a restaurant. It was a thing they often did. Barbara frequently worked late, and they both liked a semi-swanky Polynesian place in Skokie called Hai-Nun, a dark, teak-and-bamboo hideaway where the drinks were all doubles and eventually, when you were too drunk to negotiate your way to a table, you could order a platter of fried specialties and sober up eating dinner at the bar.

For a while an acquaintance of Austin's, a commodities trader named Ned Coles, had stood beside them at the bar and made chitchat about how the salad days on the Board of Trade were a thing of the past, and then about the big opportunities in Europe after 1992 and how the U.S. was probably going to miss the boat, and then about how the Fighting Illini were sizing up at the skilled positions during spring drills, and finally about his ex-wife, Suzie, who was moving to Phoenix the next week so she could participate more in athletics. She was interested, Ned Coles said, in taking part in iron-woman competitions.

"Can't she be an iron woman in Chicago?" Barbara said. She

barely knew Ned Coles and was bored by him. Ned's wife was also "kidnapping" their two kids to Arizona, which had Ned down in the dumps but not wanting to make a fuss.

"Of course she can," Ned said. Ned was a heavy, beet-faced man who looked older than forty-six. He had gone to Harvard, then come home to work for his old man's company and quickly become a drunk and a nuisance. Austin had met him in MBA night school fifteen years ago. They didn't see each other socially. "But that's not the big problem," Ned went on.

"What's the big problem?" Austin said, muddling an ice cube in his gin.

"Moi-même," Ned said, and looked grim about it. "She contends I'm a force field of negativism that radiates into all the north suburbs. So I have to move to Indiana for her to stay. And that's way too big a sacrifice." Ned laughed humorlessly. He knew a lot of Indiana jokes that Austin had already heard. Indiana, to Ned Coles, was the place where you caught sight of the flagship of the Polish navy and visited the Argentine war heroes memorial. He was old Chicago, and also, Austin thought, an idiot. He wished Ned's wife a good journey to Arizona.

When Ned wandered off into the restaurant, leaving them alone at the lacquered teak bar, Barbara grew quiet. Both of them were drinking gin, and in silence they let the bartender pour them another two on the rocks. Austin knew he was a little drunk now and that Barbara was probably more drunk than he was. He sensed a problem could be lurking—about what he wasn't sure. But he longed for the feeling he'd had when he put the phone down with Joséphine Belliard that morning. Ebullience. To be fiercely alive. It had been a temporary feeling, he understood perfectly well. But he longed for it now all the more achingly on account of its illusory quality, its innocent smallness. Even realists, he thought, needed a break now and then.

"Do you remember the other night?" Barbara began as if she were choosing her words with extreme precision. "You were in Paris, and I was back here at home. And I asked you if you thought you might be taking me for granted?" She focused on the rim of her glass, but unexpectedly her eyes cast up and found his. There was one other couple in the bar, and the bartender had seated himself on a stool at the end and was reading a newspaper. This was the dinner hour, and many people were in the restaurant section. Someone had ordered a dish that required fire to be brought from the kitchen to their table, and Austin could see the yellow flame lick up at the ceiling, hear the loud *sssss* and the delighted diners say, "Oooo."

"I didn't think that was true," Austin said resolutely in answer to her question.

"I know you didn't," Barbara said and nodded her head slowly. "And maybe that's exactly right. Maybe I was wrong." She stared at her glass of gin again. "What *is* true, though, Martin, and what's worse—about you, anyway—is that you take *yourself* for granted." Barbara kept nodding her head without looking at him, as if she'd discovered an interesting but worrisome paradox in philosophy. When Barbara got mad at him, particularly if she was a little drunk, she nodded her head and spoke in this overly meticulous way, as if she'd done considerable thinking on the subject at hand and wished to illuminate her conclusions as a contribution to common sense. Austin called this habit "reading the ingredients on the Molotov cocktail," and he hated it and wished Barbara wouldn't do it, though there was never a good moment to bring the subject up.

"I'm sorry, but I don't think I know what you mean by that," he said in the most normal voice he could manufacture.

Barbara looked at him curiously, her perfect Lambda Chi beauty-queen features grown as precise and angular as her words. "What I mean is that you think—about yourself—that you can't be changed, as if you're *fixed*. On your insides, I mean. You think of yourself as a given, that what you go off to some foreign country and do won't have any effect on you, won't leave you different. But that isn't true, Martin. Because you *are* different. In fact, you're unreachable, and you've been becoming that way for a long time. For two or three years, at least. I've just tried to get along with you and make you happy, because making you happy has always made me happy. But now it doesn't, because you've changed and I don't feel like I can reach you or that you're even aware of what you've become, and frankly I don't even much care. All this just occurred to me while I was ordering a title search this afternoon. I'm sorry it's such a shock."

Barbara sniffed and looked at him and seemed to smile. She wasn't about to cry. She was cold-eyed and factual, as if she were reporting the death of a distant relative neither of them remembered very well.

"I'm sorry to hear that," Austin said, wanting to remain as calm as she was, though not as cold. He didn't exactly know what this meant or what could've brought it about, since he didn't think he'd been doing anything wrong. Nothing had happened two or three years ago that he could remember. Joséphine Belliard had had a small effect on him, but it would pass the way anything passed. Life seemed to be going on. He thought, in fact, that he'd been acting about as normal as he could hope to act.

But did this mean that she had taken all she intended to and was through with him? That would be a shock, he thought, something he definitely didn't want. Or did she only mean to say he needed to shape up and become more reachable, go back to some nice way he'd been that she approved of—some way he would've said he still was. Or maybe she was saying she intended to make her own changes now, be less forgiving, less interested in him, less loving, take more interest in herself; that their marriage was going to start down a new, more equitable road—something else he didn't like the sound of.

He sat thoughtfully in the silence she was affording him for just this purpose. He certainly needed to offer a response. He needed intelligently and forthrightly to answer her charges and demonstrate sympathy for her embattled position. But also he needed to stand up for himself, while offering a practical way out of this apparent impasse. Much, in other words, was being asked of him. He was, it seemed, expected to solve everything: to take *both* positions—hers and his—and somehow join them so that everything was either put back to a way it had been or else made better so that both of them were happier and could feel that if life was a series of dangerous escarpments you scaled with difficulty, at least you eventually succeeded, whereupon the plenteous rewards of happiness made all the nightmares worthwhile.

It was an admirable view of life, Austin thought. It was a sound, traditional view, absolutely in the American grain, and one that sent everybody to the altar starry-eyed and certain. It was a view Barbara had always maintained and he'd always envied. Barbara was in the American grain. It was one of the big reasons he'd been knocked out by her years ago and why he knew she would be the best person he or anyone else could ever love. Only he didn't see at that moment what he could do to make her wishes come true, if he in fact knew anything about what her wishes were. So that what he said, after admitting he was sorry to hear what she'd already said, was: "But I don't think there's anything I can do about it. I wish there was. I'm really sorry."

"Then you're just an asshole," Barbara said and nodded again very confidently, very conclusively. "And you're also a womanizer and you're a creep. And I don't want to be married to any of those things anymore. So." She took a big emptying swig out of her glass of gin and set the thick tumbler down hard on its damp little napkin coaster. "So," she said again, as if appreciating her own self-assured voice, "fuck you. And good-bye." With that, she got up and walked very steadily and straight out of the Hai-Nun (so straight that Austin didn't wonder about whether she was in any condition to drive) and disappeared around the bamboo corner just as another fat lick of yellow flame swarmed into the dark dining-room air and another hot, loud sizzling sound went up, and another "Oooo" was exhaled from the dazzled diners, a couple of whom even clapped.

This was certainly an over-response on Barbara's part, Austin felt. In the first place, she knew nothing about Joséphine Belliard, because there was nothing to know. No incriminating facts. She was only guessing, and unfairly. In all probability she was just feeling bad about herself and hoping to make him responsible for it.

In the second place, it wasn't easy to tell the truth about how you felt when it wasn't what someone you loved wanted to be the truth. He'd done his best by saying he wasn't sure what he could do to make her happy. That had been a place to start. He'd sensed her opening certitude had just been a positioning strategy and that while a big fight might've been brewing, it would've been one they could settle over the course of the evening, ending with apologies, after which they could both feel better, even liberated. It had gone like that in the past when he'd gotten temporarily distracted by some woman he met far from home. Ordinary goings-on, he thought.

Though women were sometimes a kind of problem. He enjoyed their company, enjoyed hearing their voices, knowing about their semi-intimate lives and daily dramas. But his attempts at knowing them often created a peculiar feeling, as if on the one hand he'd come into the possession of secrets he didn't want to keep, while on the other, some other vital portion of life—his life with Barbara, for instance—was left not fully appreciated, gone somewhat to waste.

But Barbara had stepped out of all bounds with this leaving. Now they were both alone in separate little cocoons of bitterness and self-explanation, and that was when matters did not get better but worse. Everyone knew that. She had brought this situation into existence, not him, and she would have to live with the outcome, no matter how small or how large. Drinking had something to do with it, he thought. His and hers. There was a lot of tension in the air at the moment, and drinking was a natural response. He didn't think either of them had a drinking problem per se—particularly himself. But he resolved, sitting at the teak bar in front of a glass of Beefeater's, that he would quit drinking as soon as he could.

When he walked outside into the dark parking lot, Barbara was nowhere in sight. A half hour had gone by. He thought he might find her in the car, mad or sleeping. It was eight-thirty. The air was cool, and Old Orchard Road was astream with automobiles.

When he drove home, all the lights were off and Barbara's car, which she'd left at her office when he picked her up, was not in the garage. Austin walked in through the house, turning on lights until he got to their bedroom. He opened the door gingerly, so as not to wake Barbara if she was there, flung across the top covers, asleep. But she wasn't there. The room was dark except for the digital clock. He was alone in the house, and he didn't know where his wife was, only that she was conceivably leaving him. Certainly she'd been angry. The last thing she had said was "fuck you." Then she'd walked out—something she hadn't done before. Someone, he understood, might conclude she was leaving him.

Austin poured himself a glass of milk in the brightly lit kitchen and considered testifying to these very moments and facts, as well as to the unpleasant episode in the Hai-Nun and to the final words of his wife, in a court of law. A divorce court. He featured himself sitting at a table with his lawyer, and Barbara at a table with her lawyer, both of them, eyes straight ahead, facing a judge's bench. In her present state of mind Barbara wouldn't be persuaded by his side of the story. She wouldn't have a change of heart or decide just to forget the whole thing in the middle of a courtroom once he'd looked her square in the eye and told only the truth. Still, divorce was certainly not a good solution, he thought.

Austin walked up to the sliding glass door that gave on to the backyard and to the dark and fenceless yards of his neighbors, their soft house lights and the reflection of his own kitchen cabinets and himself holding his glass of milk and of the breakfast table and chairs, all combined in a perfect half-lit diorama.

On the other hand, he thought (the first being a messy divorce attempt followed by sullen reconciliation once they realized they lacked the nerve for divorce), *he was out.*

He hadn't left. *She* had. *He* hadn't made any threats or complaints or bitter, half-drunk, name-calling declarations or soap-operaish exits into the night. *She* had. *He* hadn't wanted to be alone. *She* had wanted to be alone. And as a result *he* was free. Free to do anything he wanted, no questions asked or answered, no suspicions or recriminations. No explanatory half-truths. It was a revelation.

In the past, when he and Barbara had had a row and he had felt like just getting in the car and driving to Montana or Alaska to work for the forest service—never writing, never calling, though not actually going to the trouble of concealing his identity or whereabouts—he'd found he could never face the moment of actual leaving. His feet simply wouldn't move. And about himself he'd said, feeling quietly proud of the fact, that he was no good at departures. There was in leaving, he believed, the feel of betrayal—of betraying Barbara. Of betraying himself. You didn't marry somebody so you could leave, he'd actually said to her on occasion. He could never in fact even seriously think about leaving. And about the forest service he could only plot as far as the end of the first day—when he was tired and bruised from hard work, his mind emptied of worries. But after that he was confused about what would be happening next—another toilsome day like the one before. This had meant, he understood, that he didn't want to leave; that his life, his love for Barbara, were simply too strong. Leaving was what weak people did. Again his college classmates were called upon to be the bad examples, the cowardly leavers. Most of them had been divorced, strewn kids of all ages all over the map, routinely and grimly posted big checks off to Dallas and Seattle and Atlanta, fed on regret. They had left and now they were plenty sorry. But his love for Barbara was simply worth more. Some life force was in him too strongly, too fully, to leave—which meant something, something lasting and important. This force, he felt, was what all the great novels ever written were about.

Of course, it had occurred to him that what he might be was just a cringing, lying coward who didn't have the nerve to face a life alone; couldn't fend for himself in a complex world full of his own acts' consequences. Though that was merely a conventional way of understanding life, another soap-opera view—about which he knew better. He was a stayer. He was a man who didn't have to do the obvious thing. He would be there to preside over the messy consequences of life's turmoils. This was, he thought, his one innate strength of character.

Only now, oddly, he was in limbo. The "there" where he'd promised to stay seemed to have suddenly separated into pieces and receded. And it was invigorating. He felt, in fact, that although Barbara had seemed to bring it about, he may have caused all this himself, even though it was probably inevitable—destined to happen to the two of them no matter what the cause or outcome.

He went to the bar cart in the den, poured some scotch into his milk, and came back and sat in a kitchen chair in front of the sliding glass door. Two dogs trotted across the grass in the rectangle of light that fell from the window. Shortly after, another two dogs came through—one the springer spaniel he regularly heard yapping at night. And then a small scruffy lone dog, sniffing the ground behind the other four. This dog stopped and peered at Austin, blinked, then trotted out of the light.

Austin had been imagining Barbara checked into an expensive hotel downtown, drinking champagne, ordering a Cobb salad from room service and thinking the same things he'd been thinking. But what he was actually beginning to feel now, and grimly, was that when push came to shove, the aftermath of almost anything he'd done in a very long time really *hadn't* given him any pleasure. Despite good intentions, and despite loving Barbara as he felt few people ever loved anybody and feeling that he could be to blame for everything that had gone on tonight, he considered it unmistakable that he could do his wife no good now. He was bad for her. And if his own puny inability to satisfy her candidly expressed and at least partly legitimate grievances was not adequate proof of his failure, then her own judgment certainly was: "You're an asshole," she'd said. And he concluded that she was right. He *was* an asshole. And he was the other things too, and hated to think so. Life didn't veer—you discovered it *had* veered, later. Now. And he was as sorry about it as anything he could imagine ever being sorry about. But he simply couldn't help it. He didn't like what he didn't like and couldn't do what he couldn't do.

What he *could* do, though, was leave. Go back to Paris. Imme-

diately. Tonight if possible, before Barbara came home, and before
he and she became swamped all over again and he had to wade
back into the problems of his being an asshole, and their life. He
felt as if a fine, high-tension wire strung between his toes and the
back of his neck had been forcefully plucked by an invisible finger, causing him to feel a chilled vibration, a bright tingling that
radiated into his stomach and out to the ends of his fingers.

He sat up straight in his chair. He was leaving. Later he would
feel awful and bereft and be broke, maybe homeless, on welfare and
sick to death from a disease born of dejection. But now he felt
incandescent, primed, jittery with excitement. And it wouldn't
last forever, he thought, probably not even very long. The mere
sound of a taxi door closing in the street would detonate the whole
fragile business and sacrifice his chance to act.

He stood and quickly walked to the kitchen and telephoned
for a taxi, then left the receiver dangling off the hook. He walked
back through the house, checking all the doors and windows to
be certain they were locked. He walked into his and Barbara's
bedroom, turned on the light, hauled his two-suiter from under
the bed, opened it and began putting exactly that in one side, two
suits, and in the other side underwear, shirts, another pair of
shoes, a belt, three striped ties, plus his still-full dopp kit. In
response to an unseen questioner, he said out loud, standing in
the bedroom: "I really didn't bring much. I just put some things
in a suitcase."

He closed his bag and brought it to the living room. His pass-
port was in the secretary. He put that in his pants pocket, got a
coat out of the closet by the front door—a long rubbery rain
jacket bought from a catalog—and put it on. He picked up his
wallet and keys, then turned and looked into the house.

He was leaving. In moments he'd be gone. Likely as not he
would never stand in this doorway again, surveying these rooms,
feeling this way. Some of it might happen again, okay, but not all.
And it was so easy: one minute you're completely in a life, and the
next you're completely out. Just a few items to round up.

A note. He felt he should leave a note and walked quickly back to the kitchen, dug a green Day-Glo grocery-list pad out of a drawer, and on the back scribbled, "Dear B," only then wasn't sure what to continue with. Something meaningful would take sheets and sheets of paper but would be both absurd and irrelevant. Something brief would be ironic or sentimental, and demonstrate in a completely new way what an asshole he was—a conclusion he wanted this note to make the incontrovertible case against. He turned the sheet over. A sample grocery list was printed there, with blank spaces provided for pencil checks.

> Pain . . . .
> Lait . . . .
> Cereal . . . .
> Oeufs . . . .
> Veggies . . . .
> Hamburger . . . .
> Lard . . . .
> Fromage . . . .
> Les Autres . . . .

He could check "Les Autres," he thought, and write "Paris" beside it. Paris was certainly *autres.* Though *only* an asshole would do that. He turned it over again to the "Dear B" side. Nothing he could think of was right. Everything wanted to stand for their life, but couldn't. Their life was their life and couldn't be represented by anything but their life, and not by something scratched on the back of a grocery list.

His taxi honked outside. For some reason he reached up and put the receiver back on the hook, and almost instantly the phone started ringing—loud, brassy, shrill, unnerving rings that filled the yellow kitchen as if the walls were made of metal. He could hear the other phones ringing in other rooms. It was suddenly intolerably chaotic inside the house. Below "Dear B" he furiously scribbled, "I'll call you. Love M," and stuck the note under the jangling phone. Then he hurried to the front door, grabbed his suitcase, and exited his empty home into the soft spring suburban night.

5

During his first few dispiriting days back in Paris, Austin did not call Joséphine Belliard. There were more pressing matters: to arrange, over terrible phone connections, to be granted a leave of absence from his job. "Personal problems," he said squeamishly to his boss, and felt certain his boss was concluding he'd had a nervous breakdown. "How's Barbara?" Fred Carruthers said cheerfully, which annoyed him.

"Barbara's great," he said. "She's just fine. Call her up yourself. She'd like to hear from you." Then he hung up, thinking he'd never see Fred Carruthers again and didn't give a shit if he didn't, except that his own voice had sounded desperate, the one way he didn't want it to sound.

He arranged for his Chicago bank to wire him money— enough, he thought, for six months. Ten thousand dollars. He called up one of the two people he knew in Paris, a former Lambda Chi brother who was a homosexual and a would-be novelist, living someplace in Neuilly. Dave, his old frat bro, asked him if he was a homosexual himself now, then laughed like hell. Finally, though, Dave remembered he had a friend who had a friend— and eventually, after two unsettled nights in his old Hôtel de la Monastère, during which he'd worried about money, Austin had been given the keys to a luxurious, metal-and-velvet faggot's lair with enormous mirrors on the bedroom ceiling, just down rue Bonaparte from the Deux Magots, where Sartre was supposed to have liked to sit in the sun and think.

Much of these first days—bright, soft mid-April days—Austin was immensely jet-lagged and exhausted and looked sick and haunted in the bathroom mirror. He didn't want to see Joséphine in this condition. He had been back home only three days, then in the space of one frenzied evening had had a big fight with his wife, raced to the airport, waited all night for a flight and taken a middle-row standby to Orly seated between two French children. It was crazy. A large part of this was definitely crazy. Probably he *was* having a nervous breakdown and was too out of his head even to have a hint about it, and eventually Barbara and a psychiatrist would have to bring him home heavily sedated and in a straight-jacket. But that would be later.

"Where are you?" Barbara said coldly, when he'd finally reached her at home.

"In Europe," he said. "I'm staying awhile."

"How nice for you," she said. He could tell she didn't know what to think about any of this. It pleased him to baffle her, though he also knew it was childish.

"Carruthers might call you," he said.

"I already talked to him," Barbara said.

"I'm sure he thinks I'm nuts."

"No. He doesn't think that," she said, without offering what he did think.

Outside the apartment the traffic on rue Bonaparte was noisy, so that he moved away from the window. The walls in the apartment were dark red-and-green suede, with glistening tubular-steel abstract wall hangings, thick black carpet and black velvet furniture. He had no idea who the owner was, though he realized just at that moment that in all probability the owner was dead.

"Are you planning to file for divorce?" Austin said. It was the first time the word had ever been used, but it was inescapable, and he was remotely satisfied to be the first to put it into play.

"Actually I don't know what I'm going to do," Barbara said. "I don't have a husband now, apparently."

He almost blurted out that it was she who'd walked out, not him, she who'd actually caused this. But that wasn't entirely true, and in any case saying anything about it would start a conversation he didn't want to have and that no one *could* have at such long distance. It would just be bickering and complaining and anger. He realized all at once that he had nothing else to say, and felt jittery. He'd only wished to announce that he was alive and not dead, but was now ready to hang up.

"You're in France, aren't you?" Barbara said.

"Yes," Austin said. "That's right. Why?"

"I supposed so." She said this as though the thought of it disgusted her. "Why not, I guess. Right?"

"Right," he said.

"So. Come home when you're tired of whatever it is, whatever her name is." She said this very mildly.

"Maybe I will," Austin said.

"Maybe I'll be waiting, too," Barbara said. "Miracles still happen. I've had my eyes opened now, though."

"Great," he said, and he started to say something else, but he thought he heard her hang up. "Hello?" he said. "Hello? Barbara, are you there?"

"Oh, go to hell," Barbara said, and then she did hang up.

For two days Austin took long, exhausting walks in completely arbitrary directions, surprising himself each time by where he turned up, then taking a cab back to his apartment. His instincts still seemed all wrong, which frustrated him. He thought the Place de la Concorde was farther away from this apartment than it was, and in the wrong direction. He couldn't always remember which way the river ran. And unhappily he kept passing the same streets and movie theater playing *Cinema Paradiso* and the same news kiosk, over and over, as if he continually walked in a circle.

He called his other friend, a man named Hank Bullard, who'd once worked for Lilienthal but had decided to start an air-conditioning business of his own in Vitry. He was married to a Frenchwoman and lived in a suburb. They made plans for a lunch, then Hank canceled for business reasons—an emergency trip out of town. Hank said they should arrange another date but didn't specifically suggest one. Austin ended up having lunch alone in an expensive brasserie on the Boulevard du Montparnasse, seated behind a glass window, trying to read *Le Monde* but growing dis-

couraged as the words he didn't understand piled up. He would
read the *Herald Tribune*, he thought, to keep up with the world,
and let his French build gradually.

There were even more tourists than a week earlier when he'd
been here. The tourist season was beginning, and the whole place,
he thought, would probably change and become unbearable. The
French and the Americans, he decided, looked basically like each
other; only their language and some soft, almost effeminate quality he couldn't define distinguished them. Sitting at his tiny, round
boulevard table, removed from the swarming passersby, Austin
thought this street was full of people walking along dreaming of
doing what he was actually doing, of picking up and leaving everything behind, coming here, sitting in cafés, walking the streets, possibly deciding to write a novel or paint watercolors, or just to start
an air-conditioning business, like Hank Bullard. But there was a
price to pay for that. And the price was that doing it didn't feel
the least romantic. It felt purposeless, as if he himself had no purpose, plus there was no sense of a future now, at least as he had
always experienced the future—as a palpable thing you looked
forward to confidently even if what it held might be sad or tragic
or unwantable. The future was still there, of course; he simply
didn't know how to imagine it. He didn't know, for instance,
exactly what he was in Paris for, though he could perfectly recount
everything that had gotten him here, to this table, to his plate of
moules meunières, to this feeling of great fatigue, observing tourists,
all of whom might dream whatever he dreamed but in fact knew
precisely where they were going and precisely why they were
here. Possibly they were the wise ones, Austin thought, with their
warmly lighted, tightly constructed lives on faraway landscapes.
Maybe he had reached a point, or even gone far beyond a point
now, when he no longer cared what happened to himself—the
crucial linkages of a good life, he knew, being small and subtle and
in many ways just lucky things you hardly even noticed. Only you
could fuck them up and never know quite how you'd done it.
Everything just started to go wrong and unravel. Your life could
be on a track to ruin, to your being on the street and disappearing

from view entirely, and you, in spite of your best efforts, your best hope that it all go differently, you could only stand by and watch it happen.

For the next two days he did not call Joséphine Belliard, although he thought about calling her all the time. He thought he might possibly bump into her as she walked to work. His garish little roué's apartment was only four blocks from the publishing house on rue de Lille, where, in a vastly different life, he had made a perfectly respectable business call a little more than a week before.

He walked down the nearby streets as often as he could—to buy a newspaper or to buy food in the little market stalls on the rue de Seine, or just to pass the shop windows and begin finding his way along narrow brick alleys. He disliked thinking that he was only in Paris because of Joséphine Belliard, because of a woman, and one he really barely knew but whom he nevertheless thought about constantly and made persistent efforts to see "accidentally." He felt he was here for another reason, too, a subtle and insistent, albeit less specific one he couldn't exactly express to himself but which he felt was expressed simply by his being here and feeling the way he felt.

Not once, though, did he see Joséphine Belliard on the rue de Lille, or walking along the Boulevard St.-Germain on her way to work, or walking past the Café de Flore or the Brasserie Lipp, where he'd had lunch with her only the week before and where the sole had been full of grit but he hadn't mentioned it.

Much of the time, on his walks along strange streets, he thought about Barbara; and not with a feeling of guilt or even of loss, but normally, habitually, involuntarily. He found himself shopping for her, noticing a blouse or a scarf or an antique pendant or a pair of emerald earrings he could buy and bring home. He found himself storing away things to tell her—for instance, that the Sorbonne was actually named after somebody named Sorbon, or that France was seventy percent nuclear, a headline he deciphered off the front page of *L'Express* and that coursed around his mind like an electron with no polarity other than Barbara, who, as it happened, was a supporter of nuclear power. She occupied, he recognized, the place of final consequence—the destination for practically everything he cared about or noticed or imagined. But now, or at least for the present time, that situation was undergoing a change, since being in Paris and waiting his chance to see Joséphine lacked any customary destination, but simply started and stopped in himself. Though that was how he wanted it. And that was the explanation he had not exactly articulated in the last few days: he wanted things, whatever things there were, to be for him and only him.

On the third day, at four in the afternoon, he called Joséphine Belliard. He called her at home instead of her office, thinking she wouldn't be at home and that he could leave a brief, possibly inscrutable recorded message, and then not call her for a few more days, as though he was too busy to try again any sooner. But when her phone rang twice she answered.

"Hi," Austin said, stunned at the suddenness of Joséphine being on the line and only a short distance from where he was standing, and sounding unquestionably like herself. It made him feel vaguely faint. "It's Martin Austin," he managed to say feebly.

He heard a child scream in the background before Joséphine could say more than hello. *"Nooooon!"* the child, certainly Léo, screamed again.

"Where are you?" she said in a hectic voice. He heard something go crash in the room where she was. "Are you in Chicago now?"

"No, I'm in Paris," Austin said, grappling with his composure and speaking very softly.

"Paris? What are you doing *here*?" Joséphine said, obviously surprised. "Are you on business again now?"

This, somehow, was an unsettling question. "No," he said, still very faintly. "I'm not on business. I'm just here. I have an apartment."

"Tu as un appartement!" Joséphine said in even greater surprise. "What for?" she said. "Why? Is your wife with you?"

"No," Austin said. "I'm here alone. I'm planning on staying for a while."

"*Oooo-laaa,*" Joséphine said. "Do you have a big fight at home? Is that the matter?"

"No," Austin lied. "We didn't have a big fight at home. I decided to take some time away. That's not so unusual, is it?"

Léo screamed again savagely. "*Ma-man!*" Joséphine spoke to him patiently. "*Doucement, doucement,*" she said. "*J'arrive. Une minute. Une minute.*" One minute didn't seem like very much time, but Austin didn't want to stay on the phone long. Joséphine seemed much more French than he remembered. In his mind she had been almost an American, only with a French accent. "Okay. So," she said, a little out of breath. "You are here now? In Paris?"

"I want to see you," Austin said. It was the moment he'd been waiting for—more so even than the moment when he would finally see her. It was the moment when he would declare himself to be present. Unencumbered. Available. Willing. That mattered a great deal. He actually slipped his wedding ring off his finger and laid it on the table beside the phone.

"Yes?" Joséphine said. "What . . ." She paused, then resumed. "What do you like to do with me? When do you like? What?" She was impatient.

"Anything. Anytime," Austin said, and suddenly felt the best he'd felt in days. "Tonight," he said. "Or today. In twenty minutes."

"In twenty minutes! Come on. No!" she said and laughed, but in an interested way, a pleased way—he could tell. "No, no, no," she said. "I have to go to my lawyer in one hour. I have to find my neighbor now to stay with Léo. It is impossible now. I'm divorcing. You know this already. It's very upsetting. Anyway."

"I'll stay with Léo," Austin said rashly.

Joséphine laughed. "*You'll* stay with him! You don't have children, do you? You said this." She laughed again.

"I'm not offering to adopt him," Austin said. "But I'll stay with him for an hour. Then you can have your neighbor come, and I'll take you to dinner. How's that?"

"He doesn't like you," Joséphine said. "He likes only his father best. He doesn't even like me."

"I'll teach him some English," Austin said. "I'll teach him to say 'Chicago Cubs.'" He could feel enthusiasm already leaching off. "We'll be great friends."

"What is Chicago Cubs?" Joséphine said.

"It's a baseball team." And he felt, just for an instant, bleak. Not because he wished he was home, or wished Barbara was here, or wished really anything was different. Everything was how he'd hoped it would be. He simply wished he hadn't mentioned the Cubs. This was over-confident, he thought. It was the wrong thing to say. A mistake.

"So. Well," Joséphine said, sounding businesslike. "You come here, then? I go to my lawyers to sign my papers. Then maybe we have a dinner together, yes?"

"Absolutely," Austin said, bleakness vanished. "I'll come right away. I'll start in five minutes." On the dark suede wall, under a little metal track light positioned to illuminate it, was a big oil painting of two men, naked and locked in a strenuous kiss and embrace. Neither man's face was visible, and their bodies were weight lifters' muscular bodies, their genitals hidden by their embroiled pose. They were seated on a rock, which was very crudely painted in. It was like Laocoön, Austin thought, only corrupted. He'd wondered if one of the men was the one who owned the apartment, or possibly the owner was the painter or the painter's lover. He wondered if either one of them was alive this afternoon. He actually hated the painting and had already decided to take it down before he brought Joséphine here. Which was what he meant to do—bring her here, tonight if possible, and keep her with him until morning, when they could walk up and sit in the cool sun at the Deux Magots and drink coffee. Like Sartre.

"Martin?" Joséphine said. He was about to put down the phone and go move the smarmy Laocoön painting. He'd almost forgotten he was talking to her.

"What? I'm here," Austin said. Though it might be fun to leave it up, he thought. It could be an icebreaker, something to laugh about, like the mirrors on the ceiling, before things got more serious.

"Martin, what are you doing here?" Joséphine said oddly. "Are you okay?"

"I'm here to see you, darling," Austin said. "Why do you think? I said I'd see you soon, and I meant it. I guess I'm just a man of my word."

"You are a very silly man, though," Joséphine said and laughed, not quite so pleased as before. "But," she said, "what I can do?"

"You can't do anything," Austin said. "Just see me tonight. After that you never have to see me again."

"Yes. Okay," Joséphine said. "That's a good deal. Now. You come to here. *Ciao.*"

"*Ciao,*" Austin said oddly, not really being entirely sure what *ciao* meant.

6

Near the Odéon, striding briskly up the narrow street that ended at the Palais du Luxembourg, Austin realized he was arriving at Joséphine's apartment with nothing in his hands—a clear mistake. Possibly some bright flowers would be a good idea, or a toy, a present of some minor kind which would encourage Léo to like him. Léo was four, and ill-tempered and spoiled. He was pale and had limp, wispy-thin dark hair and dark, penetrating eyes, and when he cried—which was often—he cried loudly and had the habit of opening his mouth and leaving it open for as much of the sound to come out as possible, a habit which accentuated the simian quality of his face, a quality he on occasion seemed to share with Joséphine. Austin had seen documentaries on TV that showed apes doing virtually the same thing while sitting in trees—always it seemed just as daylight was vanishing and another long, imponderable night was at hand. Possibly that was what Léo's life was like. "It is because of my divorce from his father,"

Joséphine had said matter-of-factly the one time Austin had been in her apartment, the time they had listened to jazz and he had sat and admired the golden sunlight on the building cornices. "It is too hard on him. He is a child. But." She'd shrugged her shoulders and begun to think about something else.

Austin had seen no store selling flowers, so he crossed rue Regnard to a chic little shop that had wooden toys in its window: bright wood trucks of ingenious meticulous design, bright wood animals—ducks and rabbits and pigs in preposterous detail, even a French farmer wearing a red neckerchief and a black beret. An entire wooden farmhouse was painstakingly constructed with roof tiles, little dormer windows and Dutch doors, and cost a fortune—far more than he intended to pay. Kids were fine, but he'd never wanted any for himself, and neither had Barbara. It had been their first significant point of agreement when they were in college in the sixties—the first reason they'd found to think they might be made for each other. Years ago now, Austin thought—twenty-two. All of it past, out of reach.

The little shop, however, seemed to have plenty of nice things inside that Austin *could* afford—a wooden clock whose hands you moved yourself, wooden replicas of the Eiffel Tower and the Arc de Triomphe. There was a little wood pickaninny holding a tiny red-and-green wood watermelon and smiling with bright painted-white teeth. The little pickaninny reminded Austin of Léo—minus the smile—and he thought about buying it as a piece of Americana and taking it home to Barbara.

Inside, the saleslady seemed to think he would naturally want that and started to take it out of the case. But there was also a small wicker basket full of painted eggs on the countertop, each egg going for twenty francs, and Austin picked up one of those, a bright-green enamel and gold paisley one made of perfectly turned balsa that felt hollow. They were left over from Easter, Austin thought, and had probably been more expensive. There was no reason Léo should like a green wooden egg, of course. Except *he* liked it, and Joséphine would like it too. And once the child pushed it aside in favor of whatever he liked better, Joséphine could claim it and set it on her night table or on her desk at work, and think about who'd bought it.

Austin paid the clerk for the nubbly-sided little egg and started for the door—he was going to be late on account of being lost. But just as he reached the glass door Joséphine's husband came in, accompanied by a tall, beautiful, vivacious blond woman with a deep tan and thin, shining legs. The woman was wearing a short silver-colored dress that encased her hips in some kind of elastic fabric, and she looked, Austin thought, standing by in complete surprise, rich. Joséphine's husband—short and bulgy, with his thick, dark Armenian-looking mustache and soft, swart skin— was at least a head shorter than the woman, and was dressed in an expensively shapeless black suit. They were talking in a language which sounded like German, and Bernard—the husband who had written the salacious novel about Joséphine and who provided her little money and his son precious little attention, and whom Joséphine was that very afternoon going off to secure a divorce from—Bernard was seemingly intent on buying a present in the store.

He glanced at Austin disapprovingly. His small, almost black eyes flickered with some vague recognition. Only there couldn't be any recognition. Bernard knew nothing about him, and there was, in fact, nothing to know. Bernard had certainly never laid eyes on him. It was just the way he had of looking at a person, as though he had your number and didn't much like you. Why, Austin wondered, would that be an attractive quality in a man? Suspicion. Disdain. A bullying nature. Why marry an asshole like that?

Austin had paused inside the shop door, and now found himself staring down into the display window from behind, studying the miniature Eiffel Tower and Arc de Triomphe. They were, he saw, parts of a whole little Paris made of wood, a kit a child could play with and arrange any way he saw fit. A wooden Notre Dame, a wooden Louvre, an Obélisque, a Centre Pompidou, even a little wooden Odéon, like the one a few steps down the street. The whole set of buildings was expensive as hell—nearly three thousand francs—but you could also buy the pieces separately. Austin thought about buying something to accompany the egg—give the egg to Joséphine and miniature building to Léo. He stood staring down at the little city in wood, beyond which out the window the real city of metal and stone went on unmindful.

Bernard and his blond friend were laughing at the little pickaninny holding his red-and-green watermelon. The clerk had it out of the case, and Bernard was holding it up and laughing at it derisively. Once or twice Bernard said, "a leetle neeger," then said, *"voilà, voilà,"* then the woman said something in German and both of them burst out laughing. Even the shopkeeper laughed.

Austin fingered the green egg, a lump against his leg. He considered just going up and buying the whole goddamned wooden Paris and saying to Bernard in English, "I'm buying this for *your* son, you son of a bitch," then threatening him with his fist. But that was a bad idea, and he didn't have the stomach for a row. It was remotely possible, of course, that the man might not be Bernard at all, that he only looked like the picture in Léo's room, and he would be a complete idiot to threaten him.

He slipped his hand in his pocket, felt the enamel paint of the egg and wondered if this was an adequate present, or would it be ludicrous? The German woman turned and looked at him, the smile of derisive laughter still half on her lips. She looked at Austin's face, then at his pocket where his hand was gripping the little egg. She leaned and said something to Bernard, something in French, and Bernard turned and looked at Austin across the shop, narrowed his eyes in a kind of disdainful warning. He raised his chin slightly and turned back. They both said something else, after which they both chuckled. The proprietress looked at Austin and smiled in a friendly way. Then Austin changed his mind about buying the wooden city and opened the glass door and stepped out onto the sidewalk, where the air was cool and he could see up the short hill to the park.

7

Joséphine's apartment block was an unexceptional one on a street of similar older buildings with white modernistic fronts overlooking the Jardin du Luxembourg. In the tiny, shadowy lobby, there was an elegant old Beaux Arts grillework elevator. But since Joséphine lived on the third level, Austin walked up, taking the steps two at a time, the little green paisley egg bumping against his leg with each stride.

When he knocked, Joséphine immediately threw open the door and flung her arms around his neck. She hugged him, then held her hands on his cheeks and kissed him hard on the mouth. Little Léo, who'd just been running from one room to another, waving a wooden drumstick, stopped stock-still in the middle of the floor and stared, shocked by his mother's kissing a man he didn't remember seeing before.

"Okay. Now I must go," Joséphine said, releasing his face and hurrying to the open window which overlooked the street and the park. She was putting on her eye shadow, using a tiny compact mirror and the light from outside.

Joséphine was dressed in a simple white blouse and a pair of odd, loose-fitting pants that had pictures of circus animals all over them, helter-skelter in loud colors. They were strange, unbecoming pants, Austin thought, and they fit in such a way that her small stomach made a noticeable round bulge below the waistband. Joséphine looked slightly fat and a little sloppy. She turned and smiled at him as she fixed her face. "How do you feel?" she said.

"I feel great," Austin said. He smiled at Léo, who had not stopped staring at him, holding up his drumstick like a little cigar-store Indian. The child had on short trousers and a white T-shirt that had the words BIG-TIME AMERICAN LUXURY printed across the front above a huge red Cadillac convertible which seemed to be driving out from his chest.

Léo uttered something very fast in French, then looked at his mother and back at Austin, who hadn't gotten far into the room since being hugged and kissed.

"*Non, non, Léo,*" Joséphine said, and laughed with an odd delight. "He asks me if you are my new husband. He thinks I need a husband now. He is very mixed up." She went on darkening her eyes. Joséphine looked pretty in the window light, and Austin wanted to go over right then and give her a much more significant kiss. But the child kept staring at him, holding the drumstick up and making Austin feel awkward and reluctant, which wasn't how he thought he'd feel. He thought he'd feel free and completely at ease and on top of the world about everything.

He reached in his pocket, palmed the wooden egg and knelt in front of the little boy, showing two closed fists.

"*J'ai un cadeau pour toi,*" he said. He'd practiced these words and wondered how close he'd come. "I have a nice present for you," he said in English to satisfy himself. "*Choissez le main.*" Austin tried to smile. He jiggled the correct hand, his right one, trying to capture the child's attention. "*Choissez le main, Léo,*" he said again and smiled, this time, a little grimly. Austin looked at Joséphine for encouragement, but she was still appraising herself in her mirror. She said something very briskly to Léo, who beetled his dark little brow at the two presented fists. Reluctantly he pointed his drumstick at Austin's right fist, the one he'd been jiggling. And very slowly—as though he were opening a chest filled with gold—Austin opened his fingers to reveal the bright little green egg with gold paisleys and red snowflakes. Some flecks of the green paint had already come off on his palm, which surprised him. "*Voilà,*" Austin said dramatically. "*C'est une jolie oeuf!*"

Léo stared intently at the clammy egg in Austin's palm. He looked at Austin with an expression of practiced inquisitiveness, his thin lips growing pursed as though something worried him. Very timidly he extended his wooden drumstick and touched the egg, then nudged it, with the shaped tip, the end intended to strike a drum. Austin noticed that Léo had three big gravelly warts on his tiny fingers, and instantly a cold wretchedness from his own childhood opened in him, making Léo for an instant seem frail and sympathetic. But then with startling swiftness Léo raised the drumstick and delivered the egg—still in Austin's proffered palm—a fierce downward blow, hoping apparently to smash it and splatter its contents and possibly give Austin's fingers a painful lashing for good measure.

But the egg, though the blow chipped its glossy green enamel and Austin felt the impact like a shock, did not break. And little Léo's pallid face assumed a look of controlled fury. He quickly took two more vengeful back-and-forth swipes at it, the second of which struck Austin's thumb a stinging then numbing blow, then Léo turned and fled out of the room, down the hall and through a door which he slammed behind him.

Austin looked up at Joséphine, who was just finishing at the window.

"He is very mixed up. I tell you before," she said, and shook her head.

"That didn't work out too well," Austin said, squeezing his throbbing thumb so as not to have to mention it.

"It's not important," she said, going to the couch and putting her compact in her purse. "He is angry all the time. Sometimes he hits *me*. Don't feel bad. You're sweet to bring something to him."

But what Austin felt, at that moment, was that he wanted to kiss Joséphine, and not to talk about Léo. Now that they were alone, he wanted to kiss her in a way that said he was here and it wasn't just a coincidence, that he'd had her on his mind this whole time, and wanted her to have him on her mind, and that this whole thing that had started last week in discretion and good-willed restraint was rising to a new level, a level to be taken more seriously. She could love him now. He could conceivably even love her. Much was possible that only days ago was not even dreamed of.

He moved toward where she was, repocketing the egg, his injured thumb pulsating. She was leaned over the couch in her idiotic animal pants, and he rather roughly grasped her hips— covering the faces of a yellow giraffe and a gray rhino with his hands—and pulled, trying to turn her toward him so he could give her the kiss he wanted to give her, the authoritative one that signaled his important arrival on the scene. But she jumped, as though he'd startled her, and she shouted, "Stop! What is it!" just as he was negotiating her face around in front of his. She had a lipstick tube in her hand, and she seemed irritated to be so close to him. She smelled sweet, surprisingly sweet. Like a flower, he thought.

"There's something important between us, I think," Austin said directly into Joséphine's irritated face. "Important enough to bring me back across an ocean and to leave my wife and to face the chance that I'll be alone here."

"What?" she said. She contorted her mouth and, without exactly pushing, exerted a force to gain a few inches from him. He still had her by her hips, cluttered with animal faces. A dark crust of eye shadow clung where she had inexpertly doctored her eyelids.

"You shouldn't feel under any pressure," he said and looked at her gravely. "I just want to see you. That's all. Maybe have some time alone with you. Who knows where it'll go?"

"You are very fatigued, I think." She struggled to move backward. "Maybe you can have a sleep while I'm going."

"I'm not tired," Austin said. "I feel great. Nothing's bothering me. I've got a clean slate."

"That's good," she said, and smiled but pushed firmly away from him just as he was moving in to give her the important kiss. Joséphine quickly kissed him first, though, the same hard, unpassionate kiss she'd greeted him with five minutes before and that had left him dissatisfied.

"I want to kiss you the right way, not that way," Austin said. He pulled her firmly to him again, taking hold of her soft waist and pushing his mouth toward hers. He kissed her as tenderly as he could with her back stiff and resistant, and her mouth not shaped to receive a kiss but ready to speak when the kiss ended. Austin held the kiss for a long moment, his eyes closed, his breath traveling out his nose, trying to feel his own wish for tenderness igniting an answering tenderness in her. But if there was tenderness, it was of an unexpected type—more like forbearance. And when he had pressed her lips for as many as six or eight seconds, until he had breathed her breath and she had relaxed her resistance, he stood back and looked at her—a woman he felt he might love—and took her chin between his thumb and index finger and said, "That's really all I wanted. That wasn't all that bad, was it?"

She shook her head in a perfunctory way and very softly, almost compliantly, said, "No." Her eyes were cast down, though not in a way he felt confident of, more as if she were waiting for something. He felt he should let her go; that was the thing to do. He'd forced her to kiss him. She'd relented. Now she could be free to do anything she wanted.

Joséphine hurriedly turned back toward her purse on the couch, and Austin walked to the window and surveyed the vast chestnut trees of the Jardin du Luxembourg. The air was cool and soft, and the light seemed creamy and rich in the late afternoon. He heard music, guitar music from somewhere, and the faint sound of singing. He saw a jogger running through the park gate and out into the street below, and he wondered what anyone would think who saw him standing in this window—someone glancing up a moment out of the magnificent garden and seeing a man in an apartment. Would it be clear he was an American? Or would he possibly seem French? Would he seem rich? Would his look of satisfaction be visible? He thought almost certainly that would be visible.

"I have to go to the lawyer now," Joséphine said behind him.

"Fine. Go," Austin said. "Hurry back. I'll look after little Gene Krupa. Then we'll have a nice dinner."

Joséphine had a thick sheaf of documents she was forcing into a plastic briefcase. "Maybe," she said in a distracted voice.

Austin, for some reason, began picturing himself talking to Hank Bullard about the air-conditioning business. They were in a café on a sunny side street. Hank's news was good, full of promise about a partnership.

Joséphine hurried into the hall, her flat shoes scraping the boards. She opened the door to Léo's room and said something quick and very soft to him, something that did not have Austin's name in it. Then she closed the door and entered the WC and used the toilet without bothering to shut herself in. Austin couldn't see down the hall from where he stood by the window, but could hear her pissing, the small trickle of water hitting more water. Barbara always closed the door, and he did too—it was a sound he didn't like and usually tried to avoid hearing, a sound so inert, so factual, that hearing it threatened to take away a layer of his good feeling. He was sorry to hear it now, sorry Joséphine didn't bother to close the door.

In an instant, however, she was out and down the hallway, picking up her briefcase while water sighed through the pipes. She gave Austin a peculiar, fugitive look across the room, as if she was surprised he was there and wasn't sure why he should be. It was, he felt, the look you gave an unimportant employee who's just said something inexplicable.

"So. I am going now," she said.

"I'll be right here," Austin said, looking at her and feeling suddenly helpless. "Hurry back, okay?"

"Yeah, sure. Okay," she said. "I hurry. I see you."

"Great," Austin said. She went out the door and quickly down the echoing steps toward the street.

For a while Austin walked around the apartment, looking at things—things Joséphine Belliard liked or cherished or had kept when her husband cleared out. There was an entire wall of books across one side of the little sleeping alcove she'd constructed for her privacy, using fake Chinese rice-paper dividers. The books were the sleek French soft-covers, mostly on sociological subjects, though other books seemed to be in German. Her modest bed was covered with a clean, billowy white duvet and big fluffy white pillows—no headboard, just the frame, but very neat. A copy of her soon-to-be-ex-husband's scummy novel lay on the bed table, with several pages roughly bent down. Folding a page up, he read a sentence in which a character named Solange was performing an uninspired act of fellatio on someone named Albert. He recognized the charged words: *Fellation. Lugubre.* Albert was talking about having his car repaired the whole time it was happening to him. *Un Amour Secret* was the book's insipid title. Bernard's scowling, condescending visage was nowhere in evidence.

He wondered what Bernard knew that he didn't know. Plenty, of course, if the book was even half true. But the unknown was interesting; you had to face it one way or another, he thought. And the idea of fellatio with Joséphine—nothing, up to this moment, he'd even considered—inflamed him, and he began to realize there was something distinctly sexual about roaming around examining her private belongings and modest bedroom, a space and a bed he could easily imagine occupying in the near future. Before he moved away he laid the green paisley egg on her bed table, beside the copy of her husband's smutty book. It would create a contrast, he thought, a reminder that she had choices in the world.

He looked out the bedroom window onto the park. It was the same view as the living room—the easeful formal garden with great leafy horse chestnut trees and tonsured green lawns with topiaries and yew shrubs and pale crisscrossing gravel paths, and the old École Supérieure des Mines looming along the far side and the Luxembourg Palace to the left. Some hippies were sitting crosslegged in a tight little circle on one of the grass swards, sharing a joint around. No one else was in view, though the light was cool and smooth and inviting, with birds soaring through it. A clock chimed somewhere nearby. The guitar music had ceased.

It would be pleasant to walk there with Joséphine, Austin thought, to breathe the sweet air of chestnut trees and to stare off. Life was very different here. This apartment was very different from his house in Oak Grove. *He* felt different here. Life seemed to have improved remarkably in a short period. All it took, he thought, was the courage to take control of things and to live with the consequences.

He assumed Léo to be asleep down the hall and that he could

simply leave well enough alone there. But when he'd sat leafing
through French *Vogue* for perhaps twenty minutes he heard a door
open, and seconds later Léo appeared at the corner of the hall,
looking confused and drugged in his BIG-TIME AMERICAN LUXURY
shirt with the big red Cadillac barging off the front. He still had
his little shoes on.

Léo rubbed his eyes and looked pitiful. Possibly Joséphine had
given him something to knock him out—the sort of thing that
wouldn't happen in the States. But in France, he thought, adults
treated children differently. More intelligently.

"*Bon soir,*" Austin said in a slightly ironic voice and smiled, setting the *Vogue* down.

Léo eyed him sullenly, still suspicious about hearing French
spoken by this person who wasn't the least bit French. He scanned
the room quickly for his mother's presence. Austin considered a
plan of reintroducing the slightly discredited paisley egg but
decided against it. He glanced at the clock on the bookcase: forty-
five minutes would somehow need to be consumed before
Joséphine returned. But how? How could the time be passed in a
way to make Léo happy and possibly impress his mother? The
Cubs idea wouldn't work—Léo was too young. Austin didn't
know any games or tricks. He knew nothing about children, and,
in fact, was sorry the boy was awake, sorry he was here at all.

But he thought of the park—the Jardin du Luxembourg—
available just outside the window. A nice walk in the park could
set them on the right course. He wasn't able to talk to the child,
but he could watch him while he enjoyed himself.

"*Voulez-vous aller au parc?*" Austin smiled a big, sincere smile.
"*Maintenant? Peut-être? Le parc? Oui?*" He pointed at the open
window and the cool, still evening air where swallows soared and
flittered.

Léo frowned at him and then at the window, still dazed. He
fastened a firm grip on the front of his shorts—a signal Austin
recognized—and did not answer.

"Whatta ya say? Let's go to the park," Austin said enthusiastically, loudly. He almost jumped up. Léo could understand it well enough. *Parc.* Park.

"*Parc?*" Léo said, and more cravenly squeezed his little weenie. "*Maman?*" He looked almost demented.

"*Maman est dans le parc,*" Austin said, thinking that from inside the park they would certainly see Joséphine on her way back from the lawyer's, and that it wouldn't turn out to be a complete lie— or if it did, Joséphine would eventually come back and take control of things before there was a problem. It was even possible, he thought, that he'd never see this kid after that, that Joséphine might come back and never want to see *him* again. Though a darker thought entered his mind: of Joséphine *never* coming back, deciding simply to disappear somewhere en route from the lawyer's. That happened. Babies were abandoned in Chicago all the time and no one knew what happened to their parents. He knew no one she knew. He knew no one to contact. It was a nightmarish thought.

Inside of five minutes he had Léo into the bathroom and out again. Happily, Léo attended to his own privacy while Austin stood outside the door and stared at the picture of Bernard's stuffed, bulbous face on the wall of the boy's room. He was surprised Joséphine would let it stay up. He'd suppressed an urge to tell her to stick it to Bernard, to get him in the shorts if she could, though later he'd felt queasy for conspiring against a man he didn't know.

As they were leaving the apartment, Austin realized he had no key, neither to the downstairs nor to the apartment itself, and that once the door closed he and Léo were on their own: a man, an American speaking little French, alone with a four-year-old French child he didn't know, in a country, in a city, in a park, where he was an absolute stranger. No one would think this was a good idea. Joséphine hadn't asked him to take Léo to the park—it was his own doing, and it was a risk. But everything felt like a risk at the moment, and all he needed to do was be careful.

They walked out onto rue Férou and around the corner, then down a few paces and across a wide street to a corner gate into the Luxembourg. Léo said nothing but insisted on holding Austin's

hand and leading the way as if he were taking Austin to the park
because he didn't know what else to do with him.

Once through the gold-topped gate, though, and onto the pale
gravel paths that ran in mazes through the shrubberies and trees and
planted beds where daffodils were already blooming, Léo went
running straight in the direction of a wide concrete pond where
ducks and swans were swimming and a group of older boys was
sailing miniature sailboats. Austin looked back to see which building was Joséphine's, and from which window he'd stood looking
down at this very park. But he couldn't distinguish the window,
wasn't even sure if from Joséphine's window he could see this part
of the park. For one thing, there hadn't been a pond, and here
there were plenty of people walking in the cool, sustained evening
light—lovers and married people both, by the looks of them, taking a nice stroll before going home for dinner. Probably it was
part of the park's plan, he supposed, that new parts always seemed
familiar, and vice versa.

Austin strolled down to the concrete border of the pond and
sat on a bench a few yards away from Léo, who stood raptly
watching the older boys tend their boats with long, thin sticks.
There was no wind and only the boys' soft, studious voices to listen to in the air where swallows were still darting. The little boats
floated stilly in the shallows with peanut shells and popcorn tufts.
A number of ducks and swans glided just out of reach, eyeing the
boats, waiting for the boys to leave.

Austin heard tennis balls being hit nearby, but couldn't see
where. A clay court, he felt certain. He wished he could sit and
watch people playing tennis instead of boys tending boats. Female
voices were laughing and speaking French and laughing again,
then a tennis ball was struck once more. A dense wall of what
looked like rhododendrons stood beyond a small expanse of well-
tended grass, and behind that, he thought, would be the courts.

Across the pond, seated on the opposite concrete wall, a man
in a tan suit was having his photograph taken by another man. An
expensive camera was being employed, and the second man kept
moving around, finding new positions from which to see through

his viewfinder. *"Su-perbe,"* Austin heard the photographer say. *"Très, très, très bon.* Don't move now. Don't move." A celebrity, Austin thought; an actor or a famous writer—somebody on top of the world. The man seemed unaffected, not even to acknowledge that his picture was being taken.

Léo unexpectedly turned and looked at Austin, as if he—Léo—wanted to say something extremely significant and exciting about the little boats. His face was vivid with importance. Though when he saw Austin seated on the bench, the calculation of who Austin was clouded his pale little features and he looked suddenly deviled and chastened and secretive, and turned quickly back, inching closer to the water's edge as if he intended to wade in.

He was just a kid, Austin thought calmly, a kid with divorced parents; not a little ogre or a tyrant. He could be won over with time and patience. Anyone could. He thought of his own father, a tall, patient, good-hearted man who worked in a sporting goods store in Peoria. He and Austin's mother had celebrated their fiftieth anniversary two years before, a big to-do under a tent in the city park, with Austin's brother in from Phoenix, and all the older cousins and friends from faraway states and decades past. A week later his father had had a stroke watching the news on TV and died in his chair.

His father had always had patience with his sons, Austin thought soberly. In his father's life there'd been no divorces or sudden midnight departures, yet his father had always tried to understand the goings-on of the later generation. Therefore, what would he think of all this, Austin wondered. France. A strange woman with a son. An abandoned house back home. Lies. Chaos. He'd certainly have made an attempt to understand, tried to find the good in it. Though ultimately his judgment would've been harsh and he'd have sided with Barbara, whose success in real estate he'd admired. He sought to imagine his father's very words, his verdict, delivered from his big lounger in front of the TV—the very spot where he'd breathed his last frantic breaths. But he couldn't. For some reason he couldn't re-create his father's voice, its cadences, the exact tenor of it. It was peculiar not to remember his father's voice, a voice he'd heard all his life. Possibly it had not had that much effect.

Austin was staring at the man in the tan suit across the lagoon, the man having his photograph taken. The man was up on the concrete ledge now, with his back turned, the shallow pond behind him, his legs wide apart, his hands on his hips, his tan jacket in the crook of his elbow. He looked ridiculous, unconvincing about whatever he was supposed to seem convincing about. Austin wondered if he himself would be visible in the background, a blurry, distant figure staring from across the stale lagoon. Maybe he would see himself someplace, in *Le Monde* or *Figaro*, newspapers he couldn't read. It would be a souvenir he could laugh about at some later date, when he was where? With who?

Not, in all probability, Joséphine Belliard. Something about her had bothered him this afternoon. Not her reluctance to kiss him. That was an attitude he could overcome, given time. He was good at overcoming reluctances in others. He was a persuasive man, with the heart of a salesman, and knew it. From time to time, this fact even bothered him, since given the right circumstances he felt he could persuade anybody of anything—no matter what. He had no clear idea what this persuasive quality was, though Barbara had occasionally remarked on it, often with the unflattering implication that he didn't believe in very much, or at least not in enough. It always made him uneasy that this might be true, or at least be thought of as true.

He *had* believed that he and Joséphine could have a different kind of relationship. Sexual, but not sexual at its heart. But rather, a new thing, founded on realities—the facts of his character, and hers. With Barbara, he'd felt he was just playing out the end of an old thing. Less real, somehow. Less mature. He could never really *love* Joséphine; that he had to concede, since in his deepest heart he loved only Barbara, for whatever that was worth. Yet he'd for a moment felt compelled by Joséphine, found her appealing, considered even the possibility of living with her for months or years. Anything was possible.

But seeing her in her apartment today, looking just as he knew she would, being exactly the woman he expected her to be, had made him feel unexpectedly bleak. And he was savvy enough to know that if he felt bleak now, at the very beginning, he would feel only bleaker later, and that in all likelihood life would either slowly or quickly become a version of hell for which he would bear all responsibility.

His thumb still vaguely ached. The women were laughing again on the tennis courts beyond the flowering rhododendrons. Austin could actually see a pair of woman's calves and tennis shoes, jumping from side to side as though their owner was striking a ball first forehand, then backhand, the little white feet dancing over the red surface. "*Arrête!* Stop!" a woman yelled, and sighed a loud sigh.

Frenchwomen, Austin thought, all talked like children: in high-pitched, rapid-paced, displeasingly insistent voices, which most of the time said, "*Non, non, non, non, non,*" to something someone wanted, some likely as not innocent wish. He could hear Joséphine saying it, standing in the living room of her little apartment the only other time he'd visited there—a week ago—speaking on the phone to someone, spooling the white phone cord around her finger as she said into the receiver, "*Non, non, non, non, non, non. C'est incroyable. C'est in-croy-a-ble!*" It was terrifically annoying, though it amused him now to think of it—at a distance.

Barbara had absolutely no use for Frenchwomen and made no bones about it. "Typical Froggies," she'd remark after evenings with his French clients and their wives, and then act disgusted. That was probably what bothered him about Joséphine: that she seemed such a typical bourgeois little Frenchwoman, the kind Barbara would've disliked in a minute—intractable, preoccupied, entirely stuck in her French life, with no sense of the wider world, and possibly even ungenerous if you knew her very long (as her husband found out). Joséphine's problem, Austin thought, looking around for little Léo, was that she took everything inside her life too seriously. Her motherhood. Her husband's ludicrous book. Her boyfriend. Her bad luck. She looked at everything under a microscope, as if she were always waiting to find a mistake she could magnify big enough that she'd have no choice but to go on taking life too seriously. As if that's all adulthood was—seriousness, discipline. No fun. Life, Austin thought, had to be more lighthearted. Which was why he'd come here, why he'd cut himself loose—to enjoy life more. He admired himself for it. And because of that he didn't think he could become the savior in Joséphine's life. That would be a lifelong struggle, and a lifelong struggle wasn't what he wanted most in the world.

When he looked around again, Léo was not where he'd been, standing dreamily to the side of the older boys, watching their miniature cutters and galleons glide over the still pond surface. The older boys were there, their long tending sticks in their hands, whispering among themselves and smirking. But not Léo. It had become cooler. Light had faded from the crenellated roofline of the École Supérieure des Mines, and soon it would be dark. The man having his picture taken was walking away with the photographer. Austin had been engrossed in thought and had lost sight of little Léo, who was, he was certain, somewhere nearby.

He looked at his watch. It was six twenty-five, and Joséphine could now be home. He scanned back along the row of apartment blocks, hoping to find her window, thinking he might see her there watching him, waving at him happily, possibly with Léo at her side. But he couldn't tell which building was which. One window he could see was open and dark inside. But he couldn't be sure. In any case, Joséphine wasn't framed in it.

Austin looked all around, hoping to see the white flash of Léo's T-shirt, the careening red Cadillac. But he saw only a few couples walking along the chalky paths, and two of the older boys carrying their sailboats home to their parents' apartments. He still heard tennis balls being hit—*pockety pock*. And he felt cold and calm, which he knew to be the feeling of fear commencing, a feeling that could rapidly change to other feelings that could last a long, long time.

Léo was gone, and he wasn't sure where. "Leo," he called out, first in the American way, then "Lay-oo," in the way his mother said. *"Où êtes-vous?"* Passersby looked at him sternly, hearing the two languages together. The remaining sailboat boys glanced around and smiled. "Lay-oo!" he called out again, and knew his voice did not sound ordinary, that it might sound frightened. Everyone around him, everyone who could hear him, was French, and he couldn't precisely explain to any of them what was the matter here: that this was not his son; that the boy's mother was not here now but was probably close by; that he had let his attention stray a moment.

"Lay-oo," he called out again. *"Où êtes-vous?"* He saw nothing of the boy, not a fleck of shirt or a patch of his dark hair disappearing behind a bush. He felt cold all over again, a sudden new wave, and he shuddered because he knew he was alone. Léo— some tiny assurance opened in him to say—Léo, wherever he was, would be fine, was probably fine right now. He would be found and be happy. He would see his mother and immediately forget all about Martin Austin. Nothing bad had befallen him. But he, Martin Austin, was alone. He could not find this child, and for him only bad would come of it.

Across an expanse of grassy lawn he saw a park guardian in a dark-blue uniform emerge from the rhododendrons beyond which were the tennis courts, and Austin began running toward him. It surprised him that he was running, and halfway there quit and only half ran toward the man, who had stopped to permit himself to be approached.

"Do you speak English?" Austin said before he'd arrived. He knew his face had taken on an exaggerated appearance, because the guardian looked at him strangely, turned his head slightly, as though he preferred to see him at an angle, or as if he were hearing an odd tune and wanted to hear it better. At the corners of his mouth he seemed to smile.

"I'm sorry," Austin said, and took a breath. "You speak English, don't you?"

"A little bit, why not," the guardian said, and then he did smile.

He was middle-aged and pleasant-looking, with a soft suntanned face and a small Hitler mustache. He wore a French policeman's uniform, a blue-and-gold kepi, a white shoulder braid and a white lanyard connected to his pistol. He was a man who liked parks.

"I've lost a little boy here someplace," Austin said calmly, though he remained out of breath. He put the palm of his right hand to his cheek as if his cheek were wet, and felt his skin to be cold. He turned and looked again at the concrete border of the pond, at the grass crossed by gravel paths, and then at a dense tangle of yew bushes farther on. He expected to see Léo there, precisely in the middle of this miniature landscape. Once he'd been frightened and time had gone by, and he'd sought help and strangers had regarded him with suspicion and wonder—once all these had taken place—Léo could appear and all would be returned to calm.

But there was no one. The open lawn was empty, and it was nearly dark. He could see weak interior lights from the apartment blocks beyond the park fence, see yellow automobile lights on rue Vaugirard. He remembered once hunting with his father in Illinois. He was a boy, and their dog had run away. He had known the advent of dark meant he would never see the dog again. They were far from home. The dog wouldn't find its way back. And that is what had happened.

The park guardian stood in front of Austin, smiling, staring at his face oddly, searchingly, as if he meant to adduce something— if Austin was crazy or on drugs or possibly playing a joke. The man, Austin realized, hadn't understood anything he'd said, and was simply waiting for something he would understand to begin.

But he had ruined everything now. Léo was gone. Kidnapped. Assaulted. Or merely lost in a hopelessly big city. And all his own newly won freedom, his clean slate, was in one moment squandered. He would go to jail, and he *should* go to jail. He was an awful man. A careless man. He brought mayhem and suffering to the lives of innocent, unsuspecting people who trusted him. No punishment could be too severe.

Austin looked again at the yew bushes, a long, green clump, several yards thick, the interior lost in tangled shadows. That was where Léo was, he thought with complete certainty. And he felt relief, barely controllable relief.

"I'm sorry to bother you," he said to the guardian. "*Je regrette.* I made a mistake." And he turned and ran toward the clump of yew bushes, across the open grass and the gravel promenade and careful beds in bright-yellow bloom, the excellent park. He plunged in under the low scrubby branches, where the ground was bare and raked and damp and attended to. With his head ducked he moved swiftly forward. He called Léo's name but did not see him, though he saw a movement, an indistinct fluttering of blue and gray, heard what might've been footfalls on the soft ground, and then he heard running, like a large creature hurrying in front of him among the tangled branches. He heard laughter beyond the edge of the thicket, where another grassy terrace opened—the sound of a man laughing and talking in French, out of breath and running at once. Laughing, then more talking and laughing again.

Austin moved toward where he'd seen the flutter of blue and gray—someone's clothing glimpsed in flight, he thought. There was a strong old smell of piss and human waste among the thick roots and shrubby trunks of the yew bushes. Paper and trash were strewn around in the foulness. From outside it had seemed cool and inviting here, a place to have a nap or make love.

And Léo was there. Exactly where Austin had seen the glimpse of clothing flicker through the undergrowth. He was naked, sitting on the damp dirt, his clothes strewn around him, turned inside out where they had been jerked off and thrown aside. He looked up at Austin, his eyes small and perceptive and dark, his small legs straight out before him, smudged and scratched, his chest and arms scratched. Dirt was on his cheeks. His hands were between his legs, not covering or protecting him but limp, as if they had no purpose. He was very white and very quiet. His hair was still neatly combed. Though when he saw Austin, and that it was Austin and not someone else coming bent at the waist, furious, breathing stertorously, stumbling, crashing arms-out through the rough branches and trunks and roots of that small place, he gave a shrill, hopeless cry, as though he could see what was next, and who it would be, and it terrified him even more. And his cry was all he could do to let the world know that he feared his fate.

8

In the days that followed there was to be a great deal of controversy. The police conducted a thorough and publicized search for the person or persons who had assaulted little Léo. There were no signs to conclude he had been molested, only that he'd been lured into the bushes by someone and roughed up there and frightened badly. A small story appeared in the back pages of *France-Dimanche* and said the same things, yet Austin noticed from the beginning that all the police used the word *"moleste"* when referring to the event, as though it were accurate.

The group of hippies he'd seen from Joséphine's window was generally thought to contain the offender. It was said that they lived in the park and slept in the clumps and groves of yews and ornamental boxwoods, and that some were Americans who had been in France for twenty years. But none of them, when the police brought them in to be identified, seemed to be the man who had scared Léo.

For a few hours following the incident there was suspicion among the police that Austin himself had molested Léo and had approached the guardian only as a diversion after he'd finished with the little boy—trusting that the child would never accuse him. Austin had patiently and intelligently explained that he had not molested Léo and would never do such a thing, but understood that he had to be considered until he could be exonerated—which was not before midnight, when Joséphine entered the police station and stated that Léo had told her Austin was not the man who had scared him and taken his clothes off, that it had been someone else, a man who spoke French, a man in blue and possibly gray clothing with long hair and a beard.

When she had told this story and Austin had been allowed to leave the stale, windowless police room where he'd been made to remain until matters could be determined with certainty, he'd walked beside Joséphine out into the narrow street, lit yellow through the tall wire-mesh windows of the *gendarmerie*. The street was guarded by a number of young policemen wearing flak jackets and carrying short machine pistols on shoulder slings. They calmly watched Austin and Joséphine as they stopped at the curb to say good-bye.

"I'm completely to blame for this," Austin said. "I can't tell you how sorry I am. There aren't any words good enough, I guess."

"You *are* to blame," Joséphine said and looked at him in the face, intently. After a moment she said, "It is not a game. You know? Maybe to you it is a game."

"No, it's really not," Austin said abjectly, standing in the cool night air in sight of all the policemen. "I guess I had a lot of plans."

"Plans to what?" Joséphine said. She had on the black crepe skirt she'd worn the day he'd met her, barely more than a week ago. She looked appealing again. "Not for me! You don't have any plans for me. I don't want you. I don't want any man anymore." She shook her head and crossed her arms tightly and looked away, her dark eyes shining in the night. She was very, very angry. Possibly, he thought, she was even angry at herself. "You are a fool," she said, and she spat accidentally when she said it. "I hate you. You don't know anything. You don't know who you are." She looked at him bitterly. "Who are you?" she said. "Who do you think you are? You're nothing."

"I understand," Austin said. "I'm sorry. I'm sorry about all of this. I'll make sure you don't have to see me again."

Joséphine smiled at him, a cruel, confident smile. "I don't care," she said and raised her shoulder in the way Austin didn't like, the way Frenchwomen did when they wanted to certify as true something that might not be. "I don't care what happens to you. You are dead. I don't see you."

She turned and began walking away down the sidewalk along the side of the *gendarmerie* and in front of the young policemen, who looked at her indifferently. They looked back at Austin, standing in the light by himself, where he felt he should stay until she had gone out of sight. One of the policemen said something to his colleague beside him, and that man whistled a single long note into the night. Then they turned and faced the other way.

Austin had a fear in the days to come, almost a defeating fear that deprived him of sleep in his small, risqué apartment above the rue Bonaparte. It was a fear that Barbara would die soon, followed then by a feeling that she *had* died, which was succeeded by a despair of something important in his life having been lost, exterminated by his own doing but also by fate. What *was* that something? he wondered, awake in the middle of the night. It wasn't Barbara herself. Barbara was alive and on the earth, and able to be reunited with if he wanted to try and if she did. And it wasn't his innocence. That had been dispensed with long before. But he *had* lost something, and whatever it was, Barbara seemed associated. And he felt if he could specify it, possibly he could begin to pull things together, see more clearly, even speak to her again, and, in a sense, repatriate himself.

Not to know what that something was, though, meant that he was out of control, perhaps meant something worse about him. So that he began to think of his life, in those succeeding days, almost entirely in terms of what was wrong with him, of his problem, his failure—in particular his failure as a husband, but also in terms of his unhappiness, his predicament, his ruin, which he wanted to repair. He recognized again and even more plainly that his entire destination, everything he'd ever done or presumed or thought, had been directed toward Barbara, that everything good was there. And it was there he would need eventually to go.

Behind Joséphine, of course, was nothing—no fabric or mystery, no secrets, nothing he had curiosity for now. She had seemed to be a compelling woman; not a great object of sexuality, not a source of wit—but a force he'd been briefly moved by in expectation that he could move her nearer to him. He remembered kissing her in the car, her soft face and the great swelling moment of wondrous feeling, the great thrill. And her voice saying, *"Non, non, non, non, non,"* softly. That was what Bernard could never get over losing, the force that had driven him to hate her, even humiliate her.

For his part he admired her, and mostly for the way she'd dealt with him. Proportionately. Intelligently. She had felt a greater sense of responsibility than he had; a greater apprehension of life's importance, its weight and permanence. To him, it *had* all seemed less important, less permanent, and he could never even aspire to her sense of life—a European sense. As Barbara had said, he took himself for granted; though unlike what Joséphine had said, he knew himself quite well. In the end, Joséphine took herself for granted, too. They were, of course, very different and could never have been very happy together.

Though he wondered again in his dreamy moments after the fear of Barbara's dying had risen off and before he drifted to sleep, wondered what was ever possible between human beings. How could you regulate life, do little harm and still be attached to others? And in that context, he wondered if being *fixed* could be a misunderstanding, and, as Barbara had said when he'd seen her the last time and she had been so angry at him, if he had changed slightly, somehow altered the important linkages that guaranteed his happiness and become detached, unreachable. Could you *become* that? Was it something you controlled, or a matter of your character, or a change to which you were only a victim? He wasn't sure. He wasn't sure about that at all. It was a subject he knew he would have to sleep on many, many nights.

ROCK SPRINGS

Edna and I had started down from Kalispell, heading for Tampa-St. Pete where I still had some friends from the old glory days who wouldn't turn me in to the police. I had managed to scrape with the law in Kalispell over several bad checks—which is a prison crime in Montana. And I knew Edna was already looking at her cards and thinking about a move, since it wasn't the first time I'd been in law scrapes in my life. She herself had already had her own troubles, losing her kids and keeping her ex-husband, Danny, from breaking in her house and stealing her things while she was at work, which was really why I had moved in in the first place, that and needing to give my little daughter, Cheryl, a better shake in things.

I don't know what was between Edna and me, just beached by the same tides when you got down to it. Though love has been built on frailer ground than that, as I well know. And when I came in the house that afternoon, I just asked her if she wanted to go to Florida with me, leave things where they sat, and she said, "Why not? My datebook's not that full."

Edna and I had been a pair eight months, more or less man and wife, some of which time I had been out of work, and some when I'd worked at the dog track as a lead-out and could help with the rent and talk sense to Danny when he came around. Danny was afraid of me because Edna had told him I'd been in prison in Florida for killing a man, though that wasn't true. I had once been in jail in Tallahassee for stealing tires and had gotten into a fight on the county farm where a man had lost his eye. But I hadn't done the hurting, and Edna just wanted the story worse than it was so Danny wouldn't act crazy and make her have to take her kids back, since she had made a good adjustment to not having them, and I already had Cheryl with me. I'm not a violent person and would never put a man's eye out, much less kill someone. My former wife, Helen, would come all the way from Waikiki Beach to testify to that. We never had violence, and I believe in crossing the street to stay out of trouble's way. Though Danny didn't know that.

But we were half down through Wyoming, going toward I-80 and feeling good about things, when the oil light flashed on in the car I'd stolen, a sign I knew to be a bad one.

I'd gotten us a good car, a cranberry Mercedes I'd stolen out of an ophthalmologist's lot in Whitefish, Montana. I stole it because I thought it would be comfortable over a long haul, because I thought it got good mileage, which it didn't, and because I'd never had a good car in my life, just old Chevy junkers and used trucks back from when I was a kid swamping citrus with Cubans.

The car made us all high that day. I ran the windows up and down, and Edna told us some jokes and made faces. She could be lively. Her features would light up like a beacon and you could see her beauty, which wasn't ordinary. It all made me giddy, and I drove clear down to Bozeman, then straight on through the park to Jackson Hole. I rented us the bridal suite in the Quality Court in Jackson and left Cheryl and her little dog, Duke, sleeping while Edna and I drove to a rib barn and drank beer and laughed till after midnight.

It felt like a whole new beginning for us, bad memories left behind and a new horizon to build on. I got so worked up, I had a tattoo done on my arm that said FAMOUS TIMES, and Edna bought a Bailey hat with an Indian feather band and a little turquoise-and-silver bracelet for Cheryl, and we made love on the seat of the car in the Quality Court parking lot just as the sun was burning up on the Snake River, and everything seemed then like the end of the rainbow.

It was that very enthusiasm, in fact, that made me keep the car one day longer instead of driving it into the river and stealing another one, like I should've done and *had* done before.

Where the car went bad there wasn't a town in sight or even a house, just some low mountains maybe fifty miles away or maybe a hundred, a barbed-wire fence in both directions, hardpan prairie, and some hawks riding the evening air seizing insects.

I got out to look at the motor, and Edna got out with Cheryl and the dog to let them have a pee by the car. I checked the water and checked the oil stick, and both of them said perfect.

"What's that light mean, Earl?" Edna said. She had come and stood by the car with her hat on. She was just sizing things up for herself.

"We shouldn't run it," I said. "Something's not right in the oil."

She looked around at Cheryl and Little Duke, who were peeing on the hardtop side-by-side like two little dolls, then out at the mountains, which were becoming black and lost in the distance. "What're we doing?" she said. She wasn't worried yet, but she wanted to know what I was thinking about.

"Let me try it again."

"That's a good idea," she said, and we all got back in the car.

When I turned the motor over, it started right away and the red light stayed off and there weren't any noises to make you think something was wrong. I let it idle a minute, then pushed the accelerator down and watched the red bulb. But there wasn't any light on, and I started wondering if maybe I hadn't dreamed I saw it, or that it had been the sun catching an angle off the window chrome, or maybe I was scared of something and didn't know it.

"What's the matter with it, Daddy?" Cheryl said from the backseat. I looked back at her, and she had on her turquoise bracelet and Edna's hat set back on the back of her head and that little black-and-white Heinz dog on her lap. She looked like a little cowgirl in the movies.

"Nothing, honey, everything's fine now," I said.

"Little Duke tinkled where I tinkled," Cheryl said, and laughed.

"You're two of a kind," Edna said, not looking back. Edna was usually good with Cheryl, but I knew she was tired now. We hadn't had much sleep, and she had a tendency to get cranky when she didn't sleep. "We oughta ditch this damn car first chance we get," she said.

"What's the first chance we got?" I asked, because I knew she'd been at the map.

"Rock Springs, Wyoming," Edna said with conviction. "Thirty miles down this road." She pointed out ahead.

I had wanted all along to drive the car into Florida like a big success story. But I knew Edna was right about it, that we shouldn't take crazy chances. I had kept thinking of it as my car and not the ophthalmologist's, and that was how you got caught in these things.

"Then my belief is that we ought to go to Rock Springs and negotiate ourselves a new car," I said. I wanted to stay upbeat, like everything was panning out right.

"That's a great idea," Edna said, and she leaned over and kissed me hard on the mouth.

"That's a great idea," Cheryl said. "Let's pull on out of here right now."

The sunset that day I remember as being the prettiest I'd ever seen. Just as it touched the rim of the horizon, it all at once fired the air into jewels and red sequins the precise likes of which I had never seen before and haven't seen since. The West has it all over everywhere for sunsets, even Florida, where it's supposedly flat but where half the time trees block your view.

"It's cocktail hour," Edna said after we'd driven awhile. "We ought to have a drink and celebrate something." She felt better thinking we were going to get rid of the car. It certainly had dark troubles and was something you'd want to put behind you.

Edna had out a whiskey bottle and some plastic cups and was measuring levels on the glove-box lid. She liked drinking, and she liked drinking in the car, which was something you got used to in

Montana, where it wasn't against the law, but where, strangely enough, a bad check would land you in Deer Lodge Prison for a year.

"Did I ever tell you I once had a monkey?" Edna said, setting my drink on the dashboard where I could reach it when I was ready. Her spirits were already picked up. She was like that, up one minute and down the next.

"I don't think you ever did tell me that," I said. "Where were you then?"

"Missoula," she said. She put her bare feet on the dash and rested the cup on her breasts. "I was waitressing at the AmVets. This was before I met you. Some guy came in one day with a monkey. A spider monkey. And I said, just to be joking, 'I'll roll you for that monkey.' And the guy said, 'Just one roll?' And I said, 'Sure.' He put the monkey down on the bar, picked up the cup, and rolled out boxcars. I picked it up and rolled out three fives. And I just stood there looking at the guy. He was just some guy passing through, I guess a vet. He got a strange look on his face— I'm sure not as strange as the one I had—but he looked kind of sad and surprised and satisfied all at once. I said, 'We can roll again.' But he said, 'No, I never roll twice for anything.' And he sat and drank a beer and talked about one thing and another for a while, about nuclear war and building a stronghold somewhere up in the Bitterroot, whatever it was, while I just watched the monkey, wondering what I was going to do with it when the guy left. And pretty soon he got up and said, 'Well, good-bye, Chipper'—that was the monkey's name, of course. And then he left before I could say anything. And the monkey just sat on the bar all that night. I don't know what made me think of that, Earl. Just something weird. I'm letting my mind wander."

"That's perfectly fine," I said. I took a drink of my drink. "I'd never own a monkey," I said after a minute. "They're too nasty. I'm sure Cheryl would like a monkey, though, wouldn't you, honey?" Cheryl was down on the seat playing with Little Duke. She used to talk about monkeys all the time then. "What'd you ever do with that monkey?" I said, watching the speedometer. We were having to go slower now because the red light kept fluttering on. And all I could do to keep it off was go slower. We were going maybe thirty-five and it was an hour before dark, and I was hoping Rock Springs wasn't far away.

"You really want to know?" Edna said. She gave me a quick glance, then looked back at the empty desert as if she was brooding over it.

"Sure," I said. I was still upbeat. I figured I could worry about breaking down and let other people be happy for a change.

"I kept it a week." And she seemed gloomy all of a sudden, as if she saw some aspect of the story she had never seen before. "I took it home and back and forth to the AmVets on my shifts. And it didn't cause any trouble. I fixed a chair up for it to sit on, back of the bar, and people liked it. It made a nice little clicking noise. We changed its name to Mary because the bartender figured out it was a girl. Though I was never really comfortable with it at home. I felt like it watched me too much. Then one day a guy came in, some guy who'd been in Vietnam, still wore a fatigue coat. And he said to me, 'Don't you know that a monkey'll kill you? It's got more strength in its fingers than you got in your whole body.' He said people had been killed in Vietnam by monkeys, bunches of them marauding while you were asleep, killing you and covering you with leaves. I didn't believe a word of it, except that when I got home and got undressed I started looking over across the room at Mary on her chair in the dark watching me. And I got the creeps. And after a while I got up and went out to the car, got a length of clothesline wire, and came back in and wired her to the doorknob through her little silver collar, then went back and tried to sleep. And I guess I must've slept the sleep of the dead—though I don't remember it—because when I got up I found Mary had tipped off her chair-back and hanged herself on the wire line. I'd made it too short."

Edna seemed badly affected by that story and slid low in the seat so she couldn't see out over the dash. "Isn't that a shameful story, Earl, what happened to that poor little monkey?"

"I see a town! I see a town!" Cheryl started yelling from the backseat, and right up Little Duke started yapping and the whole car fell into a racket. And sure enough she had seen something I hadn't, which was Rock Springs, Wyoming, at the bottom of a long hill, a little glowing jewel in the desert with I-80 running on the north side and the black desert spread out behind.

"That's it, honey," I said. "That's where we're going. You saw it first."

"We're hungry," Cheryl said. "Little Duke wants some fish, and I want spaghetti." She put her arms around my neck and hugged me.

"Then you'll just get it," I said. "You can have anything you want. And so can Edna and so can Little Duke." I looked over at Edna, smiling, but she was staring at me with eyes that were fierce with anger. "What's wrong?" I said.

"Don't you care anything about that awful thing that happened to me?" Her mouth was drawn tight, and her eyes kept cutting back at Cheryl and Little Duke, as if they had been tormenting her.

"Of course I do," I said. "I thought that was an awful thing." I didn't want her to be unhappy. We were almost there, and pretty soon we could sit down and have a real meal without thinking somebody might be hurting us.

"You want to know what I did with that monkey?" Edna said.

"Sure I do," I said.

"I put her in a green garbage bag, put it in the trunk of my car, drove to the dump, and threw her in the trash." She was staring at me darkly, as if the story meant something to her that was real important but that only she could see and that the rest of the world was a fool for.

"Well, that's horrible," I said. "But I don't see what else you could do. You didn't mean to kill it. You'd have done it differently if you had. And then you had to get rid of it, and I don't know what else you could have done. Throwing it away might seem unsympathetic to somebody, probably, but not to me. Sometimes that's all you can do, and you can't worry about what somebody else thinks." I tried to smile at her, but the red light was staying on if I pushed the accelerator at all, and I was trying to gauge if we could coast to Rock Springs before the car gave out completely. I looked at Edna again. "What else can I say?" I said.

"Nothing," she said, and stared back at the dark highway. "I should've known that's what you'd think. You've got a character that leaves something out, Earl. I've known that a long time."

"And yet here you are," I said. "And you're not doing so bad. Things could be a lot worse. At least we're all together here."

"Things could always be worse," Edna said. "You could go to the electric chair tomorrow."

"That's right," I said. "And somewhere somebody probably will. Only it won't be you."

"I'm hungry," said Cheryl. "When're we gonna eat? Let's find a motel. I'm tired of this. Little Duke's tired of it too."

Where the car stopped rolling was some distance from the town, though you could see the clear outline of the interstate in the dark with Rock Springs lighting up the sky behind. You could hear the big tractors hitting the spacers in the overpass, revving up for the climb to the mountains.

I shut off the lights.

"What're we going to do now?" Edna said irritably, giving me a bitter look.

"I'm figuring it," I said. "It won't be hard, whatever it is. You won't have to do anything."

"I'd hope not," she said and looked the other way.

Across the road and across a dry wash a hundred yards was what looked like a huge mobile-home town, with a factory or a refinery of some kind lit up behind it and in full swing. There were lights on in a lot of the mobile homes, and there were cars moving along an access road that ended near the freeway overpass a mile the other way. The lights in the mobile homes seemed friendly to me, and I knew right then what I should do.

"Get out," I said, opening my door.

"Are we walking?" Edna said.

"We're pushing."

"I'm not pushing." Edna reached up and locked her door.

"All right," I said. "Then you just steer."

"You're pushing us to Rock Springs, are you, Earl? It doesn't look like it's more than about three miles."

"I'll push," Cheryl said from the back.

"No, hon. Daddy'll push. You just get out with Little Duke and move out of the way."

Edna gave me a threatening look, just as if I'd tried to hit her. But when I got out she slid into my seat and took the wheel, staring angrily ahead straight into the cottonwood scrub.

"Edna can't drive that car," Cheryl said from out in the dark. "She'll run it in the ditch."

"Yes, she can, hon. Edna can drive it as good as I can. Probably better."

"No she can't," Cheryl said. "No she can't either." And I thought she was about to cry, but she didn't.

I told Edna to keep the ignition on so it wouldn't lock up and to steer into the cottonwoods with the parking lights on so she could see. And when I started, she steered it straight off into the trees, and I kept pushing until we were twenty yards into the cover and the tires sank in the soft sand and nothing at all could be seen from the road.

"Now where are we?" she said, sitting at the wheel. Her voice was tired and hard, and I knew she could have put a good meal to use. She had a sweet nature, and I recognized that this wasn't her fault but mine. Only I wished she could be more hopeful.

"You stay right here, and I'll go over to that trailer park and call us a cab," I said.

"What cab?" Edna said, her mouth wrinkled as if she'd never heard anything like that in her life.

"There'll be cabs," I said, and tried to smile at her. "There's cabs everywhere."

"What're you going to tell him when he gets here? Our stolen car broke down and we need a ride to where we can steal another one? That'll be a big hit, Earl."

"I'll talk," I said. "You just listen to the radio for ten minutes and then walk on out to the shoulder like nothing was suspicious. And you and Cheryl act nice. She doesn't need to know about this car."

"Like we're not suspicious enough already, right?" Edna looked up at me out of the lighted car. "You don't think right, did you know that, Earl? You think the world's stupid and you're smart. But that's not how it is. I feel sorry for you. You might've *been* something, but things just went crazy someplace."

I had a thought about poor Danny. He was a vet and crazy as a shit-house mouse, and I was glad he wasn't in for all this. "Just get the baby in the car," I said, trying to be patient. "I'm hungry like you are."

"I'm tired of this," Edna said. "I wish I'd stayed in Montana."

"Then you can go back in the morning," I said. "I'll buy the ticket and put you on the bus. But not till then."

"Just get on with it, Earl." She slumped down in the seat, turning off the parking lights with one foot and the radio on with the other.

The mobile-home community was as big as any I'd ever seen. It was attached in some way to the plant that was lighted up behind it, because I could see a car once in a while leave one of the trailer streets, turn in the direction of the plant, then go slowly into it. Everything in the plant was white, and you could see that all the trailers were painted white and looked exactly alike. A deep hum came out of the plant, and I thought as I got closer that it wouldn't be a location I'd ever want to work in.

I went right to the first trailer where there was a light, and knocked on the metal door. Kids' toys were lying in the gravel around the little wood steps, and I could hear talking on TV that suddenly went off. I heard a woman's voice talking, and then the door opened wide.

A large Negro woman with a wide, friendly face stood in the

doorway. She smiled at me and moved forward as if she was going to come out, but she stopped at the top step. There was a little Negro boy behind her peeping out from behind her legs, watching me with his eyes half closed. The trailer had that feeling that no one else was inside, which was a feeling I knew something about.

"I'm sorry to intrude," I said. "But I've run up on a little bad luck tonight. My name's Earl Middleton."

The woman looked at me, then out into the night toward the freeway as if what I had said was something she was going to be able to see. "What kind of bad luck?" she said, looking down at me again.

"My car broke down out on the highway," I said. "I can't fix it myself, and I wondered if I could use your phone to call for help."

The woman smiled down at me knowingly. "We can't live without cars, can we?"

"That's the honest truth," I said.

"They're like our hearts," she said, her face shining in the little bulb light that burned beside the door. "Where's your car situated?"

I turned and looked over into the dark, but I couldn't see anything because of where we'd put it. "It's over there," I said. "You can't see it in the dark."

"Who all's with you now?" the woman said. "Have you got your wife with you?"

"She's with my little girl and our dog in the car," I said. "My daughter's asleep or I would have brought them."

"They shouldn't be left in the dark by themselves," the woman said and frowned. "There's too much unsavoriness out there."

"The best I can do is hurry back." I tried to look sincere, since everything except Cheryl being asleep and Edna being my wife was the truth. The truth is meant to serve you if you'll let it, and I wanted it to serve me. "I'll pay for the phone call," I said. "If you'll bring the phone to the door I'll call from right here."

The woman looked at me again as if she was searching for a truth of her own, then back out into the night. She was maybe in her sixties, but I couldn't say for sure. "You're not going to rob me, are you, Mr. Middleton?" She smiled like it was a joke between us.

"Not tonight," I said, and smiled a genuine smile. "I'm not up to it tonight. Maybe another time."

"Then I guess Terrel and I can let you use our phone with Daddy not here, can't we, Terrel? This is my grandson, Terrel Junior, Mr. Middleton." She put her hand on the boy's head and looked down at him. "Terrel won't talk. Though if he did he'd tell you to use our phone. He's a sweet boy." She opened the screen for me to come in.

The trailer was a big one with a new rug and a new couch and a living room that expanded to give the space of a real house. Something good and sweet was cooking in the kitchen, and the trailer felt like it was somebody's comfortable new home instead of just temporary. I've lived in trailers, but they were just snailbacks with one room and no toilet, and they always felt cramped and unhappy—though I've thought maybe it might've been me that was unhappy in them.

There was a big Sony TV and a lot of kids' toys scattered on the floor. I recognized a Greyhound bus I'd gotten for Cheryl. The phone was beside a new leather recliner, and the Negro woman pointed for me to sit down and call and gave me the phone book. Terrel began fingering his toys and the woman sat on the couch while I called, watching me and smiling.

There were three listings for cab companies, all with one number different. I called the numbers in order and didn't get an answer until the last one, which answered with the name of the second company. I said I was on the highway beyond the interstate and that my wife and family needed to be taken to town and I would arrange for a tow later. While I was giving the location, I looked up the name of a tow service to tell the driver in case he asked.

When I hung up, the Negro woman was sitting looking at me with the same look she had been staring with into the dark, a looked that seemed to want truth. She was smiling, though. Something pleased her and I reminded her of it.

"This is a very nice home," I said, resting in the recliner, which felt like the driver's seat of the Mercedes, and where I'd have been happy to stay.

"This isn't *our* house, Mr. Middleton," the Negro woman said. "The company owns these. They give them to us for nothing. We have our own home in Rockford, Illinois."

"That's wonderful," I said.

"It's never wonderful when you have to be away from home, Mr. Middleton, though we're only here three months, and it'll be easier when Terrel Junior begins his special school. You see, our son was killed in the war, and his wife ran off without Terrel Junior. Though you shouldn't worry. He can't understand us. His little feelings can't be hurt." The woman folded her hands in her lap and smiled in a satisfied way. She was an attractive woman, and had on a blue-and-pink floral dress that made her seem bigger than she could've been, just the right woman to sit on the couch she was sitting on. She was good nature's picture, and I was glad she could be, with her little brain-damaged boy, living in a place where no one in his right mind would want to live a minute. "Where do *you* live, Mr. Middleton?" she said politely, smiling in the same sympathetic way.

"My family and I are in transit," I said. "I'm an ophthalmologist, and we're moving back to Florida, where I'm from. I'm setting up practice in some little town where it's warm year-round. I haven't decided where."

"Florida's a wonderful place," the woman said. "I think Terrel would like it there."

"Could I ask you something?" I said.

"You certainly may," the woman said. Terrel had begun pushing his Greyhound across the front of the TV screen, making a scratch that no one watching the set could miss. "Stop that, Terrel Junior," the woman said quietly. But Terrel kept pushing his bus on the glass, and she smiled at me again as if we both understood something sad. Except I knew Cheryl would never damage a television set. She had respect for nice things, and I was sorry for the lady that Terrel didn't. "What did you want to ask?" the woman said.

"What goes on in that plant or whatever it is back there beyond these trailers, where all the lights are on?"

"Gold," the woman said and smiled.

"It's what?" I said.

"Gold," the Negro woman said, smiling as she had for almost all the time I'd been there. "It's a gold mine."

"They're mining gold back there?" I said, pointing.

"Every night and every day." She smiled in a pleased way.

"Does your husband work there?" I said.

"He's the assayer," she said. "He controls the quality. He works three months a year, and we live the rest of the time at home in Rockford. We've waited a long time for this. We've been happy to have our grandson, but I won't say I'll be sorry to have him go. We're ready to start our lives over." She smiled broadly at me and then at Terrel, who was giving her a spiteful look from the floor. "You said you had a daughter," the Negro woman said. "And what's her name?"

"Irma Cheryl," I said. "She's named for my mother."

"That's nice. And she's healthy, too. I can see it in your face." She looked at Terrel Junior with pity.

"I guess I'm lucky," I said.

"So far you are. But children bring you grief, the same way they bring you joy. We were unhappy for a long time before my husband got his job in the gold mine. Now, when Terrel starts to school, we'll be kids again." She stood up. "You might miss your cab, Mr. Middleton," she said, walking toward the door, though not to be forcing me out. She was too polite. "If *we* can't see your car, the cab surely won't be able to."

"That's true." I got up off the recliner, where I'd been so comfortable. "None of us have eaten yet, and your food makes me know how hungry we probably all are."

"There are fine restaurants in town, and you'll find them," the Negro woman said. "I'm sorry you didn't meet my husband. He's a wonderful man. He's everything to me."

"Tell him I appreciate the phone," I said. "You saved me."

"You weren't hard to save," the woman said. "Saving people is what we were all put on earth to do. I just passed you on to whatever's coming to you."

"Let's hope it's good," I said, stepping back into the dark.

"I'll be hoping, Mr. Middleton. Terrel and I will both be hoping."

I waved to her as I walked out into the darkness toward the car where it was hidden in the night.

The cab had already arrived when I got there. I could see its little red-and-green roof lights all the way across the dry wash, and it made me worry that Edna was already saying something to get us in trouble, something about the car or where we'd come from, something that would cast suspicion on us. I thought, then, how I never planned things well enough. There was always a gap between my plan and what happened, and I only responded to things as they came along and hoped I wouldn't get in trouble. I was an offender in the law's eyes. But I always *thought* differently, as if I weren't an offender and had no intention of being one, which was the truth. But as I read on a napkin once, between the idea and the act a whole kingdom lies. And I had a hard time with my acts, which were oftentimes offender's acts, and my ideas, which were as good as the gold they mined there where the bright lights were blazing.

"We're waiting for you, Daddy," Cheryl said when I crossed the road. "The taxicab's already here."

"I see, hon," I said, and gave Cheryl a big hug. The cabdriver was sitting in the driver's seat having a smoke with the lights on inside. Edna was leaning against the back of the cab between the taillights, wearing her Bailey hat. "What'd you tell him?" I said when I got close.

"Nothing," she said. "What's there to tell?"

"Did he see the car?"

She glanced over in the direction of the trees where we had hid the Mercedes. Nothing was visible in the darkness, though I could hear Little Duke combing around in the underbrush tracking something, his little collar tinkling. "Where're we going?" she said. "I'm so hungry I could pass out."

"Edna's in a terrible mood," Cheryl said. "She already snapped at me."

"We're tired, honey," I said. "So try to be nicer."

"She's never nice," Cheryl said.

"Run go get Little Duke," I said. "And hurry back."

"I guess *my* questions come last here, right?" Edna said.

I put my arm around her. "That's not true."

"Did you find somebody over there in the trailers you'd rather stay with? You were gone long enough."

"That's not a thing to say," I said. "I was just trying to make things look right, so we don't get put in jail."

"So *you* don't, you mean." Edna laughed a little laugh I didn't like hearing.

"That's right. So I don't," I said. "I'd be the one in Dutch." I stared out at the big, lighted assemblage of white buildings and white lights beyond the trailer community, plumes of white smoke escaping up into the heartless Wyoming sky, the whole company of buildings looking like some unbelievable castle, humming away in a distorted dream. "You know what all those buildings are there?" I said to Edna, who hadn't moved and who didn't really seem to care if she ever moved anymore ever.

"No. But I can't say it matters, because it isn't a motel and it isn't a restaurant."

"It's a gold mine," I said, staring at the gold mine, which, I knew now, was a greater distance from us than it seemed, though it seemed huge and near, up against the cold sky. I thought there should've been a wall around it with guards instead of just lights and no fence. It seemed as if anyone could go in and take what they wanted, just the way I had gone up to that woman's trailer and used the telephone, though that obviously wasn't true.

Edna began to laugh then. Not the mean laugh I didn't like, but a laugh that had something caring behind it, a full laugh that enjoyed a joke, a laugh she was laughing the first time I laid eyes

on her, in Missoula in the East Gate Bar in 1979, a laugh we used
to laugh together when Cheryl was still with her mother and I
was working steady at the track and not stealing cars or passing
bogus checks to merchants. A better time all around. And for some
reason it made me laugh just hearing her, and we both stood there
behind the cab in the dark, laughing at the gold mine in the
desert, me with my arm around her and Cheryl out rustling up
Little Duke and the cabdriver smoking in the cab and our stolen
Mercedes-Benz, which I'd had such hopes for in Florida, stuck up
to its axle in sand, where I'd never get to see it again.

"I always wondered what a gold mine would look like when I
saw it," Edna said, still laughing, wiping a tear from her eye.

"Me too," I said. "I was always curious about it."

"We're a couple of fools, aren't we, Earl?" she said, unable to
quit laughing completely. "We're two of a kind."

"It might be a good sign, though," I said.

"How could it be? It's not our gold mine. There aren't any
drive-up windows." She was still laughing.

"We've seen it," I said, pointing. "That's it right there. It may
mean we're getting closer. Some people never see it at all."

"In a pig's eye, Earl," she said. "You and me see it in a pig's eye."

And she turned and got in the cab to go.

The cabdriver didn't ask anything about our car or where it was,
to mean he'd noticed something queer. All of which made me
feel like we had made a clean break from the car and couldn't be
connected with it until it was too late, if ever. The driver told us a
lot about Rock Springs while he drove, that because of the gold
mine a lot of people had moved there in just six months, people
from all over, including New York, and that most of them lived
out in the trailers. Prostitutes from New York City, who he called
"B-girls," had come into town, he said, on the prosperity tide,
and Cadillacs with New York plates cruised the little streets every
night, full of Negroes with big hats who ran the women. He told
us that everybody who got in his cab now wanted to know where

the women were, and when he got our call he almost didn't come because some of the trailers were brothels operated by the mine for engineers and computer people away from home. He said he got tired of running back and forth out there just for vile business. He said that *60 Minutes* had even done a program about Rock Springs and that a blowup had resulted in Cheyenne, though nothing could be done unless the boom left town. "It's prosperity's fruit," the driver said. "I'd rather be poor, which is lucky for me."

He said all the motels were sky-high, but since we were a family he could show us a nice one that was affordable. But I told him we wanted a first-rate place where they took animals, and the money didn't matter because we had had a hard day and wanted to finish on a high note. I also knew that it was in the little nowhere places that the police look for you and find you. People I'd known were always being arrested in cheap hotels and tourist courts with names you'd never heard of before. Never in Holiday Inns or TraveLodges.

I asked him to drive us to the middle of town and back out again so Cheryl could see the train station, and while we were there I saw a pink Cadillac with New York plates and a TV aerial being driven slowly by a Negro in a big hat down a narrow street where there were just bars and a Chinese restaurant. It was an odd sight, nothing you could ever expect.

"There's your pure criminal element," the cabdriver said and seemed sad. "I'm sorry for people like you to see a thing like that. We've got a nice town here, but there're some that want to ruin it for everybody. There used to be a way to deal with trash and criminals, but those days are gone forever."

"You said it," Edna said.

"You shouldn't let it get *you* down," I said to him. "There's more of you than them. And there always will be. You're the best advertisement this town has. I know Cheryl will remember you and not *that* man, won't you, honey?" But Cheryl was asleep by then, holding Little Duke in her arms on the taxi seat.

The driver took us to the Ramada Inn on the interstate, not far from where we'd broken down. I had a small pain of regret as we drove under the Ramada awning that we hadn't driven up in a cranberry-colored Mercedes but instead in a beat-up old Chrysler taxi driven by an old man full of complaints. Though I knew it was for the best. We were better off without that car; better, really, in any other car but that one, where the signs had turned bad.

I registered under another name and paid for the room in cash so there wouldn't be any questions. On the line where it said "Representing" I wrote "Ophthalmologist" and put "M.D." after the name. It had a nice look to it, even though it wasn't my name.

When we got to the room, which was in the back where I'd asked for it, I put Cheryl on one of the beds and Little Duke beside her so they'd sleep. She'd missed dinner, but it only meant she'd be hungry in the morning, when she could have anything she wanted. A few missed meals don't make a kid bad. I'd missed a lot of them myself and haven't turned out completely bad.

"Let's have some fried chicken," I said to Edna when she came out of the bathroom. "They have good fried chicken at Ramadas, and I noticed the buffet was still up. Cheryl can stay right here, where it's safe, till we're back."

"I guess I'm not hungry anymore," Edna said. She stood at the window staring out into the dark. I could see out the window past her some yellowish foggy glow in the sky. For a moment I thought it was the gold mine out in the distance lighting the night, though it was only the interstate.

"We could order up," I said. "Whatever you want. There's a menu on the phone book. You could just have a salad."

"You go ahead," she said. "I've lost my hungry spirit." She sat on the bed beside Cheryl and Little Duke and looked at them in a sweet way and put her hand on Cheryl's cheek just as if she'd had a fever. "Sweet little girl," she said. "Everybody loves you."

"What do you want to do?" I said. "I'd like to eat. Maybe *I'll* order up some chicken."

"Why don't you do that?" she said. "It's your favorite." And she smiled at me from the bed.

I sat on the other bed and dialed room service. I asked for chicken, garden salad, potato and a roll, plus a piece of hot apple pie and iced tea. I realized I hadn't eaten all day. When I put down the phone I saw that Edna was watching me, not in a hateful way or a loving way, just in a way that seemed to say she didn't understand something and was going to ask me about it.

"When did watching me get so entertaining?" I said and smiled at her. I was trying to be friendly. I knew how tired she must be. It was after nine o'clock.

"I was just thinking how much I hated being in a motel without a car that was mine to drive. Isn't that funny? I started feeling like that last night when the purple car wasn't mine. That purple car just gave me the willies, I guess, Earl."

"One of those cars *outside* is yours," I said. "Just stand right there and pick it out."

"I know," she said. "But that's different, isn't it?" She reached and got her blue Bailey hat, put it on her head, and set it way back like Dale Evans. She looked sweet. "I used to like to go to motels, you know," she said. "There's something secret about them and free—I was never paying, of course. But you felt safe from everything and free to do what you wanted because you'd made the decision to be there and paid that price, and all the rest was the good part. Fucking and everything, you know." She smiled at me in a good-natured way.

"Isn't that the way this is?" I was sitting on the bed, watching her, not knowing what to expect her to say next.

"I don't guess it is, Earl," she said and stared out the window. "I'm thirty-two and I'm going to have to give up on motels. I can't keep that fantasy going anymore."

"Don't you like this place?" I said and looked around at the room. I appreciated the modern paintings and the lowboy bureau and the big TV. It seemed like a plenty nice enough place to me, considering where we'd been.

"No, I don't," Edna said with real conviction. "There's no use in my getting mad at you about it. It isn't your fault. You do the best you can for everybody. But every trip teaches you something. And I've learned I need to give up on motels before some bad thing happens to me. I'm sorry."

"What does that mean?" I said, because I really didn't know what she had in mind to do, though I should've guessed.

"I guess I'll take that ticket you mentioned," she said, and got up and faced the window. "Tomorrow's soon enough. We haven't got a car to take me anyhow."

"Well, that's a fine thing," I said, sitting on the bed, feeling like I was in shock. I wanted to say something to her, to argue with her, but I couldn't think what to say that seemed right. I didn't want to be mad at her, but it made me mad.

"You've got a right to be mad at me, Earl," she said, "but I don't think you can really blame me." She turned around and faced me and sat on the windowsill, her hands on her knees. Someone knocked on the door, and I just yelled for them to set the tray down and put it on the bill.

"I guess I *do* blame you," I said, and I was angry. I thought about how I could've disappeared into that trailer community and hadn't, had come back to keep things going, had tried to take control of things for everybody when they looked bad.

"Don't. I wish you wouldn't," Edna said and smiled at me like she wanted me to hug her. "Anybody ought to have their choice in things if they can. Don't you believe that, Earl? Here I am out here in the desert where I don't know anything, in a stolen car, in a motel room under an assumed name, with no money of my own, a kid that's not mine, and the law after me. And I have a choice to get out of all of it by getting on a bus. What would you do? I know exactly what you'd do."

"You think you do," I said. But I didn't want to get into an argument about it and tell her all I could've done and didn't do. Because it wouldn't have done any good. When you get to the point of arguing, you're past the point of changing anybody's mind, even though it's supposed to be the other way, and maybe for some classes of people it is, just never mine.

Edna smiled at me and came across the room and put her arms

around me where I was sitting on the bed. Cheryl rolled over and looked at us and smiled, then closed her eyes, and the room was quiet. I was beginning to think of Rock Springs in a way I knew I would always think of it, a lowdown city full of crimes and whores and disappointments, a place where a woman left me, instead of a place where I got things on the straight track once and for all, a place I saw a gold mine.

"Eat your chicken, Earl," Edna said. "Then we can go to bed. I'm tired, but I'd like to make love to you anyway. None of this is a matter of not loving you, you know that."

Sometime late in the night, after Edna was asleep, I got up and walked outside into the parking lot. It could've been anytime because there was still the light from the interstate frosting the low sky and the big red Ramada sign humming motionlessly in the night and no light at all in the east to indicate it might be morning. The lot was full of cars all nosed in, a couple of them with suitcases strapped to their roofs and their trunks weighed down with belongings the people were taking someplace, to a new home or a vacation resort in the mountains. I had laid in bed a long time after Edna was asleep, watching the Atlanta Braves on television, trying to get my mind off how I'd feel when I saw that bus pull away the next day, and how I'd feel when I turned around and there stood Cheryl and Little Duke and no one to see about them but me alone, and that the first thing I had to do was get hold of some automobile and get the plates switched, then get them some breakfast and get us all on the road to Florida, all in the space of probably two hours, since that Mercedes would certainly look less hid in the daytime than the night, and word travels fast. I've always taken care of Cheryl myself as long as I've had her with me. None of the women ever did. Most of them didn't even seem to like her, though they took care of me in a way so that I could take care of her. And I knew that once Edna left, all that was going to get harder. Though what I wanted most to do was not think about it just for a little while, try to let my mind go limp so it could be strong for the rest of what there was. I thought that the difference between a successful life and an unsuccessful one, between me at that moment and all the people who owned the cars that were nosed into their proper places in the lot, maybe between me and that woman out in the trailers by the gold mine, was how well you were able to put things like this out of your mind and not be bothered by them, and maybe, too, by how many troubles like this one you had to face in a lifetime. Through luck or design they had all faced fewer troubles, and by their own characters, they forgot them faster. And that's what I wanted for me. Fewer troubles, fewer memories of trouble.

I walked over to a car, a Pontiac with Ohio tags, one of the ones with bundles and suitcases strapped to the top and a lot more in the trunk, by the way it was riding. I looked inside the driver's window. There were maps and paperback books and sunglasses and the little plastic holders for cans that hang on the window wells. And in the back there were kids' toys and some pillows and a cat box with a cat sitting in it staring up at me like I was the face of the moon. It all looked familiar to me, the very same things I would have in my car if I had a car. Nothing seemed surprising, nothing different. Though I had a funny sensation at that moment and turned and looked up at the windows along the back of the motel. All were dark except two. Mine and another one. And I wondered, because it seemed funny, what would you think a man was doing if you saw him in the middle of the night looking in the windows of cars in the parking lot of the Ramada Inn? Would you think he was trying to get his head cleared? Would you think he was trying to get ready for a day when trouble would come down on him? Would you think his girlfriend was leaving him? Would you think he had a daughter? Would you think he was anybody like you?

MY MOTHER, IN MEMORY

My mother's name was Edna Akin, and she was born in 1910, in the far northwest corner of the state of Arkansas—Benton County—in a place whose actual location I am not sure of and never have been. Near Decatur or Centerton, or a town no longer a town. Just a rural place. That is near the Oklahoma line there, and in 1910 it was a rough country, with a frontier feel. It had only been ten years since robbers and outlaws were in the landscape. Bat Masterson was still alive and not long gone from Galina.

I remark about this not because of its possible romance, or because I think it qualifies my mother's life in any way I can relate now, but because it seems like such a long time ago and such a far-off and unknowable place. And yet my mother, whom I loved and knew quite well, links me to that foreignness, that other thing that was her life and that I really don't know so much about and never did. This is one quality of our lives with our parents that is often overlooked and so, devalued. Parents link us—closeted as we are in our lives—to a thing we're not but they are; a separateness, perhaps a mystery—so that even together we are alone.

The act and practice of considering my mother's life is, of course, an act of love. And my incomplete memory of it, my inadequate relation to the facts, should not be thought incomplete love. I loved my mother the way a happy child does, thoughtlessly and without doubts. And when I became an adult and we were adults who knew one another, we regarded each other highly; could say "I love you" when it seemed necessary to clarify our dealings, but without pausing over it. That seems perfect to me now and did then, too.

My mother's life I am forced to piece together. We were not a family for whom history had much to offer. This fact must have to do with not being rich, or with being rural, or incompletely educated, or just inadequately aware of many things. For my mother there was simply little to history, no heroics or self-dramatizing—just small business, forgettable residues, some of them mean. The Depression had something to do with it, too. My mother and father were people who lived for each other and for the day. In the thirties, after they were married, they lived, in essence, on the road. They drank some. They had a good time. They felt they had little to look back on, and didn't look.

My father's family came from Ireland and were Protestants. This was in the 1870s, and an ocean divided things. But about my mother's early life I don't know much. I don't know where her father came from, or if he too was Irish, or Polish. He was a carter, and my mother spoke affectionately about him, if elliptically and without a sense of responsibility to tell anything at all. "Oh," she would say, "my daddy was a good man." And that was it. He died of cancer in the 1930s, I think, but not before my mother had been left by her mother and had lived with him a time. This was before 1920. My sense is that they lived—daughter and father—in the country, back near where she was born—rural again—and that to her it had been a good time. As good as any. I don't know what she was enthusiastic for then, what her thoughts were. I cannot hear her voice from that time long ago, though I would like to be able to.

Of her mother there is much to say—a story of a kind. She was from the country, with brothers and sisters. There was Indian blood on that side of the family, though it was never clear what tribe of Indian. I know nothing about her parents, though I have a picture of my great-grandmother and my grandmother with her new, second husband, sitting in an old cartage wagon, and my mother in the back. My great-grandmother is old then, witchy looking;

my grandmother, stern and pretty in a long beaver coat; my mother, young, with piercing dark eyes aimed to the camera.

At some point my grandmother had left her husband and taken up with the younger man in the picture—a boxer and roustabout. A pretty boy. Slim and quick and tricky. "Kid Richard" was his ring name. (I, oddly enough, am *his* namesake.) This was in Fort Smith now. Possibly 1922. My grandmother was older than Kid Richard, whose real name was Bennie Shelley. And to quickly marry him and keep him, she lied about her age, took a smooth eight years off, and began to dislike having her pretty daughter— my mother—around to date her.

And so for a period—everything in her life seemed to happen for a period and never for long—my mother was sent to live at the Convent School of St. Ann's, also in Fort Smith. It must've seemed like a good idea to her father up in the country, because he paid her tuition, and she was taught by nuns. I don't exactly know what her mother—whose name was Essie or Lessie or just Les—did during that time, maybe three years. She was married to Bennie Shelley, who was from Fayetteville and had family there. He worked as a waiter, and then in the dining-car service on the Rock Island. This meant living in El Reno and as far out the line as Tucumcari, New Mexico. He quit boxing, and my grandmother ruled him as strictly as she could because she felt she could go a long way with him. He was her last and best choice for something. A ticket out. To where, I'm not sure.

My mother often told me that she'd liked the sisters of St. Ann's. They were strict. Imperious. Self-certain. Dedicated. Humorous. It was there, I think, as a boarding student, that my mother earned what education she ever did—the ninth grade, where she was an average good student and was liked, though she smoked cigarettes and was punished for it. I think if she had never told me about the nuns, if that stamp on her life hadn't been made, I might never have ordered even this much of things. St. Ann's cast a shadow into later life. In her heart of hearts my mother was a secret Catholic. A forgiver. A respecter of rituals and protocols. Reverent about the trappings of faith; respecter of inner disciplines. All I think about Catholics I think because of her, who was never one at all, but who lived among them at an early age and seemingly liked what she learned and those who taught her. Later in life, when she had married my father and gone to meet his mother, she would always feel she was thought of as a Catholic and that his family never truly took her in as they might have another girl.

But when her father, for reasons I know nothing about, stopped her tuition, her mother—now demanding they be known as sisters—took her out of St. Ann's. And that was it for school, forever. She was not a welcome addition to her mother's life, and I have never known why they took her back. It is just one of those inexplicable acts that mean everything.

They moved around. To K.C. To El Reno again. To Davenport and Des Moines—wherever the railroad took Ben Shelley, who was going forward in the dining-car service and turning himself into a go-getter. In time, he would leave the railroad and go to work as a caterer at the Arlington Hotel in Hot Springs. And there he put my mother to work in the cigar shop, where a wider world opened an inch. People from far away were here for the baths, Jews from Chicago and New York. Foreigners. Rich people. She met baseball players, became friends with Dizzy Dean and Leo Durocher. And during that time, sometime when she was seventeen, she must've met my father.

I, of course, know nothing about their courtship except that it took place—mostly in Little Rock, probably in 1927. My father was twenty-three. He worked as a produce stocker for a grocery concern there. I have a picture of him with two other young clerks in a grocery store. He is wearing a clean, white apron and a tie, and is standing beside a bin of cabbages. I don't even know where this is. Little Rock. Hot Springs—one of these. It is just a glimpse. What brought him down from the country to Little Rock I'll never know, nor what he might've had on his mind then. He died in 1960, when I was only sixteen. And I had not by then thought to ask.

But I have thought of them as a young couple. My mother,

black-haired, dark-eyed, curvaceous. My father, blue-eyed like me, big, gullible, honest, gentle. I can think a thought of them together. I can sense what they each must've sensed pretty fast—here was a good person, suddenly. My mother knew things. She had worked in hotels, been to boarding school and out. Lived in cities. Traveled some. But my father was a country boy who quit school in the seventh grade. The baby of three children, all raised by their mother—the sheltered son of a suicide. I can believe my mother wanted a better life than working for her ambitious step-father and contrary mother, at jobs that went no place; that she may have believed she'd not been treated well, and thought of her life as "rough"; that she was tired of being her mother's sister; that it was a strange life; that she was in danger of losing all expectation; that she was bored. And I can believe my father simply saw my mother and wanted her. Loved her. And that was how that went.

They were married in Morrilton, Arkansas, by a justice of the peace, in 1928, and arrived at my father's home in Atkins the next morning, newlyweds. I have no correct idea what anyone thought or said about any of that. They acted independently, and my mother never felt the need to comment. Though my guess is they heard disapproval.

I think it is safe to say my parents wanted children. How many they wanted or how soon after they were married I do not know. But it was their modest boast that my father had a job throughout the Depression. And I think there was money enough. They lived in Little Rock, and for a while my father worked as a grocer, and then, in 1932, he was fired, and went to work selling starch for a company out of Kansas City. The Faultless Company. Huey Long had worked for them, too. It was a traveling job, and most of the time they just traveled together. New Orleans. Memphis. Texarkana. They lived in hotels, spent their off-hours and off-days back in Little Rock. But mostly they traveled. My father called on groceries, wholesalers, prisons, hospitals, conducted schools for newlyweds on how to starch clothes without boiling the starch. My mother, typically, never characterized that time except to say he and she had "fun" together—that was her word for it—and had begun to think they couldn't have a child. No children. I do not even know if that mattered so much. It was not their way to fight fate, but to see life as okay. This time lasted fifteen years. An entire life lived then. A loose, pick-up-and-go life. Drinking. Cars. Restaurants. Not paying much attention. There were friends they had in New Orleans, Memphis, in Little Rock, and on the road. They made friends of my grandmother and Bennie, who was not much older than my father—four years, at most. I think they were just caught up in their life, a life in the South, in the thirties, just a kind of swirling thing that didn't really have a place to go. There must've been plenty of lives like that then. It seems a period now to me. A specific time, the Depression. But to them, of course, it was just their life.

Something about that time—to my mother—must've seemed unnarratable. Unworthy of or unnecessary for telling. My father, who was not a teller of stories anyway, never got a chance to recall it. And I, who wasn't trained to want the past filled in—as some boys are—just never asked. It seemed a privacy I shouldn't invade. And I know that my mother's only fleeting references to that time, as if the thirties were just a long weekend—drinking too much, wildness, rootlessness—gave me the impression something possibly untidy had gone on, some recklessness of spirit and attitude below the level of evil, but something that a son would be better off not to think about and be worried with. In essence, it had been *their* time, for their purposes and not mine. And it was over.

But looked at from the time of my birth, 1944, all that life lived childless, unexpectant, must've come to seem an odd time to her; a life encapsulatable, possibly even remembered unclearly, pointless, maybe in comparison to the pointedness of a life *with* a child. Still, an intimacy established between the two of them that they brought forward into more consequential life—a life they had all but abandoned any thought of because no children had come.

All first children, and certainly all only children, date the beginning of their lives as extra-special events. For my parents my arrival came as a surprise and coincident with the end of World War II—the event that finished the thirties in this country. And it came when my mother had been married to my father fifteen years; when, in essence, their young life was over. He was thirty-nine. She was thirty-three. They, by all accounts, were happy to have me. It may have been an event that made their life together seem conventional for once, that settled them, made them think about matters their friends had thought about years ago. Staying put. The future.

They had never owned a house or a car, although my father's job gave him a company car. They had never had to choose a "home," a place to be in permanently. But now, they did. They moved from Little Rock down to Mississippi, to Jackson, which was the geographic center of my father's territory and a place he could return most weekends with ease, since my mother wouldn't be going with him now. There was going to be a baby.

They knew no one in Jackson except the jobbers my father had called on and a salesman or two he knew off the road. I'm not sure, but I think it was not an easy transition. They rented and then bought a brick duplex next to a school. They joined a church. Found a grocery. A bus stop—though you could walk to the main street in Jackson from 736 North Congress. Also to the library and the capitol building. They had neighbors—older citizens, established families hanging on to nicer, older, larger houses in a neighborhood that was itself in transition. This was life now, for them. My father went off to work Monday morning and came back Friday night. He had never exactly done that before, but he liked it, I think. One of my earliest memories is of him moving around the sunny house on Monday mornings, whistling a tune.

And so what my beginning life was was this. A life spent with my mother—a shadow in a picture of myself. Days. Afternoons. Nights. Walks. Meals. Dressing. Sidewalks. The movies. Home. Radio. And on the weekend, my father. A nice, large, sweet man who visited us. Happy to come home. Happy to leave.

Between them, I don't know what happened. But given their characters, my best belief is that nothing did. That their life changed radically, that I was there, that the future meant something different, that there was apparently no talk of other children, that they saw far less of each other now—all meant almost nothing to how they felt about each other, or how they registered how they felt. Neither of them was an inquirer. They did not take their pulse much. Psychology was not a science they practiced. They found, if they had not known it before, that they'd signed on for the full trip. They saw life going this way now and not that way. They loved each other. They loved me. Nothing much else mattered.

I don't think my mother longed for a fulfilling career or a more active public life. I don't think my father had other women on the road. I don't think the intrusion of me into their lives was anything they didn't think of as normal and all right. I know from practice that it is my habit to seek the normal in life, to look for reasons to believe this or that is fine. In part, that is because my parents raised me that way and lived lives that portrayed a world, a private existence, that *could* be that way. I do not think even now, in the midst of my own life's concerns, that it is a bad way to see things.

So then, the part of my life that has to do with my mother.

The first eleven years—the Korean War years, Truman and Eisenhower, television, bicycles, one big snowstorm in 1949—we lived on North Congress Street, down a hill from the state capitol and across from the house where Eudora Welty had been a young girl thirty-five years before. Next door to Jefferson Davis School. I remember a neighbor stopping me on the sidewalk and asking me who I was; this was a thing that could happen to you. Maybe I was nine or seven then. But when I said my name—Richard Ford—she said, "Oh, yes. Your mother is the cute little black-headed woman up the street." And that affected me and still does. I think this was my first conception of my mother as someone else, as someone whom other people saw and considered: a cute woman, which she was not. Black-haired, which she was. She was, I know, five feet five inches tall. But I never have known if that is tall or short. I think I must have always believed it was normal. I remember this, though, as a signal moment in my life. Small but important. It alerted me to my mother's—what?—public side. To the side that other people saw and dealt with and that was there. I do not think I ever thought of her in any other way after that. As Edna Ford, a person who was my mother and also who was someone else. I do not think I ever addressed her after that except with such a knowledge—the way I would anyone I knew.

It is a good lesson to learn. And we risk never knowing our parents if we ignore it. Cute, black-headed, five-five. Some part of her was that, and it didn't harm me to know it. It may have helped, since one of the premier challenges for us all is to know our parents, assuming they survive long enough, are worth knowing, and it is physically possible. This is a part of normal life. And the more we see them fully, as the world sees them, the better all our chances are.

About my mother I do not remember more than pieces up until the time I was sixteen: 1960, a galvanizing year for us both—the year my father woke up gasping on a Saturday morning and died before he could get out of bed; me up on the bed with him, busy trying to find something to help. Shake him. Yell in his sleeping face. Breathe in his soft mouth. Turn him over onto his belly, for some reason. Feeling terror and chill. All this while she stood in the doorway to his bedroom in our new house in the suburbs of Jackson, pushing her knuckles into her temples, becoming hysterical. Eventually she just lost her control for a while.

But before that. Those pieces. They must make a difference or I wouldn't remember them so clearly. A flat tire we all three had, halfway across the Mississippi bridge at Greenville. High, up there, over the river. We stayed in the car while my father fixed it, and my mother held me so tightly to her I could barely breathe. I was six. She always said, "I smothered you when you were little. You were all we had. I'm sorry." And then she'd tell me this story. But I wasn't sorry. It seemed fine then, since we were up there. "Smothering" meant "Here is danger," "Love protects you." They are still lessons I respect. I am not comfortable on bridges now, but my guess is I never would've been.

I remember my mother having a hysterectomy and my grandfather, Ben Shelley, joking about it—to her—about what good "barbers" the nuns at St. Dominic's had been. That made her cry.

I remember once in the front yard on Congress Street something happened, something I said or did—I don't know what—but my mother began running out across the schoolyard next door. Just running away. I remember that scared me and I yelled at her, "No," and halfway across she stopped and came back. I've never known how serious she was about that, but I have understood from it that there might be reasons to run off. Alone, with a small child, knowing no one. That's enough.

There were two fights they had that I was present for. One on St. Louis Street, in the French Quarter in New Orleans. It was in front of Antoine's Restaurant, and I now think they were both drunk, though I didn't know it, or even know what drunk was. One wanted to go in the restaurant and eat. The other didn't and wanted to go back to the hotel around the corner. This was in 1955. I think we had tickets to the Sugar Bowl—Navy vs. Ole Miss. They yelled at each other, and I think my father yanked her arm, and they walked back separately. Later we all got in bed together in the Monteleone Hotel and no one stayed mad. In our family no one ever nagged or held grudges or stayed mad, though we could all get mad.

The other fight was worse. I believe it was the same year. They were drinking. My father invited friends over and my mother didn't like it. All the lights were on in the house. She swore. I remember the guests standing in the doorway outside the screen, still on the porch looking in. I remember their white faces and my mother shouting at them to get the hell out, which they did. And then my father held my mother's shoulders up against the wall by the bathroom and yelled at her while she struggled to get free. I remember how harsh the lights were. No one got hit. No one ever did except me when I was whipped. They just yelled and struggled. Fought that way. And then after a while, I remember, we were all in bed again, with me in the middle, and my father cried. "Boo hoo hoo. Boo hoo hoo." Those were the sounds he made, as if he'd read somewhere how to cry.

A long time has passed since then, and I have remembered more than I do now. I have tried to put things into novels. I have written things down and forgotten them. I have told stories. And there was more, a life's more. My mother and I rode with my father summers and sat in his hot cars in the states of Louisiana and Arkansas and Texas and waited while he worked, made his calls. We went to the coast—to Biloxi and Pensacola. To Memphis. To Little Rock almost every holiday. We *went*. That was the motif of things. We lived in Jackson, but he traveled. And every time we could we went with him. Just to be going, or when he became not so well with heart trouble we went to help him. The staying part was never stabilized. Only being with them, and mostly being with her. My mother.

And then my father died, which changed everything—many things, it's odd to say, for the better where I was concerned. But not for my mother. Where she was concerned, nothing after that would ever be quite good again. A major part of life ended for her February 20, 1960. He had been everything to her, and all that was naturally implicit became suddenly explicit in her life, and she was neither good at that nor interested in it. And in a way I see now and saw almost as clearly then, she gave up.

Not that she gave up where I was concerned. I was sixteen and had lately been in some law scrapes, and she became, I'd say, very aware of the formal features of her life. She was a widow. She was fifty. She had a son who seemed all right, but who could veer off into trouble if she didn't pay attention. And so, in her way, she paid attention.

Not long after the funeral, when I was back in school and the neighbors had stopped calling and bringing over dishes of food—

when both grief and real mourning had set in, in other words—
she sat me down and told me we were now going to have to be
more independent. She would not be able to look after me as she
had done. We agreed that I had a future, but I would have to look
after me. And as we could, we would do well to look after each
other. We were partners now, is what I remember thinking. My
father had really never been around that much, and so his actual
absence was, for me (though not for her), not felt so strongly. And
a partnership seemed like a good arrangement. I was to stay out of
jail because she didn't want to get me out. *Wouldn't get me out.* I
was to find friends I could rely on instead. I could have a car of
my own. I could go away in the summers to find a job in Little
Rock with my grandparents. This, it was understood but never
exactly stated (we were trying not to state too much then; we
didn't want *everything* to have to be explicit, since so much was
now and so little ever had been), *this* would give her time to
adjust. To think about things. To become whatever she would
have to become to get along from there on out.

   I don't exactly remember the time scheme to things. This was
1960, '61, '62. I was a tenth-grader and on. But I did not get put
in jail. I did live summers with my grandparents, who by now ran
a large hotel in Little Rock. I got a black '57 Ford, which got
stolen. I got beaten up and then got new friends. I did what I was
told, in other words. I started to grow up in a hurry.

   I think of that time—the time between my father's death and
the time I left for Michigan to go to college—as a time when I
didn't see my mother much. Though that is not precisely how it
was. She was there. I was there. But I cannot discount my own
adjustments to my father's death and absence, to my independence. I think I may have been more dazed than grieved, and it is
true my new friends took me up. My mother went to work. She
got a job doing something at a company that made school pictures. It required training and she did it. And it was only then, late
in 1960, when she was fifty, that she first felt the effects of having
quit school in 1924. But she got along, came home tired. I do not
think she had trouble. And then she left that. She became a rental

agent for a new apartment house, tried afterward to get the job as manager but didn't get it—who knows why? She took another job as night cashier in a hotel, the Robert E. Lee. This job she kept maybe a year. And after that she was the admitting clerk in the emergency room at the University of Mississippi Hospital, a job she liked very much.

And there was at least one boyfriend in all that time. A married man, from Tupelo, named Matt, who lived in the apartment building she worked at. He was a big, bluff man, in the furniture business, who drove a Lincoln and carried a gun strapped to the steering column. I liked him. And I liked it that my mother liked him. It didn't matter that he was married—not to me, and I guess not to my mother. I really have no idea about what was between them, what they did alone. And I don't care about that, either. He took her on drives. Flew her to Memphis in his airplane. Acted respectfully to both of us. She may have told me she was just passing time, getting her mind off her worries, letting someone be nice to her. But I didn't care. And we both knew that nothing she told me about him either did or didn't have to match the truth. I would sometimes think I wished she would marry Matt. And at other times I would be content to have them be lovers, if that's what they were. He had boys near my age, and later I would even meet them and like them. But this was after he and my mother were finished.

What finished them was brought on by me but was not really my doing, I think now. Matt had faded for a time. His business brought him in to Jackson, then out for months. She had quit talking about him, and life had receded to almost a normal level. I was having a hard time in school—getting a D in algebra (I'd already failed once) and having no ideas for how I could improve. My mother was cashiering nights at the Robert E. Lee and coming home by eleven.

But one night for some reason she simply didn't come home. I had a test the next day. Algebra. And I must've been in an agitated state of mind. I called the hotel to hear she had left on time. And for some reason this scared me. I got in my car and drove down to the neighborhood by the hotel, a fringe neighborhood near a black section of town. I rode the streets and found her car, a gray and pink '58 Oldsmobile that had been my father's pride and joy. It was parked under some sycamore trees, across from the apartments where she had worked as a rental agent and where Matt lived. And for some reason I think I panicked. It was not a time to panic but I did anyway. I'm not sure what I thought, but thinking of it now I seem to believe I wanted to ask Matt—if he was there— if he knew where my mother was. This may be right, though it's possible, too, I knew she was there and just wanted to make her leave.

I went in the building—it must've been midnight—and up the elevator and down the hall to his door. I banged on it. Hit it hard with my fists. And then I waited.

Matt himself opened the door, but my mother was there in the room behind him. She had a drink in her hand. The lights were on, and she was standing in the middle of the room behind him. It was a nice apartment, and both of them were shocked by me. I don't blame them. I didn't blame them then and was ashamed to be there. But I was, I think, terrified. Not that she was there. Or that I was alone. But just that I didn't know what in the hell. Where was she? What else was I going to have to lose?

I remember being out of breath. I was seventeen years old. And I really can't remember what anybody said or did except me, briefly. "Where have you been?" I said to her. "I didn't know where you were. That's all."

And that *was* all. All of that. Matt said very little. My mother got her coat and we went home in two cars. She acted vaguely annoyed at me, and I *was* mad at her. We talked that night. Eventually she said she was sorry, and I told her I didn't care if she saw Matt only that she tell me when she would be home late. And to my knowledge she never saw Matt Matthews, or any other man, again as a lover as long as she lived.

Later, years later, when she was dying, I tried to explain it all to her again—my part, what I thought, *had* thought—as if we could still open it and repair that night. All she needed to do was call me or, even years later, say she would've called me. But that was not, of course, what she did or how she saw it. She just looked a little disgusted and shook her head. "Oh, that," she said. "My God. That was just silliness. You had no business coming up there. You were out of your mind. Though I just saw I couldn't be doing things like that. I had a son to raise." And here again she looked disgusted, and at everything, I think. All the cards the fates had dealt her—a no-good childhood, my father's death, me, her own inability to vault over all of this to a better life. It was another proof of something bad, the likes of which she felt, I believe, she'd had plenty.

There are only these—snapshot instances of a time lived indistinctly, a time that whirled by for us but were the last times we would ever really live together as mother and son. We did not fight. We accommodated each other almost as adults would. We grew wry and humorous with each other. Cast glances, gave each other looks. Were never ironic or indirect or crafty with anger. We knew how we were supposed to act and took pleasure in acting that way.

She sold the new house my father had bought, and we moved into a high-rise. Magnolia Towers. I did better in school. She was switching jobs. I really didn't register these changes, though based on what I know now about such things they could not have been easy.

I did not and actually do not know about the money, how it was, then. My father had a little insurance. Maybe some was saved in a bank. My grandparents stepped forward with offers. They had made money. But there was no pension from his job; it was not that kind of company. I know the government paid money for me, a dependent child. But I only mean to say I don't know how much she needed to work; how much money needed to come through; if we had debts, creditors. It may have been we didn't, and that she went to work just to thrust herself in the direction life seemed to be taking her—independence. Solitariness. All that that means.

There were memorable moments. When my Ford was stolen we

went one winter day at dusk out to a car dealer in the country, where good deals were supposedly available, and looked at cars. She felt we should replace mine, and so did I. But when we were there looking at cheap station wagons, she saw a black Thunderbird and stared at it, and I knew that was what she wanted—for herself—that that would make her feel better. Getting my father's Olds out of our lives would be a help, and there was really no one there then to tell us not to. It was a kind of new though unasked-for freedom. And so I encouraged her. She stared a long time at it, got in and tilted the steering wheel, shut the door a few times, and then we left with the promise to think about it. In a few days, though, after we'd thought, the police found my old car, and she decided to keep the Olds.

Another time, when my girlfriend and I had been experimenting in one kind of sexual pleasure and another. And quite suddenly my girlfriend—a Texas girl—sensed somehow that she was definitely pregnant and that her life and mine were ruined. Mine, I know certainly, felt ruined. And there was evidence aplenty around of kids marrying at fourteen, having babies, being divorced. This was the South, after all.

But I once again found myself in terror, and on a Sunday afternoon I just unburdened myself to my mother; told her *all* we'd done, all we hadn't. Spoke specifically and methodically in terms of parts and positions, extents and degrees. All I wanted from her was to know if Louise *could* be pregnant, based upon what she knew about those things (how much could that really have been?). These were all matters a boy should take up with his father, of course. Though, really, whoever would? I know I wouldn't have. Such a conversation would've confused and embarrassed my poor father and me. We did not know each other that well at our closest moments. And in any case, he was gone.

But my mother I knew very well. At least I acted that way and she did, too. She was fifty-two. I was eighteen. She was practiced with me, knew the kind of boy I was. We were partners in my messes and hers. I sat on the couch and carefully told her what scared me, told her what I couldn't get worked out right in my thinking, went through it all; used the words *it, hers, in*. And she, stifling her dread, very carefully assured me that everything was going to be fine. Nobody got pregnant doing what we were doing, and I should forget about it. It was all a young girl's scare fantasies. Not to worry. And so I didn't.

Of course, she was wrong. Couldn't possibly have been wronger. My girlfriend didn't get pregnant, but only because a kind fate intervened. Thousands of people get pregnant doing what we were doing. Thousands more get pregnant doing much less. I guess my mother just didn't know that much, or else understood much more: that what was done was done now, and all the worry and explaining and getting-straight wouldn't matter. I should be more careful in the future if I was to have one. And that was about it. If Louise was pregnant, what anybody thought wouldn't matter. Best just not to worry.

And there is, of course, a lesson in that—one I like and have tried ever since and unsuccessfully to have direct me. Though I have never looked at the world through eyes like hers were then. Not yet. I have never exactly felt how little all you can do can really matter. Full understanding will come to me, and undoubtedly to us all. But my mother showed that to me first, and best, and I think I may have begun to understand it even then.

In the sixties after that I went away to college, in Michigan. It was a choice of mine and no one else's, and my mother neither encouraged nor discouraged me. Going to college in Mississippi didn't enter my mind. I wanted, I thought, to be a hotel manager like my grandfather, who had done well at it. And Michigan State was the place for that. I do not, in fact, remember my mother and me ever talking about college. She hadn't been and didn't know much about it. But the assumption was that I was simply going, and it would have to be my lookout. She was interested, but in a way that was not vital or supervisory. I don't think she thought that I would go away for good, even when it happened that Michigan State took me and I said I was going. I don't know what she thought exactly. She had other things on her mind then.

Maybe she thought Michigan wasn't so far from Mississippi, which is true and not true, or that I wouldn't stay and would come home soon. Maybe she thought I would never go. Or maybe she thought nothing, or nothing that was clear; just noticed that I was doing this and that, sending and getting letters, setting dates, and decided she would cross that bridge when the time came.

And it did come.

In September 1962, she and I got on the Illinois Central in Jackson and rode it to Chicago (our first such trip together). We transferred crosstown to the old La Salle Street Station and the Grand Trunk Western, and rode up to Lansing. She wanted to go with me. I think she wanted just to see all that. Michigan. Illinois. Cornfields. White barns. The Middle West. Wanted to see from a train window what went on there, how that was. What it all looked like, possibly to detect how I was going to fit myself among those people, live in their buildings, eat their food, learn their lingo. Why this was where I had chosen to go. Her son. This was how she saw her duty unfolding.

And, too, the ordinary may have been just what she wanted: accompanying her son to college, a send-off; to see herself and me, for a moment in time, fitted into the pattern of what other people were up to, what people in general did. If it could happen to her, to us, that way, then maybe some normal life had reconvened, since she could not have thought of her life as normal then.

So, at the end of that week, late September 1962, when I had enrolled, invaded my room, met my roomies, and she and I had spent days touring and roaming, eating motel dinners together until nothing was left to say, I stood up on a bus–stop bench beside the train tracks, at the old GTW station in Lansing, and held up my arms in the cool, snapping air for her to see me as she pulled away back toward Chicago. And I saw her, her white face recessed behind the tinted window, one palm flat to the glass for me to see. And she was crying. Good-bye, she was saying. And I waved one arm in that cool air and said, "Good-bye. I love you," and watched the train go out of sight through the warp of that bricky old factory town. And at that moment I suppose you could say I started my own life in earnest, and whatever there was left of my childhood ended.

After that the life that would take us to the end began. A fragmented, truncated life of visits long and short. Letters. Phone calls. Telegrams. Meetings in cities away from home. Conversations in cars, in airports, train stations. Efforts to see each other. Leaving dominating everything—my growing older, and hers, observed from varying distances.

She held out alone in Mississippi for a year, moved back into the house on Congress Street. She rented out the other side, worked at the hospital, where for a time, I think, the whole new life she'd been handed worked out, came together. I am speculating, as you can believe, because I was gone. But at least she said she liked her job, liked the young interns at the hospital, liked the drama of the ER, liked working even. It may have started to seem satisfactory enough that I was away. It may have seemed to her that there was a life to lead. That under the circumstances she had done reasonably well with things; could ease up, let events happen without fearing the worst. One bad thing did finally turn into something less bad.

This, at least, is what *I* wanted to think. How a son feels about his widowed mother when he is far away becomes an involved business. But it is not oversimplifying to say that he wants good to come to her. In all these years, the years of fragmented life with my mother, I was aware (as I have said) that things would never be completely all right with her again. Partly it was a matter of her choosing; partly it was a matter of her own character—of just how she could see her life without my father, with him gone and so much life left to be lived in an unideal way. Always she was resigned somewhere down deep. I could never plumb her without coming to that stop point—a point where expectation simply ceased. This is not to say she was unhappy after enough time had passed. Or that she never laughed. Or that she didn't see life as life, didn't regain and rejoin herself. All those she did. Only, not utterly, not in a way a mother, any mother, could disguise to her only son who loved her. I always saw that. Always felt it. Always felt her—what?—discomfort at life? Her resisting it? Always wished she could relent more than she apparently could; since in most ways my own life seemed to spirit ahead, and I did not like it that hers didn't. From almost the first I felt that my father's death surrendered to me at least as much as it took away. It gave me my life to live by my own designs, gave me my own decisions. A boy could do worse than to lose his father—a good father, at that— just when the world begins to display itself all around him.

But that is not the way it was with her, even as I can't exactly say how it *was*. I can say that in all the years after my father died, twenty-one years, her life never seemed quite fully engaged. She took trips—to Mexico, to New York, to California, to Banff, to islands. She had friends who loved her and whom she spoke well of. She had an increasingly easy life as her own parents died. She had us—my wife and me—who certainly loved her and included her in all we could. But when I would say to her—and I did say this—"Mother, are you enjoying your life? Are things all right?" she would just look at me impatiently and roll her eyes. "Richard," she'd say. "I'm never going to be ecstatic. It's not in my nature. You concentrate on your life. Leave mine alone. I'll take care of me."

And that, I think, is mostly what she did after his death and my departure, when she was on her own: she maintained herself, made a goal of that. She became brisk, businesslike, more self-insistent. Her deep voice became even deeper, assumed a kind of gravity. She drank in the evenings to get a little drunk, and took up an attitude (particularly toward men, whom she began to see as liabilities). She made her situation be the custom and cornerstone of her character. Would not be taken advantage of by people, though I suspect no one wanted to. A widow had to look out, had to pay attention to all details. No one could help you. A life lived efficiently wouldn't save you, no; but it would prepare you for what you couldn't really be saved from.

Along the way she also maintained me and my wife, at a distance and as we needed it. She maintained her mother, who finally grew ill, then crippled, but never appreciative. She maintained her stepfather—moved, in fact, back to Little Rock. She sold her house, hers and my father's first house, and lived with my grandparents in the hotel, and later—after Ben died—in apartments here and there in the town. She became a daughter again at fifty-five, one who looked after her elderly mother. They had money enough. A good car. A set of friends who were widowed, too—people in their stratum. They accompanied each other. Went to eat in small groups, played canasta afternoons, spoke on the phone, watched TV, planned arguments; grew bored, impatient, furious. Had cocktails. Laughed about men. Stared. Lived a nice and comfortable life of waiting.

Our life during this time—my mother's and mine—consisted of my knowledge of what her life was like. And visits. We lived far away from each other. She in Little Rock. I, and then I and Kristina, in New York, California, Mexico, Chicago, Michigan again, New Jersey, Vermont. To us she arrived on trains and planes and in cars, ready to loan us money and to take us to dinner. To buy us this and that we needed. To have a room painted. To worry about me. To be there for a little while wherever we were and then to go home again.

It must be a feature of anyone's life to believe that particular circumstances such as these are not exactly typical of what the mass of other lives are like. Not better. Not worse. Only peculiar in some way. Our life, my mother's and mine, seemed peculiar. Or possibly it is just imperfect that it seemed. Being away. Her being alone. Our visits and departings. All this consumed twenty years of both our lives—her last twenty, my second, when whatever my life was to be was beginning. It never felt exactly right to me that during all these years I could not see my mother more, that we did not have a day-to-day life. That the repairs we made to things after my father's death could not be shared entirely. I suppose that nowhere in time was there a moment when life for us rejoined itself as it had been before he died. This imperfection underlay everything. And when she left again and again and again, she would cry. And that is what she cried about. That we would never rejoin, that that was gone. This was all there was. Not quite enough.

Not a full enough repaying of all that time together lost. She told me once that in an elevator a woman had asked her, "Mrs. Ford, do you have any children?" And she had said, "No." And then thought to herself, "Well, yes, I do. There's Richard."

Our conversations over these years had much to do with television, with movies we had seen and hadn't, with books she was reading, with baseball. The subject of Johnny Bench came up often, for some reason. My wife and I took her to the World Series, where she rooted for the team we didn't like and complained about the seats we'd moved mountains to get—for her, we thought. We took her on the Universal Tour. We took her back to Antoine's. We drove her to California and to Montreal. To Maine. To Vermont. To northern Michigan. To wherever we went that we could take her. We, she and I, observed each other. She observed my wife and my marriage and liked them both. She observed my efforts to be a writer and did not fully understand them. "But when are you going to get a job and get started?" she asked me once. She observed the fact that we had no children and offered no opinion. She observed her life and ours and possibly did not completely see how one gave rise to the other.

I observed that she grew older; saw that life was not entirely to her liking and that she made the most of its surfaces—taking a job once in a while, then finally retiring. I observed that she loved me; would sometimes take me aside early on a morning when we could be alone together as two adults and say: "Richard, are *you* happy?" And when I told her I was, she would warn, "You must be happy. That's so important."

And that is the way life went on. Not quite pointlessly. But not pointedly, either. Maybe this is typical of all our lives with our parents—a feeling that some goal should be reached, then a recognition of what that goal inevitably is, and then returning attention to what's here and present today. To what's only here.

Something, some essence of life, is not coming clear through these words. There are not words enough. There are not events enough. There is not memory enough to give a life back and have it be right, exact. In one way, over these years apart, my mother and I lived toward one another the way people do who like each other and want to see each other more. Like friends. I have not even said about her that she didn't interfere. That she agreed my life with Kristina had retired a part of her motherhood. That she didn't cultivate random judgments. That she saw her visits as welcome, which they were. Indeed, she saw that what we'd made of things—she and I—was the natural result of prior events that were themselves natural. She was now, as before, not a psychologist. Not a quizzer. She played the cards she was dealt. By some strange understanding, we knew that this was life. This is what we would have. We were fatalists, mother and son. And we made the most of it.

In 1973, my mother discovered she had breast cancer. It must've been the way with such things, and with people of her background. A time of being aware that something was there. A time of worry and growing certainty. A mention to a friend, who did nothing. Finally a casual mention to me, who saw to it immediately that she visit a doctor, who advised tests and did not seem hopeful.

What I remember of that brief period, which took place in Little Rock, is that following the first doctor visit, when all the tests and contingencies were stated and planned, she and I and Kristina took the weekend together. She would "go in" on Monday. But Saturday we drove up to the country, visited my father's family, his cousins whom she liked, his grave. She stated she was "going in for tests," and they—who were all older than she was— put a good face on it. We drove around in her Buick and just spent the time together. It was, we knew somehow, the last of the old time, the last of the period when we were just ourselves, just the selves we had made up and perfected, given all that had gone before. Something in those tests was about to change everything, and we wanted to act out our conviction that, yes, this has been a life, this adroit coming and going, this health, this humor, this affection expressed in fits and starts. This has been a thing. Nothing would change that. We could look back, and it would seem like we were alive enough.

Death starts a long time before it ever ends. And in it, in its very self, there is life that has to be lived out efficiently. And we did this. We found to none of our surprise that the life we had confirmed that weekend could carry us on. There were seven years to go, but we didn't know it. And so we carried on. We went back to being away. To visiting. To insisting on life's being life, in the conviction that it could easily be less. And to me it seems like the time that had gone on before. Not exactly. But mostly. Talking on the phone. Visits, trips, friends, occasions. A more pointed need to know about "how things were," and a will to have them be all right for now.

My mother, I think, made the very best of her bad problems. She had a breast removed. She had some radiation. She had to face going back to her solitary life. And all this she did with a minimum of apparent fear and a great deal of dignity and resignation. It seemed as if her later years had been a training for bad news. For facing down disasters. And I think she appreciated this and was sharply aware of how she was dealing with things.

This was the first time I ever thought seriously that my mother might come to live with me, which was a well-discussed subject all our life, there having been precedent for it and plenty of opportunity to take up a point of view. My mother's attitude was very clear. She was against it. It ruined lives, spoiled things, she thought, and said no in advance. She had lived with her mother, and that had eventuated in years of dry unhappiness. Bickering. Impossibilities. Her mother had resented her, she said, hated being looked after. Turned meaner. Vicious. It was a no-win, and she herself expected nothing like that, wanted me to swear off the idea. Which I did. We laughed about how high and dry I would leave her. How she would be in the poorhouse, and I'd be someplace living it up.

But she was practical. She made arrangements. Someplace called Presbyterian Village, in Little Rock, would be her home when she was ready, she said. She'd paid money. They'd promised to do their duty. And that was that. "I don't want to have to be at anybody's mercy," she said, and meant it. And my wife and I thought that was a good arrangement all the way around.

So then it was back to regular life, or life as regular as could be. We had moved to New Jersey by then. We had a house. And there were plenty of visits, with my mother doing most of the visiting—walking out in our shady yard, afternoons, talking to our neighbors as if she knew them, digging in the flower beds. She seemed healthy. In high spirits. Illness and the possibility of illness had made her seize her life harder. She wanted to do more, it seemed. Take cruises. Visit Hawaii. Go. She had new friends, younger than she was. Loud, personable Southerners. We heard about them by name. Blanche. Herschel. Mignon. People we never met, who drank and laughed and liked her and were liked by her. I had pictures in my mind.

The year was counted from medical exam to medical exam, always these in the late winter, not long after my birthday. But every year there was good news after worrying. And every year there was a time to celebrate and feel relief. A reprieve.

I do not mean to say that any of our lives then were lived outside the expectation and prism of death. No one, I think, can lose his parent and not live out his life waiting for the other one to drop dead or begin to die. The joy of surviving is tainted by squeamish certainty that you can't survive. And I read my mother's death in almost all of her life during those days. I looked for illness. Listened to her complaints too carefully. Planned her death obscurely, along with my own abhorrence of it—treated myself to it early so that when the time came I would not, myself, go down completely.

At first there were backaches. It is hard to remember exactly when. The spring, 1981—six years since her first operation. She came to New Jersey to visit, and something had gone wrong. She was seventy, but pain had come into her life. She looked worn down, invaded by hurting. She'd seen doctors in Little Rock, but none of this had to do with her cancer, she said they said. It was back trouble. Parts were just wearing out. She went home, but in the summer she hurt more. I would call her and the phone would ring a long time, and then her answering voice would be weak, even barely audible. "I hurt, Richard," she'd tell me, wherever I was. "The doctor is giving me pills. But they don't always work." I'll come down there, I'd say. "No. I'll be fine," she'd say. "Do what you have to do." And the summer managed past that way, and the fall began.

I started a job in Massachusetts, and then one morning the phone rang. It was just at light. I don't know why anyone would call anyone at that hour unless a death was involved; but this wasn't the case. My mother had come to the hospital the night before, in an ambulance. She was in pain. And when she got there her heart had paused, briefly, though it had started again. She was better, a nurse said over the phone from Little Rock. I said I'd come that day, from Massachusetts; find people to teach my classes, drive to the airport in Albany. And that's how I did it.

In Little Rock it was still summer. A friend of my mother's, a man named Ed, met me and drove me in. We went by old buildings, over railroad tracks and across the Arkansas River. He was in a mood to comfort me: this would not turn out well, he said. My mother had been sicker than I knew; had spent days in her apartment without coming out. She had been in bed all summer. It was something I needed to prepare myself for. Her death.

But really it was more than her death. Singular life itself—hers in particular, ours—was moving into a new class of events now. These things could be understood, is what he meant to say to me. And to hold out against them was hopeless and also maybe perverse. This all was becoming a kind of thing that happens. It was inevitable, after all. And it was best to see it that way.

Which, I suppose, is what I then began to do. That ride in the car, across town, to the hospital, was the demarking line for me. A man I hardly knew suggested to me how I should look at things; how I should consider my own mother, my own life. Suggested, in essence, I begin to see *myself* in all this. Stand back. Be him or like him. It was better. And that is what I did.

My mother, it turned out, was feeling better. But something very unusual had happened to her. Her heart had stopped. There had been congestion in her lungs, the doctor told me and her. He had already performed some more tests, and the results weren't good. He was a small, curly-headed, bright-eyed young man. He was soft-spoken, and he liked my mother, remembered how she'd looked when she first came to see him. "Healthy," he said, and he was confused now by the course of a disease he supposedly knew about. I do not remember his name now. But he came into her room, sat down in the chair with some papers, and told us bad news. Just the usual bad news. The back pain was cancer, after all. She was going to die, but he didn't know when she would. Sometime in the next year, he imagined. There didn't seem to be any thought of recovering. And I know he was sorry to know it and to say it, and in a way his job may even have been harder than ours was then.

I do not really remember what we said to him. I'm sure we asked very good questions, since we were both good when the chips were down. I do not remember my mother crying. I know I did not cry. We knew, both of us, what class of events *this* was, this message. This was the message that ended one long kind of uncertainty. And I cannot believe we both, in our own ways, did not feel some relief, as if a curiosity had been satisfied and other matters begun. The real question—how serious is this?—can be answered and over with in a hurry. It is actually an odd thing. I wonder if doctors know how odd it is.

But still, in a way, it did not change things. The persuasive powers of normal life are strong after all. To accept less than life when it is not absolutely necessary is stupid.

I think we had talks. She was getting out of the hospital again, and at least in my memory I stayed around and got out with her before I had to go back to my job. We made plans for a visit. More going. She would come to Massachusetts when she was strong enough. We could still imagine a future, and that was exactly all we asked for.

I went back to teaching, and talked to her most days, though the thought that she was getting worse, that bad things were going on then and I couldn't stop them, made me miss some days.

It became an awful time, then, when life felt ruined, futureless, edging toward disappointments.

She stayed out of the hospital during that time, took blood transfusions, which seemed to make her feel better, though they were ominous. I think she went out with her friends. Had company. Lived as if life could go on. And then in early October she came north. I drove down to New York, picked her up and drove us back to my rented house in Vermont. It was misty, and most of the leaves were down. And in the house it was cold and bleak, and I took her out to dinner in Bennington just to get warm. She said she had had another transfusion for the trip and would stay with me until its benefits wore off and she was weak again.

And that was how we did that. Just another kind of regular life between us. I went to school, did my work, came home nights. She stayed in the big house with my dog. Read. Cooked lunches for herself. Watched the World Series. Watched Sadat be assassinated. Looked out the window. At night we talked. I did my school work, went out not very much. With my wife, who was working in New York and commuting up on weekends, we went on country drives, invited visitors, paid visits, lived together as we had in places far and wide all those years. I don't know what else we were supposed to do, how else that time was meant to pass.

On a sunny day in early November, when she had been with me three weeks and we were, in fact, out of things to do and talk about, she sat down beside me on the couch and said, "Richard, I'm not sure how much longer I can look out after myself. I'm sorry. But it's just the truth."

"Does that worry you?" I said.

"Well," my mother said, "yes. I'm not scheduled to go into Presbyterian Village until way next year. And I'm not quite sure what I'm going to be able to do until then."

"What would you like to do?" I said.

"I don't exactly know," she said. And she looked worried then, looked away out the window, down the hill, where the trees were bare and it was foggy.

"Maybe you'll start to feel better," I said.

"Well, yes. I could. I suppose that's not impossible," she said.

"I think it's possible," I said. "I do."

"Well. Okay," my mother said.

"If you don't," I said, "if by Christmas you don't feel you can do everything for yourself, you can move in with us. We're moving back to Princeton. You can live there."

And I saw in my mother's eyes, then, a light. A *kind* of light, anyway. Recognition. Relief. Concession. Willingness.

"Are you sure about that?" she said and looked at me. My mother's eyes were very brown, I remember.

"Yes, I'm sure," I said. "You're my mother. I love you."

"Well," she said and nodded. No tears. "I'll begin to think toward that, then. I'll make some plans about my furniture."

"Well, wait," I said. And this is a sentence I wish, above all sentences in my life, I had never said. Words I wish I'd never heard. "Don't make your plans yet," I said. "You might feel better by then. It might not be necessary to come to Princeton."

"Oh," my mother said. And whatever had suddenly put a light in her eyes suddenly went away then. And her worries resumed. Whatever lay between then and later rose again. "I see," she said. "All right."

I could've not said that. I could've said, "Yes, make the plans. In whatever way all this works out, it'll be just fine. I'll see to that." But that is what I didn't say. I deferred instead to something else, to some other future, and at least in retrospect I know what that future was. And, I think, so did she. Perhaps you could say that in that moment I witnessed her facing death, saw it take her out beyond her limits, and feared it myself, feared all that I knew; and that I clung to life, to the possibility of life and change. Perhaps I feared something more tangible. But the truth is, anything we ever could've done for each other after that passed by then and was gone. And even together we were alone.

What remains can be told quickly. In a day or two I drove her to Albany. She was cold, she said, in my house, and couldn't get warm, and would be better at home. That was our story, though there was not heat enough anywhere to get her warm. She looked pale. And when I left her at the airport gate she cried again, stood and watched me go back down the long corridor, waved a hand. I waved. It was the last time I would see her that way. On her feet. In the world. We didn't know that, of course. But we knew something was coming.

And in six weeks she was dead. There is nothing exceptional about that to tell. She never got to Princeton. Whatever was wrong with her just took her over. "My body has betrayed me" is one thing I remember her saying. Another was, "My chances now are slim and none." And that was true. I never saw her dead, didn't care to, simply took the hospital's word about it when they called. Though I saw her face death that month, over and over, and I believe because of it that seeing death faced with dignity and courage does not confer either of those, but only pity and help-lessness and fear.

All the rest is just private—moments and messages the world would not be better off to know. She knew I loved her because I told her so enough. I knew she loved me. That is all that matters to me now, all that should ever matter.

And so to end.

Does one ever have a "relationship" with one's mother? No. I think not. The typical only exists in the minds of unwise people. We—my mother and I—were never bound together by guilt or embarrassment, or even by duty. Love sheltered everything. We expected it to be reliable, and it was. We were always careful to say it—"I love you"—as if a time might come, unexpectedly, when she would want to hear that, or I would, or that each of us would want to hear ourselves say it to the other, only for some reason it wouldn't be possible, and our loss would be great—confusion. Not knowing. Life lessened.

My mother and I look alike. Full, high forehead. The same chin, nose. There are pictures to show that. In myself I see her, even hear her laugh. In her life there was no particular brilliance, no celebrity. No heroics. No one crowning achievement to swell the heart. There were bad ones enough: a childhood that did not bear strict remembering; a husband she loved forever and lost; a life to follow that did not require comment. But somehow she made possible for me my truest affections, as an act of great literature would bestow upon its devoted reader. And I have known that moment with her we would all like to know, the moment of saying, "Yes. This is what it is." An act of knowing that certifies love. I have known that. I have known any number of such moments with her, known them even at the instant they occurred. And now. And, I assume, I will know them forever.

VINTAGE BOOKS BY RICHARD FORD

Independence Day

In this visionary sequel to *The Sportswriter*, Richard Ford deepens his portrait of Frank Bascombe, one of the most indelible characters in American fiction, and in doing so, gives the reader an unforgettable account of American life.
Fiction/0-679-73518-6

A Multitude of Sins

In this masterful collection of short stories, Richard Ford's distinct settings offer journeys through delicate ethical terrain, as he examines liaisons in and out and to the sides of marriage.
Fiction/0-375-72656-X

A Piece of My Heart

The story of two men—one pursuing a woman, the other pursuing his heart—drawn by chance and mystery to an uncharted island in the Mississippi River.
Fiction/0-394-72914-5

Rock Springs

In these ten stories, Richard Ford mines literary gold from the wind-scrubbed landscape of the American West—and from the guarded hopes and gnawing loneliness of the people who live there.
Fiction/0-394-75700-9

The Sportswriter

The Sportswriter introduces readers to Frank Bascombe, a former novelist turned sportswriter, who, in the course of an Easter week, loses the remnants of his familiar life.
Fiction/0-679-76210-8

The Ultimate Good Luck

Set in the teeming streets of Oaxaca, Mexico, *The Ultimate Good Luck* is a brilliantly evocative portrait of the alienation and dislocation of a Vietnam veteran.
Fiction/0-394-75089-6

Wildlife

In this heartbreaking and compelling novel, a family moves to Montana in search of opportunity and instead encounters the forces that will test it to the breaking point.
Fiction/0-679-73447-3

Women with Men

In three long stories, Richard Ford takes us from the plains of Montana to the streets of Paris to the suburbs of Chicago, where his characters experience the consolations and complications that prevail in matters of passion, romance, and love.
Fiction/0-679-77668-0